# HER LAST CHANCE

## A DI CROW NOVEL

HJ REED

INKUBATOR
BOOKS

Published by Inkubator Books

www.inkubatorbooks.com

Copyright © 2023 by HJ Reed

HJ Reed has asserted her right to be identified as the author
of this work.

ISBN (eBook): 978-1-83756-106-3
ISBN (Paperback): 978-1-83756-107-0
ISBN (Hardback): 978-1-83756-108-7

# 1

The house phone rings for the third time in twenty minutes.

I look down at my hand and try to gauge the severity of what I call 'the twitch'. It's a little less than last time, a lot less than the time before. It begins at the wrist and works its way down to my fingers and starts up seemingly at random – except when a phone rings. Then, it happens every single time, a tremor so violent I can't grip the handset, can't do anything but wait until I get back enough control to answer the damned thing.

Over the course of the last few months, various surgeons and psychiatrists have argued over whether the phenomenon is physical, psychological or a combination of both. So far they can't make their minds up. All I know is that it's one more thing to fight against, another hurdle in the obstacle course that life becomes when a bullet ploughs a furrow into your brain. A lump of metal lodged in the frontal lobe is bound to cause a few problems, and according to the experts, when it's taken out, it's very likely to cause a fair few more.

After the surgery I asked the consultant what kind of problems. He waved his arms in a vague and very large circle. 'I'm afraid it's hard to say at this stage. Every case is unique, and to tell you the truth ...' He paused and gave me an apologetic grin. 'Well, there aren't that many cases to go on, Inspector Crow. Getting shot in the head is usually fatal, you see. If you like, I can try to get hold of some literature. It might give you some idea what to expect.'

The next morning a nurse came into my room, loaded with a sheaf of scientific articles and a book the size of a Bible entitled *The handbook of Clinical Psychology*, with a couple of Post-it notes poking helpfully out of the top. After three hours of squinting at acres of small print on tissue-paper pages, I gave up. 'How the bloody hell am I supposed to deduce anything from that lot?' I asked the consultant on his afternoon round.

Again, I got the grin. 'I'm just a humble brain surgeon, Inspector. You're the detective.'

THE PHONE'S STILL RINGING, and I've still got the twitch, but it's just on the right side of manageable now. I'd feel better if I knew who was on the other end, but the screen on the handset stubbornly displays a less than helpful 'withheld'. I grit my teeth and pick up.

'Is that Mr Alexander Crow?'

I know who it is – the damned woman from the clinic. Mid-fifties, five feet two, grey trouser suit, no sense of humour. An inner switch trips; the tremor stops and is replaced with another of the foibles my rewired brain has developed. 'You can call me Al,' I say in a faux downtown New York accent. It's a bad chat-up line, one I last used on my ex-wife thirty years ago – as inappropriate then as it is now, but at least it gives me the few seconds I need to pull my thoughts into line.

There's a disapproving silence and then, 'Dr Rogers has just informed us you've missed three consecutive appointments, Mr Crow.'

'Sorry, I forgot.' I try to inject some sincerity into the lie, but it doesn't cut any ice.

'I'm afraid you can't keep missing appointments, Mr Crow. It takes up valuable clinic time, not to mention the cost. It would be very helpful if you could let us know when you are unable to attend.'

The woman's like an itch in an awkward place. 'In the first place,' I say, 'it's not "Mr", it's "Inspector".' I pause for effect, more out of habit than expectation. She knows as well as I do that it's just a matter of time – my sick leave runs out in two months, and there's no way the force is going to let me go back, not unless it's to some dingy office where I'm well out of the public eye. It's a fact I'd rather not think about, and being reminded of it by a clinic receptionist does nothing for the fragile hold I have on my temper. 'In the second place,' I say, when the silence has started to grate, 'my medical insurance has forked out enough in private health subscriptions to keep your mid-grade sodding clinic going for the next ten years, so don't talk to me about bloody cost.'

Finally, she takes the bait. 'For your information, *Mr* Crow, the Duchess of Malvern uses our services and finds them more than satisfactory.'

'You mean she's gaga as well? I'm sure she'll be delighted to know you take the issue of confidentiality so seriously.' At last I get a splutter of outrage down the line and feel a small, childish frisson of triumph. 'Just book me another appointment, will you? I'll do my best to attend. If I can't, I'll try to remember to let you know. Good afternoon.'

I hang up before she has the chance to respond, and take a moment to scrape myself back together. The woman's only doing her job, and I'm acting like a teenager caught bunking off school. By the end of the day my lack of cooperation with mental health services will have been reported to somebody or other in Human Resources, and I'll get yet another reminder that attending regular therapy sessions is a condition of my sick leave. My argument – that spending an hour a week listening to a pile of bullshit from an idiot with no idea of what it's really like on the front line – hasn't made any impression on the pen-pushers at head office. But as they've never been on the front line either, I don't suppose that's any kind of surprise.

I'm pondering the inevitability of another forced meeting with a clueless psychologist when the phone rings again. This time the display is giving me a name – Rosie. At the sight of it, my vision telescopes, and the world takes a sudden tilt as I back into an arm of the sofa and slide down onto the carpet. My daughter hasn't seen or spoken to me for five years, not even after the shooting – at least, if she did, I was unconscious at the time. When I came home from the hospital, I had a mad hope she'd call or leave some sort of message, even though what was left of the sensible part of me knew it just wasn't going to happen. If she had, it would probably have been to remind me what a crap father I am, and that brain surgery could only be an improvement. Now, nearly a year later, I'm staring at her name on the handset that's still gripped tightly between my fingers. I jab the 'talk' button before the twitch has time to set in again.

'Rosie?'

A man's voice answers. 'Inspector Crow?'

'Who the hell are you?'

'I'm sorry, Inspector, my name's Larson – John Larson. I'm calling on behalf of Rosie – your daughter?'

On behalf of? Christ – does she want to sue me for something? 'What are you doing on my daughter's phone?' I ask, and then think maybe she's had some sort of accident – she might be lying in hospital somewhere, and my first thought is that she wants to take me to court for being a crap father. Which really does make me a crap father.

'I'm sorry,' Larson says again – he's got a young, nervy voice, and I guess that whatever it is he does, he hasn't been doing it long. 'Rosie asked me to call you. She's been arrested, you see, and when I asked if there was anyone she wanted me to contact, she gave me her phone and said to call you.'

'Arrested?' My mind swerves in several directions at once. My estranged daughter is in trouble, and the first person she wants to see is me. My heart gives a little joyful bump, and then I remember just why this guy is on the other end of the line. She's always been squeaky clean, my Rosie – no drugs, no student riots, not even an unsavoury boyfriend and underage sex – not that I ever knew about, anyway. 'What do you mean, arrested? What for? What is she accused of?'

Larson gives a nervous cough. 'Look, Inspector, it's a bit complicated. It would be really useful if you could get down here, and I can explain in more detail. We're at West Hill police station. I'll meet you outside, and we can go for a coffee. I'm afraid you won't be able to see her right away, she's still being interviewed under caution, but I'm hoping she will get bail before too long.'

Bail? What the hell has she done? 'I'm on my way,' I say, and hang up. I look at my hand. It's not twitching. It's the only bit of me that isn't. I grab my coat, get to the door, and freeze. I got cleared to drive a month ago, but so far haven't quite worked up to it. I shouldn't have any trouble with routine procedural tasks, so the consultant tells me, like driving, navigating and so on – my eyesight hasn't been affected, and by some miracle I've not had any blackouts – not so far anyway, and there's no physical reason why I should start now. It's just that, for reasons I haven't quite understood yet, certain aspects of daily life are easier to deal with than others. But, damn it – my baby's in trouble, and now just isn't the time to start wondering whether or not I can remember how to change gears. 'Don't worry, sweetheart,' I mutter to myself, 'I'm coming,' and stomp out onto the drive.

## 2

I t's a fifteen-minute drive from my place to West Hill nick. I'm there in ten. I could use the staff car park – I'm still in the job, just about, so I'm entitled. Somehow, though, I don't fancy the whole bloody station knowing I'm there, with the claps on the back, and the 'How's it going, Al?' and all the rest of the stuff people come out with when they don't know what to say. I don't catch sight of anyone who might be Larson as I drive past, and I'm getting the jitters, so I park in a side street around the corner and sit, trying to get a grip.

Back at headquarters they call West Hill 'the Sinkhole'. It's the kind of place where the patrol cars go around in threes, and custody officers are issued with riot gear as standard. Nearly all new constables do a six-month stint in the Sinkhole. Those who make it through come out with a better understanding of what it must have been like at Custer's Last Stand. At least half of them decide that a career in law enforcement isn't for them after all. A very small minority of idiots believe a place like West Hill is what the press office call 'the cutting edge of real policing', where we're 'making a difference', and 'in the front line of the war on crime'. That's probably not far from the truth – I know because until eleven months ago I'd spent twenty years being one of those idiots.

The day our luck finally ran out, it was a pretty normal Friday in the Sinkhole – drugs, pimps, drunks, the usual quota of gang face-offs and stabbings. We – four rookie constables, my sergeant, Joe Bailey, and me – had wind of a drug deal in one of the mid-rise flats on the Cabot Rise estate. We weren't expecting that much trouble – Cabot Rise is one of the more respectable postcodes in the district, where the prostitutes work out of private accommodations and the drug of choice is mainly home-grown skunk. We did the usual thing, by the book – knock, shout, and ram the door, all within ten seconds so they didn't have time to flush the dope down the pan. Joe was first in. He took two paces and toppled backwards.

There are certain things I remember very clearly. One is the way the sound was slower than the bullet. I was already falling, with him on top of me, when I heard the bang. My second memory is of staring at the hole in the back of the poor bastard's skull. The third – and last – is realising that the bullet had passed right through his head and into mine. Later, I learned we'd stumbled on the biggest drugs deal to go down in West Hill for ten years – a suitcase full of Afghani smack with a street value well over a million. We never caught the shooter, or anybody else. By the time reinforcements arrived, they were all long gone. The drugs were recovered, so the DCI told me afterwards. I even got a visit in hospital from the chief constable. He said he was going to recommend me for a medal. I told him to chuck it in Joe's grave and fuck off. I got the medal anyway.

The bullet had slowed a fair bit by the time it got to me. It made a neat hole in my forehead and lodged itself in the right frontal lobe. Within days of the surgery, I was sitting up, talking, healing well, they said, and I was lucky to be alive. They were partly telling the truth – I'm still alive. As far as luck goes, I'm still trying to make up my mind. A new consultant appeared, a psychologist called Rogers, who jigged his way into my room rubbing his hands like a kid about to open a Christmas present. He introduced himself as an expert in war injuries and post-traumatic stress and told me I was probably the most exciting case he'd ever had. 'Survivors of your type of injury are very thin on the ground,' he said, with a gleeful grin that made me feel like a prize exhibit in a freak show. He must have caught sight of my fingers curling into a feeble fist underneath the spaghetti of wires attached to the back of my hand, because the grin faded, and he pulled the visitor's chair a little further from the bedside before lowering himself into it. 'I'm so sorry, Inspector Crow – Alexander, isn't it? Do you mind if …'

'As a matter of fact I do. And it's Al – to my friends, that is.'

'Right. I know this can't be much fun for you, Inspector, but the truth is, your recovery so far is exceptional. There are bound to be some glitches, but it's for your surgical consultant to take you through any physical problems. My concern is your psychological health. You've been through one hell of a mental trauma, and the long-term effects of that on mood and on your reactions to events in the course of daily living could be quite far-reaching.'

This time I did laugh out loud. 'You know,' I said, 'the funny thing about getting shot and seeing your sergeant's head blown off is it really improves your temper.'

He went on to rattle off a string of possible symptoms that researchers had come across – I might find myself using inappropriate language, or suddenly not knowing how to respond or what to say. I might suffer from mood swings, flashbacks, nightmares, tremors or unexplained phobias … it was at that point I gave him an expert demonstration of inappropriate language and carried on until he held up his hands in defeat and buggered off. When he'd gone, I covered my head with a blanket and cried like a baby for only the second time in my life. The first was when Rosie was born.

I REALISE I've been sitting in the car for around fifteen minutes, and the muscles in my fingers have welded themselves to the steering wheel. I take a few deep breaths and detach them, hearing them crack as I straighten the joints. I look up and see a couple of faces leering at me through the windscreen, kids, fourteen or so, guffawing and giving me the finger. One of them presses his face against the glass and does bad monkey imitations while the other aims a boot at my nearside headlight. I launch myself out of the car and grab monkey by the scruff. I'm big enough and ugly enough to make an impression, and the boy squeaks in surprise while his mate legs it down the road.

'I know you,' he wheezes through his constricted windpipe. 'You're filth – you can't do nothing.'

'That right?' I reply, and knee him in the groin – gently – he's only a kid, after all. After a couple of seconds I let go of his collar, and he collapses into a heap, one hand rubbing his balls, the other his neck. 'If you'd like to make a complaint, I'd be happy to escort you to the station – it's only round the corner.'

He scrambles to his feet and hobbles off to a safe distance before yelling, 'Fucking pig!' over his shoulder. I should thank the kid – for a minute I almost feel normal. Then I think of Rosie, and the jitters come back. I straighten my tie, adjust my jacket and try to pull myself together.

There's a guy at the station entrance, early thirties, mousy hair as crumpled as the grey suit he's wearing. He's fiddling with his mobile and hopping from foot to foot. When he sees me, he stops hopping and tries to stash the phone in his jacket pocket. He misses, and it hits the pavement, bounces in its rubber case and lands in the gutter. He's on one knee scrabbling for it when I reach him.

'Larson?' I ask the top of his head.

He manages to grab the phone, stuffs it in his pocket and bobs upright. If he's a lawyer, I'm the ghost of the queen bloody mother. 'Inspector Crow,' he says, with an irritating nervous smile, 'it was good of you to come.' He sticks out a hand, and I ignore it.

'Before we go any further,' I say, 'you can tell me who the bloody hell you are, and how you got hold of my daughter's phone.' He drops the hand and takes a breath, but before he can speak, I go on, 'And I should warn you, I suffer from a condition that makes me very prone to violence if I get upset. You understand?'

His head does a little dance – I can see his Adam's apple wobble up and down as he swallows. 'Yes,' he says, 'yes, of course. I didn't know what to say, to make sure you'd come. Rosie said ...'

'Never mind what Rosie said,' I snap – I'm well aware of my daughter's feelings towards me – 'just answer the question!'

'Of course,' he says again, running a hand through his hair and ruffling it even more. 'I'm John Larson. Rosie and I, we ... well, I'm her partner. We live together.'

'Jesus fucking Christ,' I can't help muttering, and Larson flinches as if I'd tried to hit him. If he carries on like this, I just might.

'The police came this morning,' he carries on. 'We were still asleep, and they banged on the door, yelling and shouting – we were terrified, and Rosie started screaming. I couldn't stop them coming in. They made me sit downstairs

while they went up to the bedroom and got her, and when
she came down, she was in handcuffs and ...'

The words are pouring out like a bad dose of Montezu-
ma's revenge. I grit my teeth and let him get it all out – no
point 'antagonising the witness' as it says in the manual. Half
my mind is picturing it all, which doesn't take much imagination, and the other half is seething at the idea that this idiot
spends his leisure time in bed with my daughter. He says
something that jolts me back into the torrent.

'Thank God Ben was with his grandmother.'

'Ben?'

'Yes, our son – surely you knew ... oh, shit, of course not.
Look, sorry. He's three now – nearly four, and he's a great kid.
We took him over to Christine's the day before yesterday so
we could have a short break. Rosie's got leave coming up and
...'

Rosie's got a kid – a boy – my grandson. And this joker is
his father.

'Anyway, I followed the police car and tried to get to see
her, but they wouldn't let me. I waited, and then somebody
came out and told me she'd been charged. Accessory to
murder, they said. I mean, what the hell's going on? Rosie,
she wouldn't hurt a fly, she's a psychiatric nurse, for God's
sake ... and then I remembered I'd borrowed her phone –
mine went dead last night, and I needed to phone a client,
and I forgot to give it back. I looked through and saw your
number, and I know you don't get on, but, well, you're a
policeman, and I didn't know what else to do ...'

He stumbles to a halt, and as he's staring at me, waiting
for me to say something, three things strike me. This kid
might be a feeble excuse for a man, but he loves Rosie, and
he's terrified for her. More important, to me, is the fact that
even though she cut me out of her life five years ago, my
number is still on Rosie's phone. The fact he felt he had to lie

to get me out here says a hell of a lot more about me than it does about him. Finally, I realise that since he started talking, the jitters have stopped, and my brain is switching through the gears quicker than a rally driver on a skidpan.

'It's all right, son,' I say. 'Let's get in there and sort this mess out.'

# 3

George Saint's one of the old crowd. We started at the Sinkhole in the same week in '94. I was out of uniform within five years, inspector in ten. He never made it past desk sergeant. I leave Larson in the lobby and go across to the front desk. George is sitting at the back table pecking at a keyboard. He doesn't look up.

'Afternoon, George.'

His head shoots round, and he bangs his knee on the table leg. 'Christ all bloody mighty!' He limps to the counter, dusting his trousers. 'It's good to see you, Al. How's it going?'

'Crap. I hear you've got Rosie downstairs. What's the story?'

'Oh.' The slight rising of the upper lip that passes for a welcoming smile slips back into its regular stonewall position. 'Sorry, Al, the upper ranks don't confide in me much these days. I wasn't on shift when they brought her in, so I didn't hear the charge.'

'Bullshit. I swear, Sergeant Saint, I just heard the clang of your halo hitting the squad room floor. Now, either you tell me what the hell's going on, or I'll come over there and break your bloody neck before you can say "panic button". What do you say?'

George's gaze sweeps the countertop, sagging jowls quivering as he tries to decide how to respond. He looks like an overweight basset hound that just cocked its leg on its owner's best sofa. I decide to help him out. 'Come on, George, it's my little girl you've got down there. I know somebody's told you to keep me out of the loop, but I'll tell you what – I won't grass if you don't.'

He rubs his stubble and leans close, folding his arms on the counter. 'Look, Al,' he says, trying to keep his voice down, face turned away from the CCTV in the ceiling above the front desk, 'it wasn't my idea, okay? The DCI thought it best to keep you out of it, seeing as ... you know ...'

'Seeing as I'm a total lunatic who's likely to torch the entire station if I don't get my own way?' I've followed his lead and turned my back to the camera just in case some constable with nothing better to do is practising his lip-reading.

'Don't be daft, Al – nobody thinks that.'

'Yes they bloody do. And if you don't tell me what I want to know, I'll do my best to prove them right. It's simple enough, just tell me why my daughter's been arrested, who's dealing with it, and when I can see her. I'm sure every Tom, Dick and idiot in the station knows, so you might as well let me join the party – much easier than catching one of the young PCs coming off shift and beating it out of them.'

George is not quite sure if I'm joking, and to be fair, neither am I. My hand has started to tremble, and the thought of Rosie in one of the hutches downstairs is triggering my aggressive tendencies. He gives a slow nod and to my relief says, 'Okay, Al. But you didn't get it from me.' I nod back, and he says, 'Two nights ago we got a shout to a flat in Cabot Rise – a domestic. A neighbour called in to say they couldn't sleep for the racket next door and could we send somebody. We were short-handed and didn't get to it for a couple of hours. You know how it is.'

'I know.' It's a sad truth that in the Sinkhole, domestic violence has about as much priority as seeing an old lady across the road at a zebra crossing.

'By the time the patrol got there, it had gone quiet. They knocked, got no reply. Then the neighbour came out and insisted they break in, sure someone was hurt in there. To cut a long story short, one of the new recruits – Jodie Simmons, only been at West Hill for a week – looked through the window and fainted. They had to wait for a ram to get inside, and when they did ...' George lets out his breath in a long sigh and shakes his head. 'They found a woman's body in the living room.'

I give him a sidelong glance. It's always a bad business when a domestic results in a death, but it's not unheard of, especially round here. George knows that as well as I do, but the way he's shuffling his feet tells me it's not quite that straightforward.

'The body was in the living room,' he repeats, and looks me in the eye, 'and the head was in the hall.'

'Bloody hell!'

'That's what the SOCO guy said when he arrived. It hadn't just rolled there either – it had been *put* there. Nice and neat, facing the door. The poor sod who was first in found it staring at him – he swore there was a smile on its face and one eye was closed as if it were winking, for Christ's sake! Jodie's not been back to the station since, poor cow – she's only been in the job six months.'

'Jesus! What kind of ...' Sometimes even my imagination gives up the struggle. I shake the image off and get back to the point. 'This is all very interesting, George, but what the hell has it got to do with my Rosie?'

The shuffling intensifies, but George isn't going to be rushed. He wants to tell his story, and I've got as much chance of diverting him as Canute had of holding back the English Channel. He carries on with dogged determination. 'The prints we picked up from the flat belong to one Harold Shaw.'

I sift through my internal black book, but the name means nothing to me. I hesitate before shaking my head. 'Doesn't ring a bell. Should it?'

'Doubtful,' George says. 'He's on record for a couple of assaults down Portishead way – his wife and a pub landlord. That was in 2010. Convicted of GBH, sentenced to five years. Two years in he was diagnosed with something – paranoid schizophrenia I think it was – and the powers that be decided prison wasn't the best place for him, so he was sectioned and transferred to Coombe Hill secure hospital. His sentence ended a good while ago, but the section stayed in place. They thought the risk of relapse was too great. Then, two days ago, he walks out the front door, makes a beeline for the Sinkhole and saws a woman's head off.'

'Like I said, very interesting, but I still don't see ...'

'He walked out because somebody signed a day release order, the head honcho was off with the senior staff on a team-building day, and none of the nurses on duty bothered to question it. The timing was perfect – if anyone with real authority had been there, he wouldn't have got as far as the bloody lavatory, never mind through three locked wards to the main exit.'

He pauses, waiting for me to ask the question. I oblige, even though the connection is dawning on me, and my stomach is challenging itself to a game of ice hockey. 'Okay, George, who signed the order for his release?'

'The most senior person on the wing that day,' he says, dropping his voice to a near whisper, 'Nurse Manager Rosemary Larson.'

Okay, so he's finally got it out. I stare at him, but all I can see in his eyes is my own reflection. Larson? The pair of them are actually married? Half of me wants to be sick, and the other half wants to hit something. My hands have bunched into fists, and I force myself to unclench my fingers. I suddenly wonder if the jitters I get have nothing to do with the injury at all – just strained muscles. I'll have to ask Rogers next time I see him.

'You all right, Al?'

George jolts my thinking back on course. The only important thing right now is Rosie. 'The hell I am,' I hiss back. 'You're saying you've arrested my daughter on a charge of accessory to murder because she signed a piece of bloody paper? Don't make me laugh! West Hill may be the arse end of policing, but even in a hole like this you can't go around arresting people without sodding evidence!' George raises an eyebrow, so I add a modifier. 'Okay then, without a strong suspicion that there might be some evidence. So where is it? All you've got is a signature that might be there for any number of reasons – shit, George, she probably just made a mistake.'

Now he's looking really uncomfortable. 'Before I say anything else, Al,' he says, drawing his hands together as if he's praying for guidance, 'I want you to promise me something. Promise you'll stay calm, okay?'

I nod, knowing full well that 'calm' is by now no more than a distant memory.

'There *is* evidence. Several of the nurses confirmed that Rosie took a particular interest in Shaw, spent a lot of time with him. It had been going on for a couple of years apparently ...'

'What do you mean, "going on"? What had been going on?'

He gives me a look, and I bite my tongue. 'When they

searched his room, they found several diaries – big on writing his memoirs, was Harry Shaw, went right back to his first year in prison. Thing is, in the last one, he talks about how Rosie's going to get him out – how and, more importantly, when. He says other things too, but you don't want to know about that, not right now anyway. The important thing is, the diary, her signature and the statements of the other nurses, all put together ...' He lifts his shoulders in a half-hearted shrug. 'Sorry, Al, but it's all pretty conclusive. When we brought her in, she denied signing the papers, denied having any sort of relationship with Shaw, denied doing any more than manage his ongoing treatment. It's not as if we need a confession, though. We had enough to charge her, and the DCI had the sheet made up before she got to the cells.'

'I want to see those diaries,' I say – my head's starting to ache with the effort of not punching a hole in the front desk – that, or George Saint's skull, 'and the statements. And I want to see my daughter – now.'

'No, Al.' George straightens up and goes on the defensive. 'No, you don't.'

Shit. I glance back to where the father of my grandson is still sitting, fidgeting in his chair and practically sucking his thumb. 'Has she got a solicitor?' I ask George.

'Carol Dodds. She was next on the rota.'

For a duty solicitor, Dodds isn't bad. I've had a few good tussles with her in my time. 'Could do worse. Will Rosie get bail?'

George shakes his head. 'The hearing's at nine tomorrow, but there's no chance.'

'I'll be there.'

'I wouldn't advise it.'

'Try to stop me!' I push myself upright and turn away before I lose it completely and mount a one-man assault on the back office. I don't think I'd get far – George is a lazy, lumbering arse who'd do anything for a quiet life, but he cares about his job, and he won't take any risks, not even for an old friend.

'Al?'

I turn back to the desk.

'I lied,' he says. 'It wasn't the DCI who told me to keep you out of it. When she was charged, I asked Rosie if she'd like anyone informed of her arrest. She said, "You can tell anyone you like, as long as it's not my rotten bastard father."'

Somehow, I manage a weak smile. 'Thanks, George. You just made my day.'

I'm out on the pavement before I register Larson trotting behind me, begging me to slow down. I stop and turn round – best to let him down gently. 'Sod off home,' I tell him, straining to keep my voice even. 'Haven't you got a kid to look after?'

He looks crestfallen. 'Christine ... she said she'd have him for – well, for as long as it takes to ...'

'Yeah, I bet she did. Always ready to pitch in, our Chrissie. Must be tough though – a toddler *and* having to look after Terry. How is he, by the way?' I don't know why I'm asking – even thinking about my ex-wife brings me out in a cold sweat. As for the man she left me for ten years ago – Terence the financial advisor, good-time guy, life and soul of the party until the 'accident' ... I reflect that life, depressing as it is, sometimes throws up something worth smiling about.

Larson looks at me as if I've just asked him if JFK is still alive. 'He left,' he says, 'just after Rosie got pregnant. For another woman, Rosie thinks, but Christine's been pretty close-mouthed about it.'

I ought to feel good about that piece of news, but somehow I don't – I just wish I'd finished off Terence the tosser when I had the chance. What kind of bastard wrecks a marriage and then walks away, for Christ's sake? If it weren't for him, I might still be on speaking terms with Rosie – and that brings me right back to here and now and my kid in trouble, her other half, for better or worse, crumbling in front of me like an overbaked sponge. I'm behaving like a shit, and if Rosie hears about it, my chances of a reconciliation when she gets out will be dead in the water. *When* she gets out ...

'Look,' I say, giving him a pat on the shoulder, 'there's nothing more you can do right now. I need to see some people, so why don't you go off and spend some time with Ben, and meet me at the magistrates' court, eight thirty sharp, in the morning?'

'You're going to help us?' He breaks into a smile, the first I've seen, and grabs my hand before I can stop him. He's got a surprisingly firm, dry grip. 'Thank you, Inspector Crow. I'm sure if Rosie knew ...'

'She can't know,' I say quickly. 'You don't tell her, and you don't tell Chrissie. That's the deal, okay?'

He looks dubious, but nods. 'If that's the way you want it, of course.'

'That's the way I want it.'

When I get back to my car, I find two slashed front tyres and the word 'Pig' etched into the paintwork of the driver's door. My mobile's in the back of a drawer in my kitchen, where it spends most of its time these days. Some things, I reflect as I start back to the station and the only accessible phone in West Hill, never change.

# 4

It's late afternoon by the time I get back home. There are two messages on the answering machine – the first is from my mechanic. It's going to take him a couple of days to repair the bodywork. The second is the clinic with a rearranged counselling appointment. Right now, I need counselling like a hole in the head. Three months ago I told Rogers the same thing. He just grinned and said, 'No, Inspector – you need counselling *for* the hole in the head.' Bloody comedian.

I put the transport problem on the back burner for the moment and pull my diary from under a pile of unopened bills on the coffee table. Carol Dodds works for Finchley Associates, one of the oldest and biggest Bristol firms with fingers in just about every legal pie, from high-profile criminal cases to no win, no fee insurance claims. At the last count Finchley had ten barristers on the premises, four of them QCs, with a flotilla of pupils and trainee solicitors flowing in their wake. It's only when I get to the full-page ad in the phone book that a little niggle I didn't realise was in the back of my mind jabs itself to the forefront like a red-hot needle. In a firm as big as Finchley – any law firm, come to that – the pupils are always the bottom feeders – they are the ones who get to stir the mud so that if anything floats, the upper ranks can cream it off without disrupting their cocktail parties. Dodds was one of those pupils once, but even in those days she was well on her way up the greasy pole. A couple of years ago, when Finchley Jnr. QC got kicked up to the bench, she took up the vacancy as the firm's youngest barrister.

I pick up the phone and grit my teeth. What is it about phones that sets off the twitch more than anything else? These days holding down a normal conversation sparks a cold sweat as I try to keep track of what I'm saying and make sure I don't drift or say something I wish I hadn't. Maybe, with phones, it's not being able to see whoever's on the other end, and aural cues aren't enough anymore. Maybe developing a random phobia is just one of the consequences Rogers tried to warn me about. I make a note to add it to the list of things to ask him at my next check-up, then dial the direct line to West Hill's front desk.

'George, it's Al.'

'Look, Al, you're not supposed to ...'

'Never mind what I'm supposed to do, just tell me, when Rosie was brought in, did she ask for a particular brief?'

There's a pause at the end of the line, and for a second I think he might have hung up, but then he says, 'No. I rang through to Finchley myself – they were on the duty roster. Why?'

'And who turned up? Was it a junior, or did Carol Dodds come straight in?'

'Dodds. I remember saying we weren't expecting royalty, and she said they were short-staffed, so she decided to come herself to save waiting for one of the pupils to come back.'

'Short-staffed, my arse!' I put the phone down and compose myself, then ring Finchley Associates.

'Inspector Crow, I wish I could say it's a pleasure.'

Carol Dodds and I have the sort of relationship every good policeman has with every good defence lawyer. 'Good to hear you too,' I say, and before she can cut me off, 'I understand you are representing my daughter.'

'I'm afraid I'm unable to discuss my caseload with you, Inspector – as you know perfectly well.'

'She's my daughter, for God's sake!' I tell myself to keep hold of my temper, but most of me isn't listening.

'She's still my client. And you are a serving police officer. Even if you weren't, I still couldn't discuss it.'

There's about as much sympathy in her tone as there is water in a block of granite. Nevertheless, she's slipped up and given me the confirmation I need, so I carry on, encouraged.

'I'm not serving,' I remind her. 'I'm on sick leave. I'm not involved with the case, and ...'

'Good,' she says. 'Let's keep it that way.'

It's clear that the subtle approach isn't going to get me any further. 'Look, *Ms* Dodds, I don't believe for one minute that you just happened to be passing by West Hill nick when Rosie was arrested, then decided to drop in and do her a favour. So why don't you tell me just what your bloody game is –'

'Word is,' Dodds interrupts, 'you're out on your ear, Inspector. That you've become unstable since that drugs bust you were in charge of a few months back – you remember the one? A colleague of yours was killed, if I remember correctly. I don't have to speak to you, and I'm extremely busy. If you will excuse me ...'

Damn the woman. 'Wait – please. Look, I'm on your side. I'm Rosie's father. I want to help.'

There's a pause and then, 'Mrs Larson doesn't want your help, Inspector.'

'Maybe not, Ms Dodds, but she needs it.' I have a sudden

inspiration. 'I'm calling at her husband's request. He asked if I would meet with you – check with him if you like.'

Another pause, and I hear a rush of air as she snorts out a breath. 'You can be sure I'll do that, Inspector.'

She hangs up, leaving me swearing at the dial tone. Jesus! Why can't I have a simple conversation with anybody these days without getting their backs up? When I think about it, though, pleasantries have never been at the top of my skills list. The phone's ringing, and I grab it before I have the chance to think. It's Dodds – she isn't wasting any time.

'I'll see you at six thirty,' she says, 'at the Spyglass – with Mr Larson or not at all.' She doesn't waste words either.

I look at my watch – it's half past five already. Then I remember I don't have a car. After weighing up the alternatives, it's clear there is only one real choice, and I root around in the drawer for my mobile – the 'dog lead' I used to call it in the days when everything was normal. It strikes me now, though, that given my new-found aversion to remote communication, it might come in handy. Luckily the battery isn't quite dead. I scroll until Rosie's name appears on the screen, and tap in a text message:

> Be here in half an hour. Crow.

I'm about to press 'send' when I realise the boy wonder probably doesn't know where I live, so I add my address, put the phone on charge, and make my way upstairs in the vain hope of finding a clean shirt.

THE SPYGLASS, a bar/restaurant on Bristol's harbourside, got its name from the eighteenth-century waterfront windows through which smugglers and their clientele kept watch for customs men and press gangs. Fast-forward a couple of centuries to the early seventies and the place got more of a reputation for tough steak than tough customers. Like many middle-income-bracket kids in those days, I was dragged along on special family occasions to gorge myself on prawn cocktail, a rubbery half duck garnished with an orange slice, apple pie and ice cream. In recent years, though, it's gone upmarket, an after-work haunt for the financial and legal crowd, serving flatbreads, tapas and Prosecco. I preferred it when it was a Berni Inn.

Larson parks up in the Mud Dock car park and leaves me to struggle out of his 1970s red MG Midget while he fiddles with the ticket machine. He's done a bit of preening since the morning – the rumpled suit has been exchanged for shabby-chic jeans, suede loafers and a white T-shirt. What the hell does Rosie see in this pretentious idiot? Then again, he did turn up on time, and at least one of us will blend in at what passes round here for a public bar. I do a quick calculation of how long he'd last in that getup in the Sinkhole, and decide it would be just slightly longer than his car. There's a giggle behind me, and I turn to find a couple of teenage girls staring, their eyes flitting from me to the MG and back again. For a fleeting instant, the face of the kid who carved his mark on my car door floats in front of my eyes. The girls stop giggling and totter away on too-high heels, whispering to each other.

Larson comes up behind me and tosses a ticket onto his windscreen. 'Sorry – damned machine kept spitting out the coins. Inspector? Are you all right?'

I realise I'm still staring after the girls and that the expression on my face probably scared them to death. 'Let's get on with this,' I say, and start walking.

The pub's fairly crowded, and it takes me a minute to spot Carol Dodds. She's laid claim to a small table by the far window with a view of the harbour, a defensive wall of files and assorted papers strewn across the surface, strategically

placed to repel boarders. Larson shoulders a path to my
elbow and hands me a small bottle of mineral water and a
glass half filled with ice and lemon, which probably cost
more than the Pinot Grigio he's clutching in his other hand. I
let him lead the way to Dodds's table, wishing to God my
glass was full of Scotch or, better still, that I wasn't here at all.
I'm under strict orders not to mix alcohol with my medica-
tion. Sometimes I ignore the advice, but right now I need to
keep control of the corridor between my brain and my
mouth, and it's already becoming a struggle.

Dodds half rises and turns the smile on full beam for
Larson's benefit. 'John, come and sit down; you look tired.'
She clears a space, sliding some of the papers back into her
briefcase. The switch flicks off as she turns to me. 'Inspector.'

I hunch into the remaining chair and have to reach over
two box files to find somewhere to put my drink.

'How is she?' Larson's asking. 'Did you see her this
afternoon?'

'Bearing up well,' Dodds says, leaning over to give his arm
a squeeze. 'Don't worry, John, she's fine – more worried about
you than anything else – and Ben of course.'

I want to say of course she's not bloody fine. She's in a ten-
foot-square cell that stinks of piss, terrified out of her wits
and listening to some drugged-up arsehole puking his guts
all over the corridor in the basement of West Hill nick. And
while my Rosie's sitting there wondering what the hell's
happening, her husband and her lawyer are sitting, patting
each other's hands and drinking overpriced cat pee in a
harbourside pub discussing how tired they are. I clamp my
mouth shut, pick up Dodds's box files and let them drop.
They hit the floor with a satisfying smack. Larson and Dodds
both turn to me, Larson blinking as if he's just crawled out of
a pothole, Dodds looking as if she's a whisker away from slap-
ping my face.

I pick up my water and take a sip. 'Sorry.'

For a few beats there's a standoff; then Dodds leans back. 'Look, Inspector, I understand this is very difficult for you.'

'Do you really?' I can't help saying, and just manage to leave it at that. Larson is switching his gaze from one of us to the other, like a kid who's not quite sure which playground bully is going to snatch his lollipop first. 'Look,' I say to Dodds, trying to sound reasonable, 'we're all after the same thing here – we all want to help Rosie. Like I said on the phone, she may not want my help, but she *needs* it. And you must know that – you wouldn't be here otherwise.'

'I'm here,' Dodds says stiffly, 'because John begged me to see you. He seems to think you can be of some use. My client, on the other hand, has specifically stated that she doesn't want you involved, which puts me in a very difficult position.' She lets out a sigh and takes a glug of her wine. 'I don't like you, Inspector, and I have serious doubts that your involvement will be anything more than a hindrance to Mrs Larson's case. However, I can't pretend the situation isn't extremely serious, and I would be failing in my duty to my client if I didn't explore all the possibilities. So if you have anything of value to offer, please do enlighten us.'

I may not like the woman, but I can't fault her logic. I look her right in the eyes. 'Do you think she did it?'

Larson stiffens and shoots me a horrified glare, but Dodds holds up a hand, and for a second I think she might even smile.

'No,' she says, 'I don't.'

'Why?'

She hesitates, fiddles with the olive bowl, drains her glass and waggles it at Larson. It takes him a minute, but eventually he gets up and reluctantly slopes off to the crowded bar. I fold my arms and wait.

'I don't need to tell you, Inspector, that whatever I say now is completely confidential.'

'You're right,' I reply. 'You don't need to tell me.'

There's another hesitation and then a curt nod. 'Three years ago, I met up with an old friend – we studied law together at Oxford.'

Oxford – where else? 'Go on,' I say.

'We had a few drinks and discussed old cases, you know?'

I know very well – I can imagine the pair of them giggling over a few bottles of whatever turns them on, talking fees and promotions and victories over the plods – that's me and ordinary law-abiding citizens – I nod and keep my mouth shut.

'She moved to Inverness after graduation and was back visiting family. She told me about a case – her first big trial. It involved a nurse who had an affair with a sectioned patient, one Steven Crossland, on a psychiatric ward. The nurse bent the rules, let the patient out on a day release. The first thing he did was break into a house in the suburbs and murder the occupant, a woman in her fifties – random killing according to the police. The nurse was arrested and charged with aiding and abetting. Her defence was that she hadn't signed the release form and knew nothing about it.'

She pauses to give me time for this to sink in. 'Details of the murder?' I ask, aware of a tremor starting up in my hands. I hide one under the table and grip my glass with the other.

'Decapitation with a wood axe.'

'And the nurse?'

Dodds shakes her head. 'The defence got nowhere. She was found guilty and got ten years.' She pauses, and I get the impression that for once she doesn't quite know how to phrase the next part of the story. 'For God's sake don't tell John this,' she says eventually. 'Two years in, she was found hanged in her cell. Verdict, suicide, unable to cope with being on the inside.'

'Shit!' I glance across to the bar. Larson is still waiting to get served. 'So when you heard about Rosie ...'

'The clerk took the call and passed it to one of my pupils. She came to me, and when I heard the details, I went straight over to West Hill. I didn't find out my client was your daughter until your desk sergeant told me. Not that it would have made any difference, you understand.'

She gives me a meaningful look, which I ignore. 'You think there's a connection between the two cases?'

She shrugs. 'That was my first thought, but I don't see how. Publicity was kept to a minimum, so a copycat is very unlikely.'

I think about this for a moment or two. 'The murder was eight years ago, yes?'

'Spring 2010 – the trial took a good few months, conviction November of that year.'

'And Harold Shaw first came to our attention some six years ago on a GBH charge. What if, before that ...'

'I've already thought of that, Inspector. There's no way Crossland and Shaw are the same person.'

'You're certain of that?'

'Absolutely. You see, Crossland was found two weeks after the beheading face down in the River Ness just downstream of Greig Street Bridge. Whether he fell or was pushed was never established. All the information I have points to the similarities between the two cases being pure coincidence.'

Out of the corner of my eye, I see Larson struggling his way back to the table with two more glasses of wine and another bottle of water. 'I don't believe in coincidence,' I tell Dodds. 'Do you?' There's an almost imperceptible shake of the head. I lower my voice. 'You don't like me, Ms Dodds. I don't particularly like you. But I think you're a good barrister, and you *know* I'm a good detective. It's like I said – Rosie may not want me, but right now she bloody well needs me. And so do you.' I get up just as Larson reaches us and plonks his burdens on the table. 'I'll be in touch,' I say to Dodds, and push my way out into the fresh air.

I'm almost at the corner when I hear a shout and turn to see Larson running up behind me. Christ, that man is getting up my nose. 'Inspector, wait – can't I give you a lift home?'

I look past him into the car park and his godawful MG. 'Have you got another car?'

He nods. 'Rosie's got a Volvo – it's in the garage at home. Why?'

'Pick me up in it – eight sharp in the morning.'

'But, Inspector ...'

'Go and finish your chat,' I say over my shoulder as I carry on towards the city centre, 'but if I were you, I'd stick to water if you're going to drive that thing home. Don't worry about me. I'll get the bus.'

# 5

L arson shifts from foot to foot, hands in the pockets of the suit he was wearing yesterday morning. I can't decide which looks more ragged, him or the suit. We're standing under a steady drizzle on the pavement outside the magistrates' court, watching an escort van with blacked-out rear windows edge its way towards the double doors at the side of the building.

'They've got my Rosie in that thing?' He's shaking his head in disbelief. I'm shaking at the sound of him calling her *my* Rosie.

'Nah,' I say, 'the judge comes in the van. They bring the prisoner in a Lamborghini.'

His eyes spark, and for a second I think he might actually square up to me, but Dodds arrives and distracts him. She ignores me and says, 'Don't worry, John, I'm going down to see her now. I'm going to ask for bail to be set, but I have to warn you, it's very unlikely to be successful. I do need to be sure you can cover a pretty substantial amount, though, just in case they go for it – up to a hundred thousand. Can you?'

He nods at once. 'Yes, of course.'

Yes – of course he can. I should have cottoned onto that yesterday – vintage sports car and pre-torn jeans from Harvey Nicols – maybe, I think, feeling a little shred of hope, what Rosie really fell in love with was the lifestyle, and Larson is just an inconvenient trade-off. Right on the back of that thought I see the alternative, and much more likely, scenario. Rosie went for Larson because he's about as different from me as anyone could get. He's well off, he's sensitive, and he might be out of his depth, but he's not a complete idiot. If this is who she's ended up with, I've got nobody else to blame. I glance across at the van. *My* Rosie – in that thing. Christ!

Dodds issues a general instruction to stay well away from the courtroom, and heads off through the main door.

'Do you think there's any chance ...' Larson stutters, reverting to his familiar feeble self, rain dripping from the end of his nose.

I grab his arm and pull him into the foyer, out of the drizzle and into a noisy gaggle of hacks, mostly local, although I recognise a couple of chancers from the *Mirror* and the *Daily Mail*. 'Not a bloody hope,' I tell him and, keeping a tight grip on his arm, pull him away from the disorderly queue of journalists waiting to be let into the courtroom.

'Why?' he's insisting. 'Surely they know she wouldn't run away or try to ... well ...' He can't bring himself to say it – try to make contact with Harold Shaw. 'And you're a policeman,' he goes on. 'Doesn't that count for anything?'

'It counts for nothing,' I snap, and then force myself to remember that this kid's only contact with the law has probably been to ask a policeman the time. I try to be gentler. 'Listen to me, son. This is a magistrates' court. They can't deal with cases like this ...'

'Why are we here, then? I thought ...'

I suck in my breath and try not to swear again. Hasn't

Dodds given him the drill? Sure she has, but he's in such a state it probably went right over his head. 'Just shut up,' I growl, 'and listen.'

He nods and zips his lips together in a thin line.

'This hearing will probably be over in under a minute. All they will do is hear the charge and refer the case to the Crown Court. The charge isn't actual murder, so Dodds is entitled to ask for bail, but they will most likely turn it down. The real bail hearing will be at the Crown Court in a couple of days. It's a good bet they'll turn it down there, too. You have to be prepared for that.' I pause and can't help adding, under my breath, 'We both do.'

There's a scuffle as the door to the courtroom opens, and the queue becomes a scrum. Larson jerks forward, stops himself and throws me a glance. For once, we're both on the same page. 'Stick to me and keep your mouth shut,' I tell him and plunge into the melee, digging in my jacket for my wallet. At the door I flash my warrant card to the usher and mutter, 'He's with me,' hoping Larson's done as he's told and has glued himself to my back. A few seconds later we're huddled in seats on the back row, shielded from the dock and the magistrate's bench by a cordon of jostling reporters. Their eagerness and snatches of conversation confirm my fears – word's got around, and they all want to be first to get to the front page with a lurid account of the demon bitch who let a crazed killer loose on West Hill. Half a dozen court artists have grabbed seats with the clearest view of the dock and are chatting amiably, words punctuated by gestures from sharpened pencils. One or two I recognise from previous cases. They won't have long to get their sketches, maybe less than a minute, but I know from experience that it's more than they need. By tomorrow morning Rosie's image will be plastered all over the downmarket rags.

I glance at Larson pasty and sweating in the seat next to

me, jaw clenched so hard I can see the muscles twitching. I grab his arm again. 'Keep quiet and keep still, you understand me?'

He doesn't respond, eyes wide and staring, fixed on the spot where Rosie will appear.

I give him a sharp shake and speak very slowly. 'I said, do you understand me?'

He jerks his head in a nod but keeps on staring. It will have to do.

Rosie's case is second up. The first is a seventeen-year-old public schoolboy who fancies himself the next Banksy, but whose depictions of the Kama Sutra on the walls of the public toilets in Millennium Square haven't quite drawn the same plaudits. There's a tedious ten-minute exchange between the district judge and the boy's family barrister, mainly concerning the father's offer to pay for the damage. The impatient shuffling among the press increases in volume until finally the kid's ushered from the court with an ASBO and a hefty fine.

As soon as he's gone, an expectant hush settles. The journalists hunch forward, the artists have their pencils poised like a graphite firing squad taking aim above their sketchpads. I feel Larson next to me, rigid as a corpse, and realise my teeth are aching from being clamped together too long. My hands are trembling again. A door opens, and suddenly my breakfast is threatening to upend itself all over the courtroom floor.

It's a little over five years since I last saw Rosie. She was nineteen, just a kid, halfway through the second year of her nursing degree at Plymouth University. I remember exactly what she was wearing that last day. She was getting ready for a party – black tights, a purple Lurex skater dress that stopped where her thighs started, little black boots with six-inch heels, wild dark hair and a tiny amethyst stud in one nostril. She looked terrible, but beautiful at the same time. My little girl, all grown up – I was afraid for her, proud of her ... she broke my heart.

Now it's breaking again. The woman who walks into the court looks nothing like my Rosie. She's wearing the clothes Dodds has no doubt told her to wear – a grey, nondescript trouser suit and flat black shoes. Her hair is scraped back in an unflattering ponytail. Her face is as grey as the suit, her eyes dazed and rimmed with red like a boxer who's taken too many punches. All that feistiness I used to know has gone, and worst of all she looks old – so much older than I thought she would. She's twenty-five now, but if I didn't know, I'd peg her at mid-thirties. But underneath it all it's still my Rosie, and I watch her take faltering steps to the dock, white fingers gripping the court officer's arm. She doesn't look up, not even once, and in a way I'm glad about that. I don't want her to see the crap that's going on around her, and I don't want her to see me. Not now, not yet – maybe not ever. As I look on, I have only one thought – the fucking bastard who put my baby here is going to pay.

Dodds has walked up to the front and is about to start her spiel, but I'm not really listening. I've zoned out, fogged with the effort of trying to disentangle one emotion from another. And that's why I don't check to make sure Larson's behaving himself, don't feel his muscles flex the split second before he launches himself over the reporters and towards the dock, yelling Rosie's name, kicking and punching at anyone in his way, tearing at the artists' pads as he stumbles over a row of seats and falls into the aisle. It must take only a second for my brain to reconnect with my body, but it seems like much longer. Then I'm on autopilot, ploughing through the gap he's made in the front row in time to land on top of him just before the court officials get there. They back off as I wave my credentials and haul Larson to his feet. For a moment everything stops, the entire court stunned into silence, and I look up, straight into Rosie's eyes. She's frozen, staring at me with a look that swerves between horror, contempt, and just plain shock.

Everything starts moving again, and there's a uniformed constable beside us, grabbing Larson's other arm. Together, we manhandle Larson out of the court and into a side room down the corridor. Thankfully he doesn't struggle, but he doesn't relax either. We push him into a chair, and I take the uniform by the arm. 'Would you mind waiting outside, Constable?' I ask him in the most reasonable tone I can manage. He looks doubtful, so I add, 'Look, it's the defendant's husband – it was just a bit too much for him, that's all. I promise I won't do anything I shouldn't. Scout's honour.' I make a little 'V for victory' sign, smile, and don't add that what I really want to do is beat seven shades out of the stupid little bugger.

The officer thinks about it and finally shoots Larson a sympathetic glance. 'I'll be just outside, sir.' He opens the door and turns back to me. 'I could try to rustle up some coffee if you like, sir. There's a machine just down the hall.'

'That would be very nice, Constable.' I close the door and flop into a chair, pulling it up until our knees are almost touching. Larson, still rigid, doesn't appear to notice. He's staring at his shoes and breathing hard through his nose, hands clenched into fists on his knees. 'Well,' I tell him, 'you picked a fine time to grow a pair of balls, son.'

His gaze snaps up to meet mine. The spark I saw earlier is well kindled now. The whine has completely gone from his voice as he says, 'My name is John. Not "son" or "tosser" or anything else you feel like calling me. It's John. Do you understand?'

I struggle to remember if I've called him a tosser out loud, and decide I haven't, which means he's a lot more perceptive than I've given him credit for. I let his declaration hang for a couple of beats, and then nod. 'Your name is John. I understand, son.'

At that he pulls back an arm – one with a fist at the end of it. I'm close enough to get hurt if he takes a swing, but he wavers and, after a few hissing breaths, drops the arm into his lap.

'I couldn't bear it,' he says, very quietly, still meeting my eye. 'I couldn't bear my Rosie like that, so' – I can see him struggling to get the right word out and know how he feels – 'so scared,' he ends, and shakes his head.

I understand at once what he means. Rosie was never scared of anything. My mind goes back to the time I took her to Weston Pier. She was two years old, and I dropped her reins to let her toddle off by herself just to see how far she'd go before she turned round to look for me. She never did – she just kept right on going, and it was me who broke first and rushed after her. 'I know,' I say. 'I couldn't bear it either.'

He called her 'my Rosie' again, but suddenly I'm too drained to feel anything but fear for my girl. We sit in silence until the door crashes open, and Dodds storms in, pushing aside the constable who's outside clutching two steaming paper cups. The hot coffee ends up down the front of his uniform, and I hear him yelp out a curse as Dodds slams the door.

She aims her mouth right at Larson. 'What the bloody hell ...'

I don't let her finish. Something deep in my brain tilts, and before I know it, I'm on my feet, and my chair's bounced off the wall so hard one of the legs has splintered. I want to tell her to just shut the fuck up, but the words won't come. In the end, though, my expression must be enough. Her mouth snaps shut, and we glare at each other for a full ten seconds, then she breathes and holds up a hand. 'Okay.' There's just one usable vacant chair left, and she flops into it. 'Okay,' she says again more quietly, and looks at Larson, who's staring blankly at his hands. 'I managed to smooth things over in there. As long as you apologise to the court, they've promised to take a lenient view under the circumstances. Are you willing to do that, John?'

He doesn't answer, but I give her a nod, partly on his behalf and partly to show that I appreciate her effort. I ask the question for both of us. 'What about Rosie?'

'Remanded in custody, and the case has been referred to the Crown Court.' She lets out a sigh. 'I said the plea would be not guilty and requested bail, but it was never going to happen. There will be a bail hearing within the next forty-eight hours – I'll let you know as soon as I do.'

She's done her best, I know that, and grudgingly tell her so. She acknowledges it with a grunt and says, without looking at me, 'Thanks for what you did in there – it could have been a lot worse, I suppose.'

That's true enough. I look at the broken chair – it could have been a lot worse in here too. 'At least,' I reply, 'thanks to you we've managed to keep vandalism off the list. That policeman outside is probably in the lavatory drying his shirt.'

She shoots me a glance, and I think I see the glimmer of a smile. 'I'd better go and see my client,' she says, getting up and straightening her skirt. 'Look after him, won't you.'

Larson hasn't said a word or looked at either of us. He's hunched into himself like a crumpled paper sack, staring at the wall. 'You can be sure of that,' I say. The question I don't ask is, who the hell is going to look after me?


AN HOUR LATER, we're back out in the rain, and I'm regretting my promise to Dodds. If I'm going to be of any use to Rosie, I need to focus, and that will be hard enough. Trying to babysit a dead-weight husband who looks like he's on the verge of a nervous breakdown is likely to shatter what little concentration I have left. He's recovered a bit since we left the court, but he still looks as if I'd only have to blow hard to knock him over.

'Sodding hell,' I mutter to myself, and start back towards the car park, not trusting myself to look back in case I say something I might regret later.

'What are we going to do now?' he asks as we ease out onto the main road.

'I know what I'm going to do, son,' I tell him, still trying hard to keep my thoughts in the right tramlines. 'I'm going to go home and get out of these wet clothes before I catch pneumonia. If you've got any sense, you'll do the same.'

He doesn't answer, just presses his lips together and drives, so we spend the rest of the journey in blessed silence. When we pull up at my place, he still doesn't speak, and I'm halfway to my front door before I realise he's out of the car and trotting after me. I spin round so fast he stumbles and almost breaks his nose on my chest.

'For Christ's sake,' I say, pulling him upright, 'I told you to bugger off home.'

I give him a light push for emphasis. He staggers, but stands his ground. 'Whatever you're going to do,' he says, 'I want to help.'

That's all I need. 'You can help me by staying out of my way. Rosie's my daughter, and ...'

'She's my bloody wife!' It's the first time I've heard him shout. 'I'm not as stupid as you think, Inspector, and maybe I'm not as useless either. Whether you like it or not, I'm not going to sit at home doing nothing.' He shrugs. 'I can't.'

I can understand that, and while he's been getting it off

his chest, I've realised that I might have a use for him after all. 'How are you with phones?' I ask.

'What?'

'Phones – you know, you dial a number and talk to whoever's on the other end. You any good at that, son?'

He blinks at me, wondering if I'm winding him up. 'I suppose so – and my name isn't 'son', it's …'

'Yes, you told me. It's John. Well, John, if you get in your car, turn left at the end of the road and take the first right, you'll find a chippie three doors down. Mine's haddock, chips and peas. I'll leave the door on the latch.' He's halfway down the path when I remember. 'John?'

'Yes, Inspector?'

'No salt and vinegar.'

# 6

I n the familiar territory of my living room, the fog lifts, and my brain slots back into something resembling logical process. A year ago I would have been right on top of the situation. I wouldn't have gone into the hearing, and I certainly wouldn't have let Larson anywhere near the courtroom. Dodds was right. The last thing Rosie needed this morning was the sight of her husband and her father rolling around on the floor like a couple of brawling drunks. I need Dodds onside, and I've just made that harder for myself. As for Rosie, if I wanted to prove to her that I'm not the thug she thinks I am, I've done a bloody fine job. Maybe I should listen to what everyone is telling me. I'm sick in the head, my judgement is off, and I can't hack it anymore. Christ, what a mess.

Larson has changed into designer track pants and a T-shirt from a holdall in the boot of his car and is in one of my armchairs, staring out the window and sipping the tea he rustled up for us after lunch. He doesn't make a bad brew, I have to admit, and I take the opportunity to study the man my daughter married a little more closely. He's good looking in the scruffy way girls go for these days, blond, toned, a regular at whatever fancy gym he pays a small mortgage to belong to. I peg him as more a treadmill and exercise bike man than weights and boxing. He might know how to make a fist, but from the look of his hands, he's never used one. I picture him with Rosie, in the kitchen smooching over pasta and glasses of Prosecco, and with my grandson, a perfect New Age dad at toddler group when Rosie's got a weekend shift. He's the husband and father I never was, and what's really pathetic is that I can't forgive him for it.

'Are you all right, Inspector?'

I've drifted off again and scramble to get the mental spaghetti back in the pan. 'Don't mind me, son ...' He stiffens. What the bloody hell is it with him? Still, if we're going to do Rosie any good, we've both got to make the effort. I hold up a hand. 'Sorry – bad habit.'

He lets out a sigh and frowns into his mug. 'And just how many of those have you got, Inspector?' He looks up, still frowning, but there's a glimmer in his eye that might be a touch of humour.

'Believe me,' I say, 'we haven't scratched the surface.'

He thinks about this, then gives me a slow nod. 'I suppose being an arsehole is part of your job description.' There's that spark again. I'm slowly starting to warm to him. He goes on, 'But I'd be grateful, Inspector, if you would try to remember that I'm a normal person, not one of your petty criminals.'

I decided a long time ago that anyone who thinks they are 'normal' is probably delusional, but let it go. Winding him up again isn't going to do anything except make me feel better. 'I'll do my best,' I say, but can't help adding, 'No promises.' Before he has a chance to object, I ask, 'Did Rosie have any friends up at the hospital? Close friends I mean, not just people she worked with?'

He scratches his head and sits back. 'One or two I think – she went out on the occasional girls' night.' He considers.

'There was one who came round to our place a few times, mostly when I was working away – Jenny, her name was, but I don't know the last name. She had a little boy around Ben's age, and they used to meet up on Rosie's days off, in the park or a coffee shop ...' He stops and lets out a groan. 'Christ! I'm talking about her in the past tense for God's sake ...'

Before I know what I'm doing, I've leaned over and patted his shoulder. 'It's okay, son. We're going to get her out of this. There's a couple of things I need to do, but while I'm gone, you can help out here. Are you any good with a computer?'

He blinks at me in surprise and nods. 'It's one of the things I *am* good at – why?'

I explain the conversation I had with Dodds last night. 'Anything you can find out about that case in Scotland might be useful, and I mean anything. It's eight years ago, but it must have made a pretty big splash at the time. You still might be able to find news reports, interviews, names of investigating officers – all that might come in handy. And before you get started, ring Dodds and tell her to bring round copies of any evidence they've got against Rosie. As the defence barrister, she's entitled to disclosure from the prosecution, and it's my bet she's nipping at their ankles for it already. Don't take no for an answer. You think you can manage that?'

'Sure. But what are you going to do?'

I give him a grin. 'What I'm best at, son. Like you said, being an arsehole is part of my job description – mainly because nine times out of ten it gets the quickest result. I take it you won't mind if I borrow your car?'

I HAVE to sit for a full five minutes behind the wheel of the Volvo before flicking the ignition key, hoping Larson isn't staring through the window wondering what the hell I'm doing. In the last twenty-four hours I've managed to negotiate the Sinkhole, a crowded pub and the sight of my daughter in a courtroom dock. Any one of those things could have brought on a brain freeze – so why is it that my faulty circuits choose to short out when I'm faced with the simple task of driving someone else's car? A year ago it wouldn't have given me any trouble despite the fact that my old rust bucket is a manual and this one's automatic. It's pretty new, too – probably no more than a few months old, and the panel's got more symbols than the bloody Rosetta Stone. The jitters come out of nowhere, and suddenly I might as well be looking at the business end of a space shuttle.

Rogers warned me this might happen now and then. He told me the way to deal with it is to relax, give it time and not fight it or get frustrated. I close my eyes and try to take deep breaths. When that doesn't work, I imagine myself as I was twenty-odd years ago, with Rosie on our first trip to the zoo. I'm lifting her in one arm so she can see the giant tortoise, and delving with my free hand for a handkerchief to wipe her face clean of the sticky remains of a chocolate ice cream. I'm telling her the story of the tortoise and the hare ...

I've become like a tortoise over the last few months – at least my brain has – but the tortoise in the story, I remind myself, was the one who won the race. I open my eyes, and the world is back to normal. Somewhere out there, a hare is running, and whatever it takes, I'm going to catch it.

EVERY SO OFTEN, life throws up a stroke of good fortune, mostly when it's least expected. I get to Portishead mid-afternoon and head not for the main police headquarters, the West Country's greatest bastion of uniformed pen-pushers, but for the small-town nick, a place very like West Hill but without the evil reputation. I'm through the door heading for the front desk, still mulling over how I'm going to get my hands on the information I need, when I hear a shout behind me.

'Inspector? Inspector Crow?'

I spin round and feel a moment of dread as I stare into a face that is totally unfamiliar. Luckily, the uniformed sergeant trotting up to me doesn't wait for a sign of recognition.

'It is you, boss!' He grabs my hand and gives it an enthusiastic pump. 'Benson – you probably don't remember me. I was one of your babies when I did my stint over in the Sinkhole, ooh, must have been ten years back. I heard you got a bravery medal after that shooting business. Good on you, boss – we were all dead proud – if anyone deserved it, it was you. But what are you doing out here in the sticks? Anything I can help you with, just say the word. I mean, you covered our arses enough times back in those days ...' He stops and lets out an embarrassed cough. 'God, I forgot – your daughter ...'

I wave a dismissive hand, not wanting to get stuck down that alley. 'Of course I remember you, Benson,' I lie, 'and it looks like you've done well for yourself. Congratulations.' And so, for once, Lady Luck is shining down in all her glory, and I'm not going to start any arguments with her. 'I suppose you've heard all the gossip?'

Benson gives a sympathetic shake of the head. 'Who hasn't? Bloody awful business by the sound of it.' I see the light go on. 'Ah, of course – you want to know about Harold Shaw. Well, you've come to the right place. I was one of the arresting officers six years or so ago – a lowly PC back then. Funny, but I never would have pegged him as the type to take anyone's head off.'

'Why not?'

Benson shrugs. 'Well, he was a nutter, that much was obvious, but ... well, there was method in his madness. He had a reason, found out his missus was getting more than free G&Ts at the local, know what I mean? Look, you want a coffee? It's one of those bloody machines, but it's not too bad. I'm on refs for the next fifteen minutes, and I can fill you in.'

I manage to nod, and might even be giving him a smile, but my head's taken a dive, and I'm five years away, staring at Terence the tosser in a heap at the bottom of my ex-wife's stairs and Rosie, in the doorway of her bedroom, dressed to kill and screaming, mascara running and making her face look like someone's beaten it to a pulp.

'What do you fancy?' Benson's asking, finger poised over the keypad of the coffee machine. 'We've got all sorts here – latte, mocha, cappu-bloody-ccino. Give me a kettle and a jar of Nescafé any day.'

I pull myself together. 'You got straight black, extra sugar?'

'Man after my own heart, boss.' He grins and jabs a few buttons. 'Mind your fingers, the cups are crap – our inspector's threatening to charge the company with GBH since he got his hand burned last week.'

I take the thin plastic cup and manage to dump it on one of the two cramped tables that pass for a staff canteen before the heat forces me to drop it on the floor. I imagine the facilities at head office down the road – waiter service, a choice of wine and nouvelle cuisine for the chief constable and his Met cronies. I'd rather have scalded fingers.

'So,' I ask as we sit down, 'about Shaw – what's the real story?'

Benson leans forward and lowers his voice, even though the only other person I've seen in the building is at the front desk, one floor up. 'I'm not saying Harry was an angel,' he says, gingerly testing the temperature of his cup, 'because he wasn't, not by a long way. But he wasn't an out-and-out thug either. Had a record stretching as far as the marina, but all petty stuff and mostly under the influence – drunk and disorderly, pub brawls, that sort of thing. It was only when he hooked up with Monica that things really started to go downhill fast.'

'Monica?'

'His missus – a nasty little piece with a record longer than Harry's. Drugs, prostitution, you name it. Her last conviction was less than a year ago, obtaining money by deception. She was lucky not to get sent down. Anyway, she led Harry a dance until he found out she was shagging the landlord at the Old Duck. He had a skin full, went over there and sorted the pair of them out. Next thing, he's up on charges, and before he knows what's hit him, he's banged up for five years. Between you and me, I don't think Monica was too upset – she'd had enough of him by that time – not keeping her in the manner to which she was accustomed.'

I feel a tremor, but this time it's got nothing to do with the hole in my brain. 'So Shaw puts his wife's lover in intensive care, but you don't think he's capable of sawing a woman's head off with a bread knife?'

Benson shakes his head. 'No, boss, I don't. Shaw was only ever violent when he was drunk – admittedly he was pissed quite a lot, but even so ... from what I've heard, it was quite a performance. Whoever did it cut the head off and placed it very carefully in front of the door – you'd have to be pretty sober to do that, I reckon.'

'Maybe he was. He'd been in a mental hospital for a long while, and I think alcohol is pretty much frowned on in those places. Booze would have interfered with the drugs anyway – especially for schizophrenia.'

'Schizophrenia?' Benson gives me an incredulous look. 'Whoever made that diagnosis needs their head looking at – if you'll pardon the pun. Not that I'm an expert, mind, but I just put him down as a miserable bugger with a soft spot for cheap Scotch. When he was sober, he was more pathetic than anything else. Monica ran rings round him – he'd have cut off his own dick if she'd asked him to, stupid sod.' He looks at his watch and pushes himself to his feet. 'Sorry, boss, I'd better get back out before my inspector comes hunting. If you need more information, you know where to find me.'

I follow him out and sit in Larson's car for a few minutes, mulling over Benson's assessment of Harold Shaw. Like he says, he's not an expert on mental health, but even though I still don't remember him, I know an observant copper when I see one. That little inner tremor is starting to vibrate a bit stronger. I fire up the engine and head back towards town.

COOMBE HILL HOSPITAL, a mile or so north of Bristol city centre, isn't the most inviting building in the world. It still has its original Victorian façade of blackened brick – the only concession to the twenty-first century is the replacement of iron bars at the windows with toughened safety glass. It takes around twenty minutes to find a parking space, during which I'm grinding my teeth with the effort of trying to stay calm. By the time I switch off the engine, I'm sweating so much my hand slips off the brake. The place seriously scares the shit out of me, mainly because for months after the shooting I had nightmares about ending up in a place like this, a drooling vegetable parked in a corridor somewhere, having my intimate bodily functions seen to by some gorilla of an attendant hell-bent on stripping any dignity I might have had left. I try to pull myself together – Rosie works here, for God's sake, so how bad can it be? Maybe I've watched *One Flew over the Cuckoo's Nest* too many times – that, or too many *Panorama* exposés. I force my legs to move, and follow the signs for main reception.

Once again, my warrant card comes in handy. So far I've managed to get away with it, but it's not going to be long before the powers that be realise they've got an officer prowling around who should be sitting at home watching TV and waiting to get booted into retirement. Jenny Pugh is a cheerful, good-looking woman in her mid-thirties, whose smile doesn't waver as she guides me to a small side room on the ground floor.

'I'm afraid I can't give you much time, Inspector,' she says, perching on the arm of a chair as if to emphasise the point, 'we're terribly short-staffed, and it's coming up to the busiest time of the day. If there's anything I can do to help poor Rosie though ...' The smile slips into a sort of professional concern. 'I'm sure she wouldn't have done anything to help that man, at least not intentionally. But I've said all this already. Have you found out something? Is that why you're here?'

I weigh up the situation and hope I'm not making a bad decision. 'Actually,' I tell her, 'this isn't official.'

Her eyes narrow.

'Don't worry,' I add quickly, 'I'm a real policeman – and I suspect I'm about to get into an awful lot of trouble with my bosses for being here. If you want to complain to my superiors, it'll just mean I'll be in the shit a bit sooner than I'd like, but go ahead if you don't feel comfortable talking to me.'

I watch the understanding dawn on her face. 'You're Rosie's dad, aren't you?'

I nod. At least she's told her friends she's *got* a dad. 'Her husband, John, got in touch with me. He thought I could help, and that's what I'm trying to do. We both want to see her where she belongs – at home, with Ben. What do you say – will you talk to me?'

'Hang on.' She gets up and leaves the room, and I hold my breath, half expecting her to come back with security. When she returns, she's alone. 'One of my colleagues is covering for me,' she says, sitting down, this time properly. 'What do you want to know?'

'Thank you, Jenny.' Rosie's got at least one good friend

here, and I'm glad. I also get the impression she's keen to say things she hasn't been able to say until now. The question is, what? 'What can you tell me about Harold Shaw?' I ask. She purses her lips – I'm right – there is something she hasn't told the official police, but she needs to tell somebody. 'It's okay,' I reassure her. 'If anyone's going to get in trouble over this, it's me. Nothing you tell me will go any further, I give you my word.' That's probably a lie, but like Larson said, being an arsehole comes with the territory. I give her an encouraging smile.

'Okay. He came to us from Millbank Prison just over three years ago, suffering with bipolar disorder – the authorities judged him a risk to himself and others, and it was thought he'd be better off in a secure treatment unit.'

'Wait a minute – I thought he was diagnosed with paranoid schizophrenia?'

There's a small hesitation, and I can see her tossing up whether to go for it. She decides. 'Not when he was admitted. That diagnosis came later – much later, around a year ago.'

'So which was it? Bipolar or schizophrenia?' Even I know enough to realise there's a big difference between the two.

'I'm not a psychiatrist, but ...'

I press my lips together, waiting.

'It's not my place to make diagnoses. They are the experts. I'm just a nurse.'

'And your opinion doesn't count for much. I understand. But you didn't agree with the psychiatrist's view?'

She shakes her head. 'I didn't know what to think. His behaviour was entirely consistent with bipolar until the new diagnosis. Then instances started to arise that could have been interpreted as hallucination, delusion, but overall I'd say his symptoms fitted more with a typical bipolar patient – periods of excitability followed by deep depression. That didn't change.'

'So who made the new diagnosis?'

'Dr Lynch – Margaret Lynch, she's the head of the unit.' Jenny gives me a wry grin. 'Very well qualified – not the kind of person you argue with. She came with very high recommendations from some clinic in Spain.'

'And you don't like her very much?'

'She's the boss. We don't have to like her as long as she's good at her job.'

I get the feeling that's as close as Jenny Pugh ever gets to an admission of hatred. 'How long has she been in charge?' I ask.

'Around eighteen months. She took over when Dr Kennedy retired. We all got on really well with him, but I suppose everything has to change – new broom, and all that.'

I change tack. 'What about Rosie? It's said she had some sort of special relationship with Shaw?'

For the first time I see Jenny's face crinkle into a real frown. 'If you call doing her job a "special relationship", then yes, she did. She looked after him, got to know him. We all have patients we build bridges with, have a particular connection with – we couldn't do our jobs otherwise. Rosie understood Harry; he opened up to her. It's a vital part of our work, to give patients the opportunity to trust, let their guard down. It's an essential part of treatment.'

'But aside from "doing her job"?'

'What they're saying is a load of rubbish! I don't care what they've found or what they think. Rosie was a good nurse and a great manager. She did nothing wrong, and I'll swear to that in any court you like!'

The vehemence in her tone is unexpected, but sends a thrill of relief through me. My Rosie did nothing wrong. I know it, Larson knows it, but now I find out that someone in this sod-awful place knows it too. Proof, though, is another thing. 'What does your boss say about all this?' I ask her.

She rolls her eyes. 'Who knows? The day it happened, she was on a management team-building day – Centre Parcs, can you believe it?'

'And when she came back?'

'The police interviewed her, of course. They took a statement, and then she went off on holiday.'

That surprises me. 'She was allowed to go on holiday – with a murder investigation going on? Where to?'

Jenny shrugs. 'They must have thought she'd told them all she could. As for where, she certainly wouldn't have told any of us about her holiday arrangements – she wasn't that sort of person. Sorry, but you'll have to find out from your colleagues. They are bound to have asked her, in case they needed her for anything else. Isn't that the way it works?'

'It's the way it's supposed to work.' I need time to absorb all this. 'I'd better let you get back to work,' I say. 'It's very good of you to talk to me. Do you mind if I get in touch again if I think of anything else?'

'No, of course not.' She delves in her uniform pocket and brings out a notepad, scribbles a phone number and tears off the sheet. 'My mobile number. Call me anytime.' She opens the door, then turns back to me. 'You know, you're not at all what I expected, Inspector Crow.'

'Really?'

She smiles. 'Stay in touch, okay?'

'I will,' I say to her retreating back.

## 7

By the time I get home, the light's beginning to fail. The curtains are still drawn back, and I can see the glow of the laptop screen on the coffee table. There's no sign of Larson though, and I feel a twinge of worry that he might have gone chasing off to make a nuisance of himself at West Hill. The last thing I need is a night spent scraping his middle-class backside out of some alley in the Sinkhole. It's a relief when I open the front door and hear clattering in the kitchen. He comes to the doorway clutching a tea towel. Of course – he's a 'new man' – where else would he be?

'Just taking a break,' he says, fiddling with the cloth, 'thought I'd do a bit of washing up. I hope you don't mind.'

'Go ahead and knock yourself out,' I tell him, 'but I'd tread carefully if I were you – the sight of a dishcloth might scare some of those mugs to death.'

He gives me a nervous smile. 'Yeah, I sort of noticed. Shall I make some coffee?'

'Good idea – as long as it's not cappu-bloody-ccino.'

'What?'

'Never mind. There's a jar in the cupboard above the

microwave. Make mine strong and black, three sugars. Then you can tell me what you've found out while I've been off being an arsehole.'

'You're welcome,' he mutters, and retreats into the kitchen.

As soon as I get into the living room, I can see he hasn't been idle. There are so many windows open on the screen I feel like I'm staring at an incident room noticeboard. None are in English. One I recognise as French, but the rest could be anything. He comes up behind me and sets down a tray with two mugs and a plate of Rich Tea. One of the mugs is full of something that looks like cat pee. I pick up the other one. 'Cheers. What the bloody hell is that?'

'Green tea with lemongrass. I called Carol Dodds. The hearing is at ten on Monday morning, and she says she'll have access to the initial witness statements by midday tomorrow. She's also trying to get copies of Shaw's journals, but that might take longer.'

I nod, trying to process the fact he carries his own tea around with him. 'So what's all this lot?' I ask, pointing at the computer screen.

He shrugs. 'I'm not sure yet. I started off with a search for any instances of violent assault related to released or escaped patients from mental institutions worldwide in the last fifteen years. It seemed a good starting point.'

'And you found?'

'Four thousand, two hundred and fifty-three.'

'Christ all bloody mighty!'

He gives me a sheepish laugh. 'Yes, I know – so I narrowed the parameters a bit, to fatal or near-fatal attacks involving knives or other sharp instruments, and only cases where the patient was on some kind of temporary release. That returned forty-three results.'

'A bit better,' I say, 'and that's what you've got here?'

'Yes.' He hesitates. 'At least I think so. I won't know until I've translated them.'

'You what?' I glance back at the screen and its jigsaw of gobbledegook and suddenly realise what I'm looking at. Some are copies of old newspaper articles, but others ... I turn back to him and see him shuffle uncomfortably. 'Where the bloody hell did you get hold of all this? I assume they are what I think they are?'

He clears his throat. 'Classified police files – yes, some of them are. Unfortunately, some of the cases are too old to have been stored on computer, or the force hasn't gotten round to digitising its records yet.'

'But ...' I'm perilously close to another brain freeze. The implications are dizzying, and at the same time my conception of squeaky-clean John Larson does a handbrake turn. 'Have you got any idea how illegal this is? And it's on my sodding computer, for Christ's sake!' My mind flits back to the staff briefing a year ago on all the cyber-detection stuff the constabulary boasts about these days.

'You want me to delete it?'

He's got me on that one. 'No, of course I bloody don't. What are you, anyway – some kind of computer whizz-kid?'

'Hardly a kid,' he replies with a shrug, 'but yes, I suppose so. I work as a freelance, writing software for games companies – at least that's what I do now, but I've learned a few other things along the way.'

'Including a couple of dozen foreign languages, I hope, if we're going to make any sense of that lot!'

This time he grins at me. 'No need for that – a friend of mine has developed a very accurate programme that translates scanned or digital text, even handwriting and audio. It's much more sophisticated than the online translators – it was commissioned by the civil service for use at international conferences and the like. She's digging me out a beta copy, and once she's sent it across, we shouldn't have any trouble.'

'So not only are we hacking into the databases of foreign police forces, we're probably breaking the Official Secrets Act as well? That's just bloody marvellous!'

'Sorry – you asked me to get information, and this is the best way I know of getting a direct, accurate view of what's going on. Unless you've got a better idea?'

I have to admit, grudgingly, that I don't. And he's right – one thing I've learned over the years is that the best way to make the force collectively curl up like startled hedgehogs is to suggest even the smallest hint of a possible miscarriage of justice. I've got more chance of getting a clean bill of health than a critical review of a closed case – top brass the world over like nothing more than covering their own backsides.

Larson is scrabbling at a jumble of papers on the carpet. He comes up with three sets of documents and sets them out on the coffee table. 'This is what I've got so far on the Inverness case.' He taps one pile. 'These are transcripts of some of the police interviews with Lucy Radcliffe, the nurse who was convicted, and these' – he points to another – 'are the notes from the court. Carol might have some input on those.'

'If she doesn't get us arrested first,' I say. 'She might be representing Rosie, but that doesn't mean she wouldn't get a kick out of dumping me in the shit the first chance she got. Or has it escaped your notice that we don't exactly kiss each other goodnight?'

He snorts out a breath and carries on, 'And this lot is newspaper reports. Where do you want to start?'

The words come out almost as a challenge, but before I can say anything, my phone rings. 'Sod it! Get that, will you?'

He stiffens and opens his mouth, but then stops and just stares. I look down. My hand has started to twitch. I grab the nearest bunch of papers, but too late. He gives a slight nod, turns away and answers the phone. 'It's a Sergeant Saint from West Hill – something about a body.'

I snatch the handset. 'George?'

'Evening, Al. Listen, I haven't got long; we're up to our ears down here. I thought you'd want to know a body's been found, and word is it's Harry Shaw.'

'Where? When? Are you sure it's Shaw?'

'Half an hour ago, fished out of Portishead Marina. No confirmation yet but from what we've heard so far, it sounds like him. Sorry, I gotta go – the local lads have decided to start their weekend entertainment early. But, Al, go careful, okay? Word's out that you're poking your nose in, so if you trip face first in the brown stuff, it wasn't me who helped you get there.'

He rings off. I shove the phone back into Larson's hand and shoot to my feet – or at least try to, but my brain doesn't quite translate the message, and the floor suddenly feels like the black run at St Moritz. 'Fuck it to hell!' I mutter as I slide back down onto the sofa. My son-in-law looks concerned, but is sensible enough to keep his mouth shut. I take a couple of deep breaths and try again, more slowly this time, and make it upright. 'I'm going out for a while,' I tell him, making for the door.

'Not in my car you're not.'

I turn to face him. He's got that glint in his eye again, and he's standing, arms loose, feet apart, as if he's expecting me to take a pop. It's only then I realise I've clenched my fists, and I'm teetering on the edge of what Rogers would call 'inappropriate behaviour'. I make a conscious effort to relax. Larson lets out a relieved breath, but the wary look doesn't leave his eyes. 'George says Harry Shaw's been found in Portishead,' I say by way of apology. 'Dead.'

'Shit!' Somehow the word doesn't sit right, coming out of his mouth. He scratches his head. 'Right. I'll drive, then.'

I glare at him, but he just shrugs. 'You wouldn't get more than a mile down the road in your state,' he points out. 'That's if you manage to start the car at all.'

It's a statement, not a question – he must have been watching me struggle earlier on, damn it. I give up. 'Yeah – so are you going to stand there or what?'


THE FAR END of Portishead Marina is lit up like a billboard for a pantomime, a jumble of brilliant arc lights and flashing blue that's probably visible from Newport high street, ten miles away across the Bristol Channel. We park up at the supermarket complex that runs across the eastern edge of the inlet. Twenty years ago there was nothing here but industrial wasteland. Now it's a playground for local yachties, the squeaky-clean, well-equipped pontoons bordered by town houses way beyond a police inspector's salary, painted up in pastel shades to give a faux Mediterranean atmosphere. Unfortunately, the illusion ends at the shoreline – not even the cleverest architects can make any impression on the banks of shifting brown sludge thrown up by the channel's powerful tides. On the other side of the marina, the old town, where the likes of Harry Shaw hang out, washes up against the boundary of new development. I imagine Monica and Harry in happier times, out on a Friday night, casing the five-hundred-grand apartments on the waterfront. At least, if it is him up there on the slipway, he finally made it to where Monica wanted to be.

As I fumble with the seat belt, Larson puts a hand on my arm. I want to bat it away but restrain myself. 'You okay, Inspector?' There's genuine concern in his voice.

'Don't you worry about me, son.' I yank the door catch and haul myself out before he can argue, and head off towards the light show at a brisk pace that I hope looks more purposeful than petulant.

Larson catches up with me at the end of the car park. 'Look, I'm sorry. You're on sick leave and ... well, I shouldn't have called you. It wasn't fair, and ...'

I stop, plant my feet and thrust my face an inch from his nose. 'Are you telling me, son, that all of a sudden you're concerned about my health? Because it's a bit bloody late to start worrying about it now.'

'Okay. Fine.' He sidesteps and carries on across the road.

For a brief moment I'm tempted to come clean, tell him what effect the damage to my brain has had on my social skills, which if I'm honest weren't that refined to start with, but the urge is fleeting. I fall in beside him. 'I got shot in the head,' I tell him, although he must know that already – everyone else does. 'It affects my balance sometimes, that's all. And that makes me irritable.'

'Really? I hadn't noticed.'

I shoot him a look – he's grinning. We're close enough to see the police tape cordoning off the final stretch of the marina, next to the sea lock. I put a restraining hand on his arm. If George is right and word's got round that I'm impersonating an officer on active duty, I've got bugger all chance of getting on the other side of the line. I'm reviewing my options when I see a burly shape dip under the tape and head towards us. It takes me a minute, but as he gets closer, I recognise the silhouette and relax.

'That you, boss?' He walks up and stands beside us, staring out at the crime scene. 'I thought you might be turning up – been keeping an eye open. And this is ...?' He waves a hand at Larson.

'John Larson, my daughter's husband. Good to see you again, Benson. What's going on up there?'

'It's Harry Shaw all right. Managed to end up in the lock

somehow. The body was found by a boat owner bringing his craft through at lock-in – he said it just popped up in front of him as the water level rose. He's still in the back of an ambulance, suffering from shock, poor devil.'

My sidekick's gone a bit pale, and I resist the urge to ask him if *he's* feeling all right. 'Do they know the cause of death yet?' I ask Benson.

He shakes his head. 'Not for certain, no, but there's a theory he was either drunk and fell in, or drunk and jumped in.'

'And your theory?'

'Loony or not, Harry Shaw never struck me as the suicidal type, pissed or sober. And you'd have to climb over a fair few railings if you wanted to drown yourself accidentally.'

'If he *did* drown,' I think out loud. What I also think, but don't say, is that both suicide and accidental death fit quite neatly with the prosecution's case against Rosie. If, on the other hand, any evidence was to emerge that he didn't get into Portishead Lock under his own steam, things could take quite a different turn.

Benson's ahead of me. 'Don't worry, boss – I've got a mate works alongside the pathologist. I'll get her to keep an eye on what's going on and let you know the score.' His radio crackles, and a woman's clipped voice spits out of it. 'Sorry,' he says. 'The DI – gotta go.' At the same time a volley of shrill protests cuts across the general hubbub down at the lock, and after a short scuffle, a dark shape emerges, gunning towards us along the quay on heels that batter the concrete like a burst from a semi-automatic. 'Oh, sodding hell,' Benson mutters under his breath, 'bloody Monica!'

He takes a step forward, arms spread as if he's trying to divert a wayward goose. I follow him and tap his shoulder. 'You get off back to the action. I'll take care of this.'

He gives me a look, eyebrow raised. 'If you say so, boss,

but don't say I didn't warn you.' He doesn't quite get out of her way quick enough though, and she manages to give him a surprisingly hefty push as she steams past, lips pressed together in a thin, determined line. 'Mind how you go, Monica,' he shouts over his shoulder, gives me a wave and sets off back towards the cordon.

I step into her path. 'And you can fucking well sod off an' all,' she says in a Yorkshire accent that's half an octave lower than it ought to be, probably because of all the screeching she's been doing up by the lock. At the same time she unhitches a shoulder bag that looks as if it's got half a brick in it. As she swings, I realise I probably won't be able to get out of the way in time, but to my surprise Larson shoots in front of me, grabs her wrist and wrenches her arm back. She lets go of the bag, which hits the ground with a soft thunk, over-balances and follows it down, lands squarely on her backside on a muddy patch of grass and deflates like a grounded blimp. 'Bloody bastard coppers,' she mutters, and bursts into noisy sobs, head in her hands.

A year ago, I would have known exactly how to handle things, but these days any unexpected response sends me into a tailspin. As I'm trying to work it out, I see Larson crouch in front of Monica. 'I'm so sorry, Mrs Shaw,' he says, and holds out a hand like a suitor at a Victorian ball. 'I'm not a policeman. Please, let me help you up.'

She stops wailing and blinks at him as if he's got two heads, and then, utterly compliant, takes his hand and lets him ease her onto her feet. He even picks up her bag and hands it to her. She hitches it back on her shoulder and wipes her eyes with the cuff of her faux-fur jacket. 'Thanks. At least someone round here's got some bloody manners.'

I catch myself wondering if his lounge lizard act is how he managed to impress my daughter, but then pull myself together and step forward. 'I *am* a policeman, Mrs Shaw, but

I'm not on duty just now. I'd like to know what happened to your husband though, and I've got a feeling we might be able to help each other.'

She shoots me a suspicious glare and stiffens, but as she gets her insults in order, Larson takes her arm and gently propels her away from the police line. 'I'm sure you could do with a drink, Mrs Shaw – I know I could.'

I see her eyes light up at that. I've got to hand it to him – he learns fast. There's a fancy restaurant-cum-wine bar a hundred metres behind us. Most of the clientele are huddled outside under the awning, watching the spectacle. We push past and find a table in a corner of the dimly lit, near-deserted bar. 'Gin and tonic,' she says before any of us have the chance to sit down. 'And make it a double if you don't mind, no ice or lemon.'

She directs the demand at me, which is fine – Larson seems to be doing a far better job of the soft soap than I could. I raise an eyebrow at him, and he asks for a Peroni. I plod over to the bar and order the drinks. After a moment's hesitation, I add a half of the guest real ale – what the hell harm can it do? I forgot to take my pills this morning, so I figure I can just about get away with it.

When I get back to the table, the pair of them are chatting away like old mates at a school reunion. Monica even gives me a bleak smile as she grabs her gin and downs half of it in one gulp.

'So you're sure your husband didn't know this woman in West Hill?' Larson asks her.

'I'll swear on anything you like.' She stares miserably into the half-empty glass, gripping it with both hands. 'He wasn't like that, my Harry, you ask anyone.'

'Even the landlord at the Old Duck?' I can't help asking.

It's Larson who shoots me the look. I tell myself to shut up and concentrate on my beer, but Monica, surprisingly calm, answers the question. 'That was my fault. We'd had a row, I got drunk and so did Harry. Things went a bit far, that's all.' She narrows her eyes at me. 'I know what you lot think about me and Harry, but it's all bollocks. Yeah, okay, so we did a bit of thieving, I'll hold my hands up to that, and Harry could be free with his fists when he'd had a drink, but only as much as every other bugger round here. You're a copper – you know how it is.'

I nod, seeing Larson's brow crease out of the corner of my eye. He doesn't move in the kind of circles where a decent Saturday night punch-up is part of the general entertainment. 'Harry still got sent down, Monica,' I remind her. 'You can't deny that.'

'Only because you bastards bullied Reggie Dwyer into pressing charges. He was in the General, for Christ's sake, drugged up to the eyeballs, didn't know what he was doing. He would've signed away his pub if you'd told him to.' She drains her glass and slams it on the table. 'They say he was sick in the head. Well, he wasn't, not my Harry. He got depressed now and again, that's all – I mean, everybody does, don't they? But he wasn't a psycho, and he would never have done what they say he did – not unless somebody drugged him up and made him do it. That bitch they've got locked up, the one they say he was shagging – she put him up to it, and when they prove it, she'll get what's coming. She won't last a week where she's going, not if I have anything to do with it, and that's a promise.'

This time it's me doing the restraining. Larson's gone as taut as a tripwire, and I have to grab his arm and squeeze until I feel him flinch. By tomorrow morning every rag in the country will have Rosie's name plastered all over it, but right now Monica Shaw doesn't know who she's talking to, and my little voice inside – the one that hasn't quite deserted me yet –

is suggesting that she and Harry are as much victims as my daughter.

'Come on, son,' I say quietly. 'We'd better be off.' I pull him to his feet and nod to Monica. 'Thanks,' I tell her. 'You've been a lot of help.'

She stares at me, confused. As I push Larson through the door, I turn to her. 'You're convinced Harry didn't commit suicide or have an accident up there, right?'

She nods.

'In that case,' I say, 'someone must have killed him. If the woman who put him up to the murder is in prison, who do you think that might have been?'

## 8

I jerk awake to a cacophony that I think, at first, is the product of a sudden glitch in my mental processes. Then I realise it's the bells of St Mary Redcliffe church around the corner, straining to make themselves heard over the din of hailstones bouncing off the guttering. It's Saturday, so they are probably practising for a wedding later in the day – enough of a reason for the heavens to open, I think bitterly. I close my eyes, remembering the day Christine and I made our vows, emerging through a curtain of steady November drizzle. It would have been our thirtieth anniversary around now, and I lie there wondering if we could have got back on track if it hadn't been for Terry. In a fleeting instant of honesty with myself, I know the answer is no – Terry didn't shatter the idyll, he just came along at the right time to pick up the pieces. At least, that's how Chrissie saw it. For me, even though ten years have gone by, the shards of our broken marriage still rip through my gut whenever they get the chance, which is usually every time I close the bedroom door and have to face the double bed with one solitary pillow propped against the middle of the headboard.

My cheerless thoughts are interrupted by a sharp rap at the front door. I grab my dressing gown, head downstairs and find Larson on the front step, holding an umbrella over a little boy bundled in a bright yellow mackintosh and red wellington boots. My son-in-law shuffles nervously. 'Sorry. Christine had a breakfast meeting, so Ben's with me until lunchtime. Nothing I could do, I'm afraid – I hope you don't mind ...'

He trails off, waiting, but I'm hardly listening. My eyes are fixed on the kid, who's staring up at me with Rosie's eyes and, when he giggles at me from behind a chubby hand, Rosie's laugh.

'Daddy, why is that man still in his pyjamas?'

Larson gives an embarrassed cough, and I realise they're both getting soaked. I stand aside, and they pile into the hall-way, shedding dripping rainwear on the mat. Little Ben plonks himself on the carpet and starts tugging at his boots. I crouch down and give him a hand. 'They're my Paddington boots,' he announces proudly. 'Mummy got them so I could splosh. They're red.'

I try to answer him, but the lump in my throat won't let any words out. I just smile and carefully line up the boots by the front door.

'What's your name?' he asks, and I catch a furrow of concern on Larson's brow.

I swallow hard and take a breath. My voice, when it finally emerges, feels like sand crumbling out of a rusty pipe. 'I'm a friend of your dad's,' I tell him. 'We work together. I'd better go and get out of my pyjamas.' I turn to Larson. 'What time is it, anyway?'

'Just gone nine. Sorry if we've disturbed you.'

Thankfully I remember there is a child present and turn my inappropriate comment into a nod before heading back to the bedroom. As I'm dressing, it strikes me that for the first time in nearly a year, I've slept through the night, and despite what's going on around me, I feel better for it, more alert than I have for months. What kind of person, I wonder, does that make me? Two people are dead, my daughter is in prison, and suddenly I feel alive. Maybe Chrissie was right the day she told me she wanted a divorce. I was incapable of leading a normal life, she said. She wanted someone who was turned on by normal things like sex, a steak dinner after a night at the pictures, maybe even a decent conversation – not some pervert whose eyes only lit up talking about drunks and murderers, blood and bodies, who came in at God knows what time every night too knackered to do anything beyond drink whisky and fall asleep on the sofa.

Back downstairs I find Ben installed at the kitchen table with a colouring book and enough crayons to reproduce Da Vinci's *Last Supper*, so engrossed he doesn't even glance up as I walk in. His father hands me a mug. 'Black, three sugars, right?'

'Right,' I admit, and make an enquiring gesture towards the lounge. He nods, and we settle ourselves in front of our laptops – this time he's brought his own, a fancy-looking thing that probably cost as much as my car. 'He looks like a great kid,' I say, more to break the awkward silence than anything else.

'Yeah.' Larson blushes, every inch the proud father. 'Sorry to spring him on you. I didn't want to waste the morning.' He sighs. 'Thank God he's too young to understand what's going on. I'll take him back to Christine's as soon as she's home. He'll be fine with his colouring for an hour or two – he's obsessed with crayons at the moment.'

A quick glance tells me he's right – head bent over the page, all I can see is a curtain of blond hair and the pink tip of Ben's tongue poking through lips pursed in concentration. 'It's okay,' I say, 'really,' and change the subject before my voice breaks again. 'Do any of your clever programs pick up patterns – sort out coincidences that might not be coincidences, for example?'

He narrows his eyes and takes a slug of his herbal tea. 'That depends. Have you something specific in mind?'

'I'm not sure, but what's in my head so far – and it could all be rubbish – is this – eight years ago in Scotland someone persuades a mentally unstable man to commit a particularly grisly murder and push the blame on an innocent nurse for supposedly letting the guy out in the first place. Then they do away with the murderer, presumably so he can't point the finger in the right direction should he ever work out what just happened. Getting on for a week ago, someone persuades Harry Shaw to lop off a woman's head, and ...'

'I get you.' Larson holds up a hand. 'And if this someone is turning up at psychiatric institutions the world over, suffering from a sort of serial killer syndrome by proxy, they must be leaving some kind of data trail, however hard they've tried to cover it up.' He thinks for a moment. 'We've got the information on possible related crimes, although we don't know yet how many of them are relevant. If I'm going to do a search along the lines you suggest, I'll need the personnel files as well, to do an analysis of all the staff comings and goings, see if anyone fits the timescales. If there's anything in this at all, we're dealing with someone who's clever enough to cover their tracks, at first sight at least, but it's very difficult not to leave some sort of electronic trail. It may take a little time though – before we can look for patterns in individuals, we have to eliminate non-relevant events.'

'Better get started, then. We've got forty odd cases to get through – if you managed to get hold of that translation program?'

He digs in his pocket and pulls out a memory stick. 'This is almost instant and very accurate. I can bring up the information, but you're the detective, so you'll have to make the decisions.'

After an hour or so, we've managed to discard a dozen of the files on our list – two gang fights, four robberies, a pub brawl, four domestics and an argument over the proceeds of crime. It's the thirteenth that makes us both sit up. The document is from a local Spanish newspaper a couple of years old and reports the case of twenty-five-year-old Alfredo Batista, committed to the Hospital Psiquiatrico San Sebastian, Malaga, suffering from severe paranoid schizophrenia. Batista was initially hospitalised following a number of violent knife attacks on horses at a local riding school – he was, apparently, convinced that all horses were, in the words of the tabloid, 'instruments of the devil'. The story goes on to report that while incarcerated Batista began a torrid affair with a teenage care assistant, Gloria Marinez, resulting in his persuading her to sneak him out of the grounds and drive him down to the coast so he could, he said, fulfil his ambition to swim by moonlight in a deserted cove.

According to Gloria's statement following her arrest, he tried to urge her to join him in the water, but she refused – she wasn't a strong swimmer and was afraid of the current. He left her on the rocks, swam out into the bay and disappeared. At this point she panicked but, realising her job was at risk, didn't call the police. She simply drove home and turned up at the hospital the next day claiming ignorance. Unfortunately for her, teenagers make poor confidantes, and two of the other care assistants were quick to pass on gossip about the affair to the police. Gloria was arrested, questioned and remanded in the local prison. Six days after Batista's escape, his corpse was washed up three kilometres south of the cove. That, sadly, was not the end of the story. A week after the discovery of Batista's body, Gloria was found dead in her cell. She hanged herself with a strip torn from her skirt.

By itself, this story would have formed no more than a tenuous connection with our investigations. However, the front page of the rag was shared with another news item – the discovery of a murder victim – a woman – in a house in downtown Malaga. Apparently dead for several days, the victim was already well on the road to decomposition, the face half-eaten by rats. An attempt had even been made by some larger mammal, probably a dog, to drag away the head, which had been severed from the body with the sharp end of a garden spade. Investigations were underway, but so far no further information was available. It was easy to see why the Spanish police hadn't linked the two cases. As far as they were concerned, Batista had swum out beyond safe limits, maybe got confused in the dark, and simply drowned, possibly within minutes – hours at the most – of entering the water. He could not, therefore, be responsible for the gruesome find days later on the other side of the city.

Larson pecks away feverishly at the laptop keyboard for a few minutes and then shakes his head. 'The forensic report says the body was in too bad a state to retrieve any but the victim's DNA. Is that true, do you think?'

'Maybe. Southern Spain is pretty warm, even in winter, and a lot can happen to exposed flesh in a few days with those temperatures. But if they did manage to get a result ...'

'They might have thought it was just cross-contamination, especially if the same officers were working on both cases. If they didn't want to admit that,they might just leave it off the report, right?'

'You're getting the hang of police procedure pretty well, son,' I tell him, and see his mouth twitch into the ghost of a grin. He's learning.

'So it's a contender for our list?'

'I'd say a ninety percent certainty. What we need now is to find out where this bastard was in the eight years between

Inverness and Malaga – if we can work out what route they took, it might give us more of an idea where they might go next.'

'You don't think they are still here?'

'If they are, my bet is they won't be for much longer. We won't have much time, so it might be useful to know where they are going next. All we need to do is work out the pattern.'

'Yeah, right – that's all.'

I glance across and see an expression he's not worn before – pure misery. I don't get the chance to ask him what his problem is though, as there's a rustle behind us, and we turn to see Ben in the kitchen doorway, hopping from foot to foot.

'Daddy, I want the toilet.'

Larson shakes himself and gets up. 'Okay, Ben, I'm coming.'

At the same time someone bangs on my front door, and I open it to find Tom, my mechanic, offering up my car keys and a smile that warns me not to open the envelope he's clutching in his other hand until I've got access to a stiff drink.

'Got it all done late last night,' he tells me through a display of expensive dentistry, 'and figured you wouldn't want to wait 'til Monday. You want to check her over?'

I peer over his shoulder at my old Ford Focus, the continuing deluge battering its newly valeted paintwork, and shake my head. 'I'll trust you, Tom. Besides, if I'm not happy, I can always arrest you for fraud.'

His smile gets even wider. 'You say that every time, and it hasn't happened yet. Better run – the missus followed me down. Pop the cash in sometime next week, yeah?' Halfway down the path he turns and shouts over his shoulder, 'And your next service is a couple of thousand overdue – make an appointment when you come in.'

Back inside, Larson is looking even more unhappy. 'What?' I ask him, less than charitably – my mind is still on the bill, which I toss into the general mess on the dining table.

'I've just had a call,' he says, fidgeting in a way that reminds me of our first meeting outside West Hill station, 'Carol's secretary. She has some documents and says to collect them right away while she's still in the office. I ought to go – it might be something important.'

'You'd better be off, then. Something else?'

He's still fidgeting. 'Thing is, I tried to ring Christine, and she's not back yet. Do you think you could ... I'll be no more than fifteen minutes – twenty tops ...'

The penny drops, and I feel a sudden flutter of apprehension. 'You want me to keep an eye on Ben.'

He nods. 'I'll be as quick as I can.'

I look at the little boy, who is gazing up at me, sucking his index finger, his other hand curled in a death grip round his father's thumb. He pulls his finger out of his mouth and asks, his voice uncertain, 'Will you colour with me?'

'Yeah, sure, if you show me what to do.'

A smile – Rosie's smile – lights up his face. He lets go of Larson to take my hand and gives it a mighty tug, propelling me towards the kitchen. 'Come on then, let's go.'

'Thanks.' Larson scoops up his laptop – just in case there's a holdup, he says – and heads for the door.

'Don't be long,' I mouth at him, and give my attention to my grandson, who has manoeuvred me to the kitchen table and is pressing a bright green crayon into my hand.

Within minutes, I'm transported back to Rosie's childhood. The page contains the simple outline of a flower, and there's something unexpectedly soothing about filling the spaces between thick, black, toddler-friendly lines with the vivid primary colours of the wax sticks. Ben is a perfect companion, intent on his picture of a sandcastle, less concerned than me with staying within the lines, but rapt and silent except for the occasional comment on his masterpiece.

'I want some blue now,' he decides, and I pass him the crayon, my mind drifting in some sort of dream world, hovering between past and present, unable to separate Ben from my memories of Rosie, her lips and cheeks daubed with purple, red and yellow wax smudges.

When a tune suddenly starts up from nowhere, I sit up, blinking like an idiot, momentarily confused.

'Daddy's phone,' Ben says helpfully, and carries on with his picture.

'What?'

'Daddy's phone,' he says again, and jabs a crayon in the direction of the lounge.

'Oh.' I follow my ears to the sofa and find a state-of-the-art smartphone behind one of the cushions, trilling out the prelude to *Also Sprach Zarathustra* – the opening theme from the old 1968 movie *2001: A Space Odyssey*. Yep – that's definitely Larson's style and almost as irritating as the fact he's forgotten to take his mobile with him. I squint at the screen and almost drop the thing. The name on the display reads 'Christine'. 'Bloody hell!' I mutter under my breath. The ridiculous tune seems to go on forever while I hold the phone as if it's a grenade and I've just pulled out the pin. Eventually it stops, but my sigh of relief is interrupted by my house phone and its louder, but far more sensible burr. There's a moment of indecision – it can't be my ex-wife – she doesn't know I've been seeing Larson, and as far as I know, she doesn't have my number. I chuck the mobile back onto the sofa, flex my fingers a couple of times to forestall the jitters, and grab the handset. 'Yes?'

'Am I speaking to Detective Inspector Crow?' It's a woman's voice, low and tentative.

'Who is this?'

'My name is Sister Bryce. I'm calling from the Royal Infirmary. Do you know a John Larson?'

Oh, God! 'Yes – what's the matter? What's happened?'

'I'm sorry, Inspector, but Mr Larson was brought in forty-five minutes ago. He's been a little incoherent, but he managed to ask us to inform you. He became quite agitated, clearly thought it was important to let you know as soon as possible.'

Forty-five minutes ago? I glance at the clock and realise Ben and I have been at the kitchen table for almost two hours – Christ-all-bloody-mighty!

'What's happened?' I ask again, my heart starting to race. 'Some kind of accident? Is he badly injured? What?'

There's a pause, and when she answers, I pick up a hesitation, a reluctance in her tone. 'Look, it's a bit ... is there any way you could come to the hospital, Inspector? It would be best if you spoke with the doctor. I'm sorry, but I don't think I can give you more information over the phone.'

'Oh, Jesus f...' Ben tugs at my trouser leg, and I pull myself up. 'I'll be over in fifteen minutes,' I finish, and hang up.

## 9

The cab spits us out at the main entrance to the infirmary, and I hoist a tired and slightly grizzly Ben into my arms. I know he's picking up on my own anxiety, but there's nothing I can do about it. 'I want Daddy,' he mumbles for the fiftieth time, clutching the carrier bag containing his crayons and colouring book to his chest like a shield.

'I know, son,' I tell him. 'We'll find him, don't worry.' He doesn't hear me though – he's fallen asleep, thumb in mouth, head slumped against my shoulder.

I announce myself at reception and am ushered down several corridors to a small relatives' room, where I perch rigidly on a plastic chair, trying not to disturb my grandson. After a short wait the door opens and an exhausted-looking kid in a white coat, no older, I guess, than Rosie, shuffles in and holds out a hand. 'Inspector Crow? I'm sorry to keep you waiting.'

His voice is ominously hushed. I glance down at Ben to make sure he isn't faking sleep – my suspicious nature, I suppose – before hissing, 'Never mind that, just tell me what the hell is going on.' I realise I've dropped into interrogation mode and might as well have threatened to arrest him for withholding evidence. 'Sorry – I'm just a bit ...'

'That's okay, I understand. It's difficult, I know. Mr Larson is sleeping at the moment, but you should be able to see him in an hour or so.'

'He's going to be okay?' It's only when relief starts to wash through that I become aware of just how wound up I've been.

'He should be – physically at least. It was a close thing, but we managed to get him on the pump in time, and he couldn't have been in the water more than a minute. He's a lucky man, Inspector.'

*Pump? Water? 'Physically at least'?* I take a deep breath. 'I'm sorry, Dr ...'

'Caldwell.'

'Dr Caldwell, do you think we could start at the beginning? What, exactly, happened to my son-in-law?'

'Of course ...' He hesitates, measuring his words. 'It appears Mr Larson took a large overdose of amitriptyline – that's a form of antidepressant, very dangerous in high doses.'

'He what?' It takes a supreme effort to keep my voice down. 'You said he was in the water? What water?'

'The call came in from the Nova Scotia pub down by Underfall boatyard – a chap outside having a smoke noticed Mr Larson by the ferry stage. He said he saw him wobbling a bit, and then he fell into the harbour. Luckily the harbour-master was a few feet away in a RIB and managed to grab him before he went down. The ambulance was there within five minutes and got him up to us pretty quickly. He was vomiting when they arrived too, which probably saved his life.'

Nothing makes sense. Even leaving aside the drugs, Larson was headed for Queen's Square. Underfall Yard is more than a mile away, right on the other side of the floating harbour. Caldwell is talking again.

'Inspector Crow, can you think of any reason why Mr Larson would want to end his life? I know it's a difficult question, but it would really help us decide how to proceed when he wakes up.'

My mind is scattering down several alleys at once. I shake my head. 'I'm sorry, Dr Caldwell, right now I can't think of any reason at all.'

He gives a sympathetic nod. 'That's okay. If anything does occur to you, just talk to one of the nurses, and they'll page me. Would you like to wait? You're welcome to stay here, or there's a coffee shop by main reception. As soon as Mr Larson is awake, someone will come and find you.'

'Thanks. I'll stay here if you don't mind, at least until the lad wakes up.'

'You're welcome,' he says, and slides out of the room. I find myself hoping he doesn't have many hours left of his shift – the poor sod looked dead on his feet.

Right on cue, Richard Strauss decides to add his two penn'orth to the proceedings, Larson's ludicrous ringtone floating up from my jacket pocket, right next to Ben's ear. The little boy's head jerks up, cheeks flushed, eyelids screwed up against the harsh fluorescent light in the ceiling. 'Where's Daddy?'

'We'll see him soon,' I try to reassure him while fumbling for the phone. It's Chrissie again. I have to answer – if I ignore her, she'll probably do something stupid like call the police. My hands are shaking so badly as I try to work out how to answer a call on the thing that it slips out of my sweating fingers and clatters to the floor, still ringing.

Before I can stop him, Ben has slid off my lap, grabbed the phone and jabbed something on the display. He welds it to his ear. 'Hello, Granny.' I stop breathing. 'I'm in hospital,' Ben carries on innocently, 'with a man, waiting for Daddy.' Pause. 'No, I don't know who he is, but he likes colouring.'

Oh, shit! I try to grab the mobile, but Ben's not playing ball. He twists away from me, and with the worsening tremor in my fingers, I've no chance of retrieving anything but air. 'It's a really big one,' he says, 'like where I had an ice cream.' There's a pause, then, 'Okay, Granny. Bye.' He gives me a beatific smile. 'Granny says she's coming to see us at the hospital. She did that when I had to have a 'jection. Do you know you get ice cream when you go to hospital?'

For a second I think I'm going to be sick. If someone handed me a mirror right now, I wouldn't be surprised to find that the remains of my hair have gone completely white – like the guy in *Les Miserables* the moment he realises he has to give himself up to the police to stop an innocent man being executed. Alone, I could have just slipped away, but I daren't leave Ben, and if I take him with me, it's only going to make matters worse. Chrissie will probably kick off an Amber Alert – child abduction by person or persons unknown. My grandson is still beaming up at me as if he's snagged a plastic duck at a fairground. I try to pull myself together.

'Do you ...' The gravel is back in my throat, and I cough several times before managing to put together something coherent. 'How about we go and find an ice cream now, while we're waiting to see your dad?'

The smile gets impossibly bigger. 'Yeah!' Then he remembers his manners. 'Yes, please! Can we get one for Daddy and one for Granny too?'

'Sure – but maybe we ought to wait until we see them, in case they melt?'

'Okay.' He tilts his head and adds in a sing-song, 'Good thinking, Batman.'

'Is that what your dad says?' I ask as he snatches up his carrier bag.

'All the time.' He skips to the door as if he's heading to a party. I follow, thinking, not for the first time, of how surviving a shot in the head isn't always all it's cracked up to be.

NO RESPECTABLE PARENT or guardian would think of taking a child anywhere these days without at least a bumper pack of wet wipes. Sadly, it's been a while since I placed myself into the category of respectable. After five minutes in the bathroom, I've managed to get most of the mess out of Ben's fingers, face and hair, but my attempts to clean the front of his sweatshirt have only succeeded in driving the sticky trails of melted ice cream further in. We emerge from the 'disabled and baby changing only' cubicle only slightly less dishevelled than when we went in, and I'm still clutching the door handle as Ben gives a loud whoop and jerks free of my other hand. I start after him, but barely manage half a step before my body freezes and my legs almost give way under me.

At the other end of the short corridor Chrissie has also stuttered to a halt. The blood drains from her cheeks as I watch, and for a horrible moment she teeters, eyes wide and uncomprehending, before folding gracefully to the grey vinyl, her head, by some miracle, landing on the shoulder bag that has already slipped from her fingers. Ben's headlong dash stops abruptly as he sees her fall. There's a moment of utter stillness, and then he races forward again, screaming, 'Granneeeeee!' at the top of his lungs.

I'm past him in two strides, on my knees, cradling her head. 'Chrissie? For Christ's sake, Christine, don't do this to me! Wake up, damn it!' For a few unbearable seconds there's no response, but then her eyelids flutter, and she comes up blinking in confusion. 'It's okay, Chrissie,' I mumble, feeling utterly inadequate. 'It's okay; you fainted, that's all.'

'Al? What the hell are ... Ben, don't do that, sweetie; you're hurting Granny's arm.' Ben is tugging wildly at Chrissie's elbow, letting out tearful sniffles. All of a sudden Chrissie's eyes focus; she pushes me away and sits up, taking Ben into her arms. 'It's fine, Ben,' she says. 'Granny fell over, that's all. I'm fine.'

'But you died, Granny. Your eyes went shut,' he protests through little hiccups.

'Of course I didn't. I just went to sleep for a minute.' She turns to me, and I brace myself, but the flood of abuse I'm expecting doesn't come. Instead, she simply says, 'So what *are* you doing here? And where's John? What's happened, is he all right?'

'He's okay, Chris. Sleeping – we should be able to see him soon.' I hesitate. 'Look – it's a long story. I don't suppose you fancy a coffee?'

She stiffens, but not at the suggestion. She's staring at my hands. They're shaking like I've got some kind of a palsy, and I try, too late, to stuff them in my pockets. 'Sorry,' I say, 'just a bit of a shock – hard day ...'

It's bloody pathetic, and we both know it. Her eyebrows come together in a frown as if she's contemplating the quickest route to the part of the hospital furthest away from me, but I was never that good at reading her, and when she does speak, it's to say, 'What I really fancy is a stiff gin, but I guess there's no chance of that around here. You'd better help me up before a nurse comes round the corner and starts getting curious.'

She's still a bit pale, but steady on her feet as we head over to the café in the foyer and find two empty tables in the back corner. She sets one of them up as Ben's art studio while I fetch two double-shot Americanos and an orange juice from the counter. By the time I get back, Ben is scratching earnestly away, his little legs swinging like pendulums under the table. I realise both Chrissie and I are staring at him with idiotic, grandparental grins.

'He's a great kid,' I venture – I seem to have said that a lot in the last couple of hours. Her grin disappears, but the hard expression that replaces it relents, melting into a resigned smile, which stabs at my entrails with more ferocity than if she'd leaned across the table and slapped my face.

'Yes,' she agrees, 'he is. John's a wonderful father.' I give her a sharp glance, but there's no accusation there. 'So, are you going to tell me what the hell's going on?'

I give her the bare bones – how I've become involved, but with no mention of our investigations, nor of my vague suspicions. I figure she's got enough to deal with as it is. I know she's not buying it. Chrissie's always been able to slice her way through my mind with the efficiency of a surgeon's scalpel. There's a long silence as she stares into her coffee, mulling things over. She glances across at Ben, who's still engrossed in his drawing, and finally back to me. 'Al?'

Her voice is a whisper, and there's an apprehension in her tone that pulls me up short. There's something she wants to tell me, and she's scared – and that terrifies me.

'Come on, Chris,' I say, trying and failing to give an encouraging smile, 'it's me you're talking to.' We used to tell each other everything, once upon a time – at least I think we did, in the halcyon days before I got promoted to CID and the normal conversations stopped, the ones that started 'How was your day at work, darling,' and ended with a gentle amble to the bedroom with the half-empty wine bottle we'd opened at dinner.

These days my throwaway line should have prodded a cynical laugh from her, but not today. She doesn't even smile. When she speaks, it's into her coffee mug. 'Al – about Terry ...'

'Oh, Jesus ...'

'Al, listen.' She snatches a gulp of her coffee, her hand

shaking almost as much as mine was earlier, the hot liquid slopping over the sides and over her fingers.

'I'm listening.'

'The day he left ... Al, the day Terry left, he told me the truth. He told me what really happened. He lied, and I believed him.' Her hands clench into tiny, ineffectual fists. 'Stupid! I was so stupid, Al, and ...'

Without thinking, I reach over and place my rough paw of a hand over hers. I feel as if I've been hit by a truck – a big, loud, beautiful truck that's just run right over the last five years and crushed them into oblivion, hurling me back to those last, precious moments before everything went to hell.

IT HAD BEEN A LONG DAY. We'd just done two drug busts in the Sinkhole, and I was late coming off shift, held up by the interviews and paperwork. Rosie had called me in the morning. She was off to a party tonight, she said, and her favourite coat was at the dry cleaners in Redcliffe, just round the corner from my house. Would I drop it over for her after work? 'Pretty please, Dad? I'll love you forever!'

'You mean your affection for me is entirely dependent on a moth-eaten vintage rag?'

'You bet, Dad – no rush, the party doesn't start 'til ten. See you later!'

'It starts *when*?'

She'd hung up. I made it round to what had once been my family home over in Sneyd Park around eight thirty, looking – and feeling – like shit. Rosie, kitted out in a combination of purple and black that made her look like a giant bruise, waved at me from the landing before disappearing into the bathroom to add the final touches. Chrissie let me in and rolled her eyes. 'Christ, Al, you look terrible. Tough day at the office, huh?'

'Something like that.'

'Look, Terry's at a business meeting, won't be back for a couple of hours. Why don't you take a quick shower in the ensuite while I make some coffee – Irish, if you like?'

That's how come Terence the Tosser came back early, slipped straight upstairs before Chrissie, busy in the kitchen, was aware of him, to find me sitting on the edge of the conjugal bed, pulling on my socks. I could smell the Scotch on his breath the minute he walked – swayed – through the door. The bastard had had a skinful, that was plain enough, and I remember hoping he'd driven himself home, just so I could haul him down to the cells on a drunk driving charge. As for where he'd been – business meeting, my arse. Underneath the alcohol another faint, but unmistakable whiff drifted across the space between us – a sickly mixture of cheap scent and sex. I watched the cogs whirr, slot into all the wrong places, the eyes, already glazed, curtain over into that peculiar madness that puts the fear of God even into hardened old coppers like me. His wasn't a normal kind of fury, the kind that leads to a brief flurry of fists and a re-establishment of the status quo. There was no emotion at all, not a flicker of heat in that glacial expression, no movement other than the gentle rocking of a man who was well on the wrong side of sober. He wasn't going to tackle me – he was too much of a coward for that, but this toe rag, I knew, was gunning for somebody. Not just somebody – he was going after Chrissie.

My mind was aware of the danger several seconds before fear kicked a hole in my exhaustion, and I was on my feet. Terry had already taken the half dozen steps out onto the landing, drunk, unsteady, but purposeful. It was one of those balcony landings framed by a wooden balustrade. He was halfway along when I reached the door, saw him catch his foot in the carpet runner and fall, his entire weight crashing into the flimsy wood. It splintered, and he went on falling.

Instinct sent me lunging forward, and for a brief instant I felt the brush of his fingers in the palm of my hand.

There are several things that no amount of brain damage will ever expunge from my memory. One is the soft thump of Terry's body hitting the parquet flooring ten feet below. Another is the scream – a wail that seemed to go on and on, that set my ears ringing until I thought they would burst. I was kneeling on the carpet and turned my head to see Rosie in the bathroom doorway with her wild hair and Goth makeup, hands covering her mouth, mascara running in black streaks down her cheeks, through her fingers and dripping onto the fabric of the purple skater dress. Her eyes, wide and terrified, were fixed on me with a sort of disbelieving horror, and I realised that she had come out of the bathroom just in time to see her stepfather plummet from the landing – from the end of my outstretched arm, the fingers of which had bunched into a fist as I tried to grab him. I staggered upright and grabbed her shoulders, shook her, shouted her name, but nothing made the screaming stop. Finally, in desperation, I did a thing I had never done in my entire life – I slapped her.

The silence was deafening. And in the middle of it, I heard Terry's voice drift up from below us, weak, but clear. 'He pushed me. The fucking bastard tried to kill me!'

I'd always figured Terry for a vile little shit. What I understood in that moment was that he was also a bloody clever, manipulative arsehole. Even so, it took a while for it to sink in just how manipulative. Rosie jerked clear of me, ran back into the bathroom and locked the door. There was nothing more I could do up there, so I made my way downstairs. Chrissie, on the floor with Terry, had called an ambulance and was clutching a phone in one hand, his wrist with the other. I opened my mouth, and she shook her head. 'Not now, Al. Just go. Get out. Please?'

So I did. I grabbed my coat and left. I never saw my daughter or my ex-wife again. At least, not until now. Terry's spine was broken in the fall. He played the innocent victim to the hilt. He wasn't going to press charges; there wasn't any point. I was a policeman after all, and everyone knew the lengths coppers would go to, to protect their own. Me and my mates, well, we'd just fit him up for something, make sure his life, what was left of it, would be even less worth living. So he carried on, day after day, year after year, dripping poison into my family's ears – Rosie's in particular, while Chrissie became his captive audience, nurse, cook, cleaner and wheelchair technician. It's only now, with her sitting in front of me, waif-thin, streaks of grey in her hair and a mouth that looks as if it hasn't really smiled in the last five years that I fully understand what Terry wanted all along. It wasn't me he set out to destroy – that was just a lucky bonus. His target had always been Chrissie. He was a man who wrecked marriages, chewed up women and spat them out. Being stuck in a wheelchair had slowed him down, but eventually he'd managed to work the charm on someone else's wife and moved on.

'AL? SAY SOMETHING – PLEASE?'

I come back into focus and give her hand a gentle squeeze. 'Why didn't you tell me, Chris? Terry left, what? Three years ago? You've waited all this time?' I want to add, 'To tell me I was right', but now is not the time for recriminations.

She shrugs. 'I was scared. Al, I'm so sorry. Are you angry?'

Am I angry? Too fucking right I'm angry. If Terry were in front of me now, I'd probably have him in the basement morgue quicker than the emergency lift could make the descent. 'No, I'm not angry. Just glad you're out of it. Does Rosie know?'

She looks down at her lap. 'I tried to tell her, but she didn't believe me. She kept saying she saw it and I didn't, and Terry wouldn't have said something like that if it wasn't true. After a while she said if I didn't drop it, she'd make sure I never saw Ben again, so I didn't mention it any more after that. God, I really messed up, didn't I? And now she's ...'

I cast an urgent glance at Ben, and Chrissie pulls herself together. 'Terry really got to her, didn't he?' I say. 'You think she still has contact with him?'

She shakes her head. 'Not face to face, I don't think, but these days, with all the online stuff, who knows?'

Her husband would, I think to myself, and make a mental note to ask him when I get the chance. I make another note – Terry, wherever he is, is going to get what's coming. Nobody treats my Chrissie like this, and nobody, but nobody tries to take Rosie away from me. Did he hurt her? I wonder. Did he try it on with my daughter? I'm trembling again, and I can see Chrissie gearing up to ask the inevitable question, the one she so diplomatically avoided earlier. Before she can speak, though, a nurse appears by our table.

'Inspector Crow? Mr Larson woke up a few minutes ago. You can see him now – room five, off the main ward on the left.'

I turn to Chrissie. 'You go – take Ben. I'll be here, if you want to ...' I can't quite manage to finish the sentence.

She nods. 'I'd like that.' She gets up and on her way round the table stoops to peck my cheek. 'Thanks.'

I watch them make their way through reception to the lifts, Ben tugging eagerly on his grandmother's hand. For a couple of precious minutes my failing brain takes a timeout, allows itself to contemplate the impossible, but, like all good things, my daydream of cosy nights back with Chrissie comes to an abrupt end with the scrape of plastic on vinyl, and the face of just about the last person I want to see right now appears on the other side of the table. Detective Chief Inspector Grace Helston is someone I respect a great deal in the normal run of things. She's pretty sharp, doesn't mind getting mucky now and then, and sticks up for her people when they need it. She's also my boss, and I knew she was going to catch up sooner or later. She dumps two fresh black coffees on the table and sits back with a non-committal smile. 'Afternoon, Al. Thought I might find you here. I don't suppose you want to bring me up to speed on this?'

I look her right in the eyes and say the only thing that comes into my head, 'Oh Jesus sodding bloody hell.'

# 10

'So what you're telling me,' Grace says, in the tone she generally reserves for juvenile shoplifters who claim the Jack Daniel's stuffed down their trousers fell in there by accident, 'is that your daughter is totally innocent, and you and her other half are hot on the trail of a serial killer whose MO is persuading mental patients to break out of hospital and decapitate women at random?' She's a whisker away from rolling her eyes.

I sit back and concentrate on keeping my hands still. 'That's about the size of it,' I say, 'although "hot on the trail" might be stretching it a bit.'

She keeps her gaze locked on my face and lets out a long sigh. 'Al, try to see this from my point of view. As far as the CPS is concerned, we've got enough on Rosie Larson to get a watertight conviction. They're not about to let it go, and if I'm being straight with you, neither am I, not without something a lot more definite. I'm not saying I can't be persuaded, but ...' She holds up her right hand and starts to count off on her fingers. 'On one side, we've got Shaw's diaries indicating an affair between him and your daughter, the signature on the release form and Rosie in the right place at the right time with pass keys for every door in the place.' She holds up her other hand. 'On the other side, we've got a couple of what look like similar crimes but with no proven connection, a father who will go to any lengths to pull his kid out of a hole – a father, I should say, who is recovering from a serious head injury and who has ... well ...'

'Outstanding psychological issues?' I suggest, quoting Rogers and giving her what I hope is a helpful smile.

'Quite. And as if that isn't enough' – she holds up her thumb, having run out of fingers – 'her husband – the one who's helping you gather this so-called evidence, has just tried to bloody well kill himself. I'm sure if you take all that to the powers that be, they'll be lapping up your every word.'

'He didn't try to kill himself,' I snap, trying not to clench my fists in frustration. 'That's one thing I can be absolutely sure of, Grace. Not Larson – he hasn't got the balls for it even if he wanted to.'

'Oh really?' She rests her elbows on the table and gives her temples a quick massage before saying, a little more gently, 'If that's so, Al, how come we found a half-empty bottle of amitriptyline in his jacket? According to the label, it was one of three bottles that went missing a fortnight ago from the pharmacy at Coombe Hill. We're examining it now, and I won't be surprised if it comes back with both his and Rosie's fingerprints all over it.'

Before I can absorb this bombshell, I catch sight of Chrissie pushing through the press of bodies in the doorway of the coffee shop, Ben toddling behind, hanging onto the hem of her jacket. Grace follows my gaze and gets to her feet. 'Listen, Al,' she says, bending to my ear, her voice low, 'keep looking. You know as well as I do that in three months you may be off the force for good, but until then, you're still one of my officers. I can't give you my support, but I'll do what I can to watch your back.' She straightens up and gives me a nod. 'She's your kid, and I can't blame you for wanting to kick every stone. I don't think for a minute you'll find anything, but if something does crawl out – something I can stuff in an evidence bag, that is – I want to be the first to know, okay?' I nod back. 'You can bet your life on that, ma'am.'

Chrissie flops into the vacated chair. 'He wants to see you. I tried to get him to rest, but he just got agitated.' She gives me a hard – and very familiar look. 'Be nice, Al. I know what you're like when you get going on something. Just ...'

I want to tell her she doesn't know the half of it, that ruffling John Larson's feathers is the last thing I'm going to worry about if it gets Rosie out of prison and safe. 'I'll be nice,' I say. 'I promise.'

She gives me a weak smile, but still looks dubious. 'I know you'll try. I need to get Ben home.' She pauses and adds, 'And I need to get Rosie home. You'll do it, Al – if anyone can. When you do, I'm sure she'll come round. Once she's had time to think things through ...'

'One step at a time, eh, Chris?' The words just about make it through the quicksand that substitutes for my brain chemistry. I can feel myself sinking and decide it's time to back off – for now, anyway. 'I'd better go before the Lone Ranger in there falls asleep on me.'

'You'll call me?'

'I'll call.'

She looks exhausted.

'Don't worry, Chris. I'll sort it – just go home, look after Ben and get some rest, okay?'

'Okay.'

I leave her still sitting there, looking lost, helpless, totally unlike the Chrissie I used to know. Or maybe not – maybe the way I remember things is wrong, or maybe I never looked properly in the first place. At least, I think as I make my way down the corridor, I'll have something to talk about at my next appointment with Rogers if I manage to force myself to turn up.

LARSON'S FACE is whiter than the starch in the pillows he's propped on, except for the grey circles round his eyes. He really does look like shit. 'Be nice,' Chrissie had said. I pull up a chair. 'Okay, son – what the fuck happened?'

He manages a sickly grin. 'I'll be fine. Thanks for asking.'

'That's good to know. Can you remember anything?'

He starts to shake his head, but stops and draws in a breath. 'Jesus, that hurts. My stomach feels as if it's been turned inside out, too. That's the pump, I suppose. Your boss just asked me the same thing. I remember getting to Queen's Square, then nothing until I woke up puking in the ambulance. Is it true, what she said about the pills? About Rosie stealing drugs? She'd never do anything like that – it's crazy.'

'I don't believe for a minute she did, son.' He starts to cough, and I pour him a glass of water from a carafe on the bedside table. 'I don't think the DCI believes it either, but she's still expecting to find Rosie's fingerprints on the bottle, and so am I. There's one clever bastard messing us about here, and we're floundering around wondering what the bloody hell they're playing at.'

His coughing fit subsides, and he hands me back the glass. 'Thanks. In other words, we know *what* they are doing, but not why – no motive, as you would say, except maybe there isn't one and whoever it is, they're just a simple nutcase?'

'Oh, I'd say they are definitely a bloody nutcase, but I think we've established they're far from simple. And I'm not altogether sure we've got the entire "what" either.'

'Meaning?'

'Meaning we've got two incidents so far, not counting this one, and three deaths in each case – the original victim, the murderer and the murderer's supposed accomplice – and joining the dots between them is, from a legal point of view, near impossible. Out of six, three of them are down as suicides. It's the same pattern here – one murder, one suicide or accidental death so far ...'

'Oh, God!' Larson shoots upright, promptly doubles up again and retches into a bowl on the other side of the bed. 'Rosie – we've got to do something about Rosie,' he gasps, wiping his mouth with his sleeve. 'The other two girls, they ...'

'I know – they're dead,' I finish for him, 'and as far as the court is concerned, Rosie's banged up and safe enough already. I'll see if I can't persuade Grace to invent a reason why she should be kept in isolation though – shouldn't be difficult after your little adventure this morning. She's only got to say the words "suicide risk" and they'll be all over her like flies on a cow pat.' I ignore his grimace at my turn of phrase and carry on, 'For now I want you to take me through everything you can remember – right from the moment you got the call. Do you think you can do that?'

He sinks back into the pillows. 'I'll try. A woman rang from Carol's office and said she had some documents for me to look at ...'

'A woman? Did she give a name?' Before he can answer, it becomes blindingly obvious how stupid I've been. I bring my fist down on the bedside table hard enough to send a spray of water out of the top of the decanter. 'Shit! Jesus, I'm a fucking idiot. I should have stopped you – I'm sorry.'

He blinks at me in surprise. 'What?'

'It's Saturday,' I explain, and when he still looks confused, I add, 'Since when did a barrister open their office on a bloody Saturday? Besides, if Dodds had come up with something she wanted you to see, she would have called you herself, not sent a message through a secretary or a clerk.' I dig into my jacket and pull out his phone, making his eyebrows rise even further into his hairline. 'You left it at my place.' I hand it to him. 'There's one way to be sure – call Dodds.'

'You think she'll want to be disturbed on a ...'

'On a Saturday? Make the call.'

She picks up after three rings. Larson puts the call on speaker. 'Get your phone to the police right now,' she says. 'There's a slim chance they will be able to trace the incoming.'

'I'm on it,' I butt in, 'but if this person is as clever as I think they are, it will be a burner, and it's probably already in a bin somewhere near Queen's Square. There's something else – Rosie is likely to be charged with the theft of the drugs from Coombe Hill. Don't be surprised if you get a phone call.'

'Damn and bugger!' There's a short silence, then, 'Crow, can you get over to my place? As it happens, there *is* something I want both of you to see, but, John, you need to stay right where you are. Is that okay?'

'It's okay,' I answer for him. 'Give me the address and around an hour. I need to pick up my car.'


DODDS'S APARTMENT in Clifton isn't quite as upmarket as I assumed it would be. Even so, the modest garden flat in Bellevue Crescent, with its views across to Brandon Hill, would likely not have left much change from half a million. The door opens to a blast of paint fumes, and it takes a moment before the figure in a paint-splotched boiler suit resolves itself into something vaguely familiar.

'Come through' – Dodds waves a paintbrush along the dust sheet covering the hallway – 'but watch the skirtings.'

I follow her through to the rustic-style kitchen and take a seat at a table piled high with folders and box files, plus two open laptops. 'I didn't peg you for a DIY enthusiast,' I can't help commenting as she tosses the brush into the sink and peels off a pair of pink Marigolds.

'Decorating is good for stress,' she replies with a humourless grin. 'You should try it sometime.'

'I'll pass, thanks – allergic to paint. What is it you want me to see?'

The grin disappears, and she leans back against the sink, studying me. 'How well do you know your daughter, Inspector?'

My first instinct is to tell her to mind her own fucking business, but her expression reminds me it *is* her business, for the moment at least. 'Until five years ago, I'd say I knew her pretty well. Now ... well, now I'm not sure I know her at all. What are you trying to suggest?'

'I'm not suggesting anything – I was hoping you might be able to answer a question for me. It may sound odd, but when she wrote anything, letters, signing cheques, anything like that – was she fussy about what she used? Biro, rollerball ...'

'Fountain pen,' I answer without even having to think about it. 'An old-fashioned fountain pen, gold, with her initials engraved on the barrel. I gave it to her the day she got her GCSE results, and she was obsessed with it, carried it with her everywhere, refused to use anything else. Why? What are you getting at?'

'Take a look at these.' She comes over to the table and pulls half a dozen sheets of paper from one of the piles. 'These are copies of all the papers Rosie signed on the day Shaw got out of the unit. We don't just have the day; the times are noted as well. She signed into the secure unit at 8.30am.' She passes me a sheet. 'Note the signature. The next one is an hour later, a list of patient medications from the pharmacy. Take a good look.'

'I'm looking. The signatures look identical to me.'

'They are. Now the third and fourth, routine sign-offs on the unit, midday and just after 2pm.'

At first, I can't see any difference. When it strikes me, though, it's obvious. 'She's used a different pen.'

Dodds nods. 'She used her fountain pen for the first two, but the subsequent signatures were written using a bog-standard biro – not a very good one either – see the blotches where the ink leaked out?'

'So? I don't see what this tells us.'

The corner of Dodds's mouth twitches. 'Bear with me. Now here's Shaw's release authorisation, the last signature on that date.'

'Using the fountain pen again. I still don't ...'

'Rosie told me she lost the pen – she used a biro because she couldn't find it, spent half the afternoon hunting for it. Crow, it's still missing, and the police didn't find it either at the unit or when they searched her house. When I tried to make something of it, your lot didn't want to know – they couldn't see the significance of what someone signed a chitty with.'

She kept it. Rosie kept the pen I gave her, still used it – treasured it. It's almost too much of a thought to hang on to.

'Crow, are you listening?'

I manage to nod. 'I'm listening.'

'You say she's been using it since she was sixteen, yes?'

I nod again, still half lost in the days when Rosie and I talked to each other.

Dodds ploughs on, relentless, 'You realise, a fountain pen is intensely personal – over time, it moulds itself to the way the owner writes, and even if the nib is changed, the style of writing is very individual. The angle, the pressure points made by the nib, the amount of ink released – the differences might be microscopic, invisible to the naked eye, but …'

'But a forensic analysis would show whether two signatures were written by the same person?' I'm back on track now, staring at Dodds with grudging admiration.

She gives me a tight smile. 'Whoever's doing this slipped up, Crow. They figured using Rosie's pen would underline her guilt. What it might well do is prove she didn't sign that release form. I've demanded an analysis, and the prosecution have no choice but to allow it. It's a small chance – but it's a chance.'

'Oh, Jesus.' For a fleeting second I want to grab Dodds and kiss her, but thankfully come to my senses. 'It's not going to be enough though, is it? We need more than that to get her out.'

'I think I may have more.' She hands me a couple of exercise books, the kind I remember from my own school days, blue covers of cheap sugar paper holding fifty or so rough lined sheets. The first book has dates printed on the front in a spidery scrawl:

*2014, July – December.*

'Shaw's journals?'

She nods. 'Two of them. There are quite a few more – keeping a diary of his thoughts was a part of the therapy, apparently. Not exactly page-turners – the handwriting is practically illegible, and the spelling hardly gets past primary school. Mostly he writes about what a failure he is and how he's let Monica down. I assume Monica is his wife?'

'That's right, and believe me, from what I've seen of Monica, she's not the easiest woman to satisfy – in any sense.' I leaf through a few of the pages. Dodds is right, his handwriting and spelling are terrible, and there's not a word more than four letters long. 'Poor sod,' I mutter, half to myself. 'He probably never wrote much more than his name until he got into prison.'

Dodds gives a snort. 'Whether he could write or not, that "poor sod" took a woman's head off – I know who I feel more sympathy for, but that's not the point. Compare that book with the other one.'

The writing is the same untidy scribble, but I can see what she's getting at straight away. 'Where the hell did he learn prose like this? I mean, he still can't spell, but, *it became a conspiracy*, and *her affection was such that I knew she would do whatever I asked* ...' I look up at Dodds. 'This isn't Harry Shaw – it's his writing, but not his words. He wasn't even copying from a book or a dictionary – the spelling is too poor. Someone dictated all this.'

'That's my guess,' Dodds agrees, 'someone with a lot of time and patience and with frequent access to Shaw. He didn't have visitors, not even his wife, so it had to be someone in the hospital, either a member of staff or another patient.'

'It's still not enough, at least not for my DCI, and if she's right about Rosie's prints being on that amitriptyline bottle, it'll be even less convincing.'

Dodds hesitates before replying. 'Until this morning I was prepared to use these diaries and the missing pen to try for bail at Monday's hearing. Now I'm not so sure it's a good idea to request bail at all.'

The same thought has been in my mind, but still I ask, 'Why not?'

Her answer isn't quite what I'm expecting. 'I'm wondering if we're not looking at this from the wrong angle, Inspector.'

'You mean there's an angle? That's more than I've been able to work out so far.' I'm starting to wish she'd just bloody well get to the point she's been working up to since I arrived.

She gives me a shrug. 'I don't know about you, but until

today I've been looking for commonalities in environment and process. The crimes themselves, the way they were committed and so on. I've assumed the motive is a fairly straightforward one – psychological or sexual gratification of some sort, and the victims are opportunistic, people in the wrong place at the wrong time. But what if that's not the case? What if the victims are connected in some way, and they are being specifically targeted?'

'How the hell can they be? They are at different ends of the country for a start, and the only thing they have in common is that they were women living alone. Maybe they had the same sort of lifestyle, could have been identified by the killer as prostitutes, but there is no evidence in our case here that the victim was on the game.'

'Oh, come on, Crow! You might have been shot in the head, but it hasn't made you stupid. Up until today I was following the same logic as you, but if we're dealing with some psychopath who gets their kicks from controlling whoever comes under their influence, where does John Larson fit in? He's not a mental patient, he doesn't work at the hospital, and this attempt to stage his supposed suicide is one hell of a risk for the killer to take. True, we still haven't got any direct evidence, at least nothing we can use, but whatever's going on, it's starting to look pretty personal to me.'

# 11

Christ knows how I get back to the hospital without either killing somebody or being arrested for dangerous driving. Somehow, my brain's managed to switch on the autopilot, and although I can't remember doing it, my official 'police' sign has found its way onto the dash as I pull up on the double yellows by the entrance to the BRI. I'll probably get a ticket anyway, but who the hell cares? I dash past the queue waiting for the lifts and take the stairs to the fourth floor. I can't believe I've been so bloody dense, and what makes me really furious is that Dodds was a step ahead of me. Not anymore, though, damn it.

By the time I reach the corridor, my chest is heaving, reminding me just how out of condition I've got over the last year. I got Dodds to call ahead, so I find Larson perched unsteadily on the edge of the bed, struggling into his jacket. His face isn't quite as grey, but he still looks as if he's recovering from a night raiding the optics behind the bar at the Dog and Duck.

'So,' I say, still wheezing and wishing I'd waited for the

lift, 'you think you can manage to haul your arse down to the car, son?'

He gives me an incredulous look and reaches for his shoes. A nurse, hovering by the next bed, gives Larson a disapproving shake of the head. 'You shouldn't be out of bed, and certainly not out of the hospital for at least another twenty-four hours.' She turns a vulturine eye on me. 'And by the look of it, neither should you – you look less fit than he is.'

She stalks off back towards the nursing station, and I hear her mutter something about 'Laurel and Hardy'. Larson has managed to tie his trainers and make it to his feet, grinning to himself.

I'm not in the mood. 'What's so bloody funny?'

'Well, she's got a point.' He sways alarmingly, and I make a grab for him before he crumples. 'We do look a bit like a comedy double act.'

'Yeah, well,' I tell him as I manhandle him down the corridor, 'before you nip out to buy a couple of bowler hats, son, just bear in mind, we may have something else in common with Stan and Ollie before long.'

'What's that?'

'It may have escaped your notice, but they're both dead.'


It's mid-afternoon when we find ourselves back where we started. My living room looks exactly as I left it, but I'm starting to wonder if that means anything. In the kitchen I find half a pint of milk and not much else. Neither of us has eaten since early morning, and whatever breakfast Larson had is at the bottom of the Floating Harbour down by Underfall Yard. There's a corner shop a couple of minutes' walk away, but I don't want to leave Larson by himself even for a second. I can't shake off the feeling I'm missing something, and after recent events it doesn't take much to spark my natural paranoia. As I'm pondering this dilemma, a sharp rap at the front door drives my blood pressure up another notch. It's probably just the local Jehovah's Witnesses, but then again ... there's another knock, and the snap of the letter box, followed by a familiar voice.

'Al? I know you're in there. Let me in, for Christ's sake; it's bloody pissing down out here!'

I start breathing again and get the door. George Saint, out of uniform and looking more animated than usual, kicks off his shoes, invites himself through to my living room and flops into my favourite armchair. 'Afternoon, Mr Larson. I hope you're feeling better.'

My son-in-law, huddled on the end of the sofa, gives him a weak smile. 'Thank you, Sergeant Saint, much better.'

'Never mind the chit-chat, George,' I butt in. 'What the sodding hell are you doing here? And I don't suppose you've brought any food?'

'I knew you'd be pleased to see me,' he replies with a grin. 'You want me to call out for Chinese?'

'Good idea – and while we're waiting, you can answer the first question.'

The grin fades a bit. 'DCI Helston thought I should widen my horizons a bit – get out from behind a desk, you know?' He pauses, working up to it. We've known each other a long time, me and George, and while there are times he responds to a kick up the arse, there are definitely occasions on which it's best to let him pick his way in his own time. It takes him a minute or two, but eventually he leans forward, hands clasped between his knees. 'Thing is, Al, the DCI knows what an unsociable bastard you can be, and you probably wouldn't want some pimply PC cluttering up the place. So ...'

'What are you saying, George? Am I under surveillance? Grace thinks I've finally lost my bloody marbles, is that it?'

'No – no, nothing like that, Al.' He shakes his head vigorously and holds up a hand. 'Nothing like that at all – the opposite in fact. Dodds rang through about half an hour ago, must have been just after she saw you, and then Helston came down and told me to get into plain clothes and get over here. She seems to think the pair of you need a minder, and just said you'd give me more details when I got here. My orders are to stick with you and lend a hand if you ask for it, act as a liaison if you like. She said she'd be in touch later, but meanwhile you're both to stay put, and so am I.'

'She thinks we need protection? Jesus bloody Christ!' Then I have another thought – a very unpleasant one. 'And Chrissie? What about Chrissie? She's on her own, George, with my three-year-old grandson, for God's sake.'

Larson has already pushed himself upright. 'I'm going to get them,' he says, almost crashing into the coffee table.

'Oh, no you're not, son,' I tell him, and wrestle him back to his seat, which doesn't take an awful lot of effort. Thankfully he's still too feeble to put up a fight.

'It's okay.' George puts on his 'nothing to see here, move along' voice. 'We're on it already. A couple of officers have gone over to pick them up and take them to Mrs Crow's mother's. One of them will stay on, just to be sure.'

'To be sure of what, George? What are you trying to say here?' The back of my neck is giving me a warning prickle, and I have to stuff my hands in my pockets to hide the jitter I know is about to start up. This is my family we're talking about – first Rosie, then Larson, and now Chrissie and Ben. Something has made Helston throw the random nutter theory out the window, and I'm pretty sure it's nothing I've said, so what does she know that I don't?

George's reply is cut off by the crackle of his police radio and Helston's voice on the line. 'George, is Al with you?'

I snatch the set out of his hand. 'I'm here, Grace – what the bloody hell's going on?'

'It's "ma'am" to you, Inspector, and don't swear over a police channel. I've got a couple of things to finish up here, and then I'll come straight over. I don't want anybody going anywhere in the meantime, got it?'

'I've got it, ma'am.'

'Good. I'll be around an hour, so get the kettle on – and I mean it, Al. Chrissie and the kid are fine, so there's nothing for you to do. Just stay put and look after your son-in-law, okay? And don't take it out on Sergeant Saint either, he's just doing as he's told, and he doesn't know any more than he's probably told you already.'

'I understand, ma'am.' She signs off, and I give George his radio back. 'I don't suppose you can call up the nearest squad car and get them to pick up that bloody Chinese?'


THE DCI TURNS up just as we're stuffing the empty foil trays back into their carriers. Larson's perked up quite a bit now he's got something in his stomach, even if it is only plain rice. I hustle George off to make the tea, and rush to grab Helston's umbrella before it drips even more water onto my already sodden hall carpet.

'Christ almighty, Al, this is turning into one hell of a fucking mess,' she remarks as she sweeps past me, tosses Larson a sympathetic nod and collapses into the chair George has just vacated. While she's getting herself settled, I can't help thinking this is the biggest gathering my house has seen in five years, and if it carries on, maybe I should set George on the door selling tickets. He comes in with a tray, sets it on the coffee table, realises there's nowhere for him to sit and trundles off to fetch a bar stool from the kitchen.

There's a brief silence, and my thoughts snap back to

Chrissie and Rosie. All of a sudden it's as though all the air has been sucked out of the room, and I can't breathe. Helston half-rises, her brow furrowed in concern, and Larson reaches for my arm. 'I'm okay, damn it,' I tell them as a major attack of the jitters threatens to take over – my knuckles have gone white with the effort of keeping my hands still. 'At least I will be if you sodding well get on with it and tell me what's going on – with all due respect, ma'am,' I add, trying to force air into my lungs.

'Jesus, Al!' The DCI sits back and runs a hand through her hair. 'Just take it easy. Your family is fine, and they'll stay that way if we have anything to do with it. But I need you thinking straight; you're no good to me if you can't hold yourself together, you understand?'

I nod, and to demonstrate, I grab my mug and manage to take a gulp of tea without spilling it. 'No problem, ma'am.'

'And we can drop the formalities now we're off air and the chief constable isn't listening in. How about you, Mr Larson – are you up to this?'

'Of course,' he replies, 'but are you sure Christine and Ben are safe?'

She gives him a reassuring smile. 'Perfectly. They're in Long Ashton with Mrs Crow's mother, and a police officer will stay with them until all this is sorted out.'

'Which brings us to the point,' I say. 'Until all *what* is sorted out? Come on, Grace, what have you found out?'

She lets out a long sigh. 'Okay. Like I said, this whole thing is starting to get very messy, and I'm hoping if we put our heads together, we can come up with something that makes sense. That means we all share what we've got so far, agreed?'

I catch a worried look from Larson and ignore it. 'Agreed.'

'Okay. Firstly, we've had a preliminary report back from Harold Shaw's post-mortem. He didn't drown. He had an injury to the head that might be consistent with a fall and, according to the pathologist, was the cause of death, but it wouldn't have been instantaneous. If the injury had been sustained falling into the lock, he would have been knocked unconscious, but there would still have been water in his lungs.'

'Mistake number two,' I mutter to myself.

'What?'

'Whoever it is, they made a mistake when they signed Shaw's release form using my daughter's fountain pen ...'

'There's no evidence of that,' Helston protests, but then gives a small shrug. 'However, I'm beginning to think there will be when the results come through of the test Carol Dodds ordered this morning. As far as Shaw is concerned though, I'm pretty much convinced the head injury wasn't an accident – blunt instrument, probably metal, but they can't say exactly until the examinations are all complete. What I can't work out is how the killer managed to get the body into the lock – it's pretty busy round there, even at night, so it would have been a huge risk to take. It would have been much safer and easier to drive a mile or so down the coast and chuck it off the cliff.'

'That wouldn't have worked,' I say. 'Assuming there is a link between the similar cases we've dug up so far, the deaths of all three mental patients have been staged to look like either suicide or accident. Harry Shaw probably never took a cliff walk in his life, not even to have sex in the bushes when he was a teenager. If his body had been found in a deserted cove down the coast, our first question would have been "how did he get there?" As it is, the initial assumption was that he got pissed, walked across from one of the bars and either fell or jumped in. There was alcohol in his system, right?'

'Right – a large amount of Scotch.'

'Which was probably ingested at a cosy little meeting

with the killer, who got him pissed, then whacked him with a hammer. It's my bet that if you take his photo round all the pubs in the area, nobody will remember seeing him – and Harry Shaw was the type landlords don't forget, especially when he'd had a skinful.'

Helston nods. 'George, get on to Portishead, would you, and ask if they can send someone round the pubs and bars. A PCSO will do – I'm sure you're right, Al, but it won't hurt to have it all in the paperwork.'

Something else suddenly strikes me. 'We've got another pattern, too. All three female victims were decapitated, but these deaths are connected by water – the Ness River, the Mediterranean and the Bristol Channel.'

'If the cases are connected.' Helston shakes her head. 'At this point we've got bugger all evidence that they are.'

She's about to say something else, but catches my eye and thinks better of it. I know what's in her mind – it's in mine too, and in Larson's, tense and silent beside me on the sofa. There's a third set of victims, and if the pattern is followed, Rosie is next on the list. That doesn't explain why Larson was pumped full of pills this morning, though, nor the sudden concern for Chrissie's welfare.

I lean forward to put my mug down, my eyes still on my boss. She's working up to something, I can tell. 'So, what haven't you told us yet, Grace?'

Her mouth twitches into a humourless smile. 'Two things.' She turns to Larson. 'First, we've picked up your car, Mr Larson. I'm afraid it's been broken into. There's no real damage, just a smashed passenger window, but ...'

'Oh, bugger it!' He gives me a look of consternation. 'My laptop was in there!'

I groan. 'Don't tell me – you had copies of everything on it?'

He bridles. 'Of course not – I'm not that stupid!'

'That's something at least,' Helston says, 'but I think it would be wise to assume that the theft wasn't random, and the killer may be in possession of sensitive information about you and your family.'

Larson grins. 'They may have the machine, but that doesn't necessarily mean they can get into it. Bloody nuisance though – it cost a fortune.'

'And the second thing?' I ask – I have the distinct feeling the DCI has left the best 'til last.

'Ah.' She looks us both up and down, trying to decide how we're going to react. 'Okay,' she says at last, 'the first victim, remember her?'

'The woman in Cabot Rise – what about her, Grace?'

'Her name was Alison Crawley, age twenty-three, been in the flat around a month, never spoke to the neighbours, hardly ever went out. According to the next-door neighbour, a Mrs Golding, she only ever had one visitor, a man, mid-fifties, height around six feet, dark hair, always wore a hat – wide brim, like an old-fashioned fedora from the description. Either they're coming back into fashion, or he wanted to obscure his face. I'm leaning towards the latter, just to be cautious. He was seen entering the flat twice, both times late at night, no one ever saw him leave, so it's not known whether he was in the habit of staying overnight. However, the post-mortem found traces of semen. She'd had sex, at most a matter of hours before she died.'

I open my mouth, but Helston holds up a hand. 'Before you ask, there was no evidence of rape, and the semen wasn't Shaw's.'

'So whose was it? Do we know?'

There's a slow nod. 'We know, Al. The semen we found on Alison Crawley matches an entry on our DNA database for your ex-wife's former boyfriend – Terence Markham.'

## 12

F or a moment I can only stare blankly at my DCI, trying to take it in. I can't for the life of me imagine Terence the tosser within a mile of the Sinkhole, never mind shagging some trollop from Cabot Rise. That's not my first concern though. 'Are you saying you have that bastard's DNA on the national database? Why? What's he done?'

'As far as we know, nothing. For the last two years he's been living just off St Michael's Hill, and if you remember, there was a spate of assaults on female students in the area some eighteen months ago. We took samples from all males between the ages of sixteen and sixty but didn't get a hit. We haven't got around to deleting the records yet.' Helston shrugs. 'Inefficiency isn't always a bad thing.'

'But ...' We both turn to Larson, who's staring out at my garden with a puzzled look on his face.

'But what?' I ask. 'Come on, son, spit it out.'

'Well, it's obvious, isn't it?' He blinks at us. 'Terry couldn't have gone to the flat, at least not without help, and if he had been there, someone must have seen him. He was in a wheel-chair – you're saying nobody noticed?'

George suddenly comes to life. 'The lad's right – the victim's flat was on the third floor, and the lift hadn't been working for weeks. Unless somebody carried him up the stairs, she must have met him somewhere else.'

'So what does Terry have to say about it?' I ask. 'I assume you've asked him.'

Helston gives a grunt of frustration. 'Not yet. According to neighbours, he's away with his personal assistant – nobody knows where. He had no itinerary, and his phone's switched off.'

Personal assistant? No prizes for guessing what that means – Jesus Christ, is there no end to the reasons I have to hate this bastard? 'You think he's got something to do with the murders? I mean, he's probably the most unpleasant person I've ever met – and that includes everyone I've ever arrested – but somehow I can't see him arranging to have his screw of the week decapitated. For one thing he's too much of a wimp, and for another he's too bloody clever.'

'That may well be your opinion, Inspector Crow' – Helston's tone has gained a touch of frost – 'but I'd say you weren't in the best position to judge. Meanwhile, we need an explanation of how his semen got inside Alison Crawley just hours before her death, and what precisely his connection was with her. I'll be putting those questions both to your daughter and your ex-wife.' She gets up and jerks a thumb towards the door. 'Come along, Inspector, you can see me out.'

In the hallway she reaches past me and closes the living room door. 'You're not going to drop this, whatever I say, are you?'

'You really need to ask that, Grace?'

She lets out a long sigh. 'In that case, Al, you're going to have to put your feelings towards Markham to one side. I know that where Rosie's concerned it's probably too much to ask, but if you're going to be any use, I need you thinking clearly – you're still a policeman, so do what they say at staff development meetings, and' – she does a passable imitation of the head of Human Resources – '*utilise your optimum skill set.*'

I can't help but smile. Right now my primary skills seem to be getting people's backs up and avoiding answering the phone. Come to think of it, nothing much has changed. And then the meaning of her little speech dawns on me. 'You want to bring me in on this?'

'Not officially – I can't. But there are certain things you can do that I can't, and I can maybe oil a few cogs here and there. This investigation is becoming a total nightmare, and if we're going to get to the bottom of it, we're going to need all the help we can get.'

'That's not what you said this morning. What's changed your mind?'

'Several things. A conversation with Carol Dodds for one. If that signature comes out as a forgery, we've got no case against your Rosie, and the CPS will have to drop it. It looks very much like Harry Shaw didn't kill himself, and your son-in-law swears he didn't deliberately take those pills. Add to that the phone call he got, supposedly from Dodds's office – it was a mobile by the way, untraceable – and the fact his laptop was nicked from his car ...'

'And the two other cases we've dug up?'

'More problematic, and I'm hoping you and John Larson can help me out there.' Before I can say anything, she goes on, 'Don't try to tell me the whizz-kid in there hasn't been delving into police filing systems – that information on the Malaga case had to come from somewhere, and not all of it was in the papers. I'm afraid I'll have to have an official word with him at some point. Hacking is a serious offence, and I can't simply ignore it.'

A raised hand stops my objection before I can spit it out.

'However, if we go through official channels, we could be hanging around for weeks, and without his input we may not have a chance. I want you to let him carry on for now, and I'll deal with the consequences later. Meanwhile, don't say a word about this conversation, Al. Larson's going through enough as it is, and my priority is to catch a killer, not a computer nerd, okay?'

There's no point arguing. 'Okay. Anything in particular you want us to look for?'

She spreads her hands. 'Your guess is as good as mine, but it would help if we had complete staff lists for both mental hospitals, with photographs if your boy can manage it.'

'We're already on it. Anything else?'

'Any connections the victims had – family, friends, lovers ... the more I see, the less I think these are random selections. Those women were singled out, and my gut is telling me it's to do with people they knew or had had some dealings with.'

'Like Terry Markham, you mean?'

She nods. 'And while you're at it, see what you can dig up on him as well – it won't do any harm.'

'Grace ... you do realise you are inciting the commission of a criminal act?'

'Bollocks, Al. Like I said, I'll deal with that problem when and if it becomes a problem. Meanwhile, I know nothing about it if anyone asks. Whoever this arsehole is, I want to catch them before any more dead bodies turn up on my patch. If that means using a few borderline tactics ...' She shrugs. 'So be it. Meanwhile, I think it would be better if Larson didn't go home. I haven't got enough manpower to put officers everywhere, so you'd better dust off your spare room.'

'Bloody hell, Grace!' The thought is bringing me out in a cold sweat. 'Is this really necessary?'

'You bet it is. I'm not taking any risks while this lunatic is still out there – you stick to Larson like glue, and if you go anywhere, Al, watch your back, you understand?'

'Looks like I don't have much choice. But you can take George away with you – I won't have him stuck in the corner like a spare garden gnome! I'm as qualified to look after Larson as he is, and I don't need anybody to look after me – not yet anyway. If he's so hard up for something to do, he can help look after Chrissie and Ben.'

She gives me a long look and finally a reluctant nod. 'Fair enough – but any hint you're losing your edge and his sleeping bag's on your sofa. Now, about Rosie ...'

My heart gives a little leap. If that signature is a forgery, Dodds has every chance of getting her out after the weekend.

'Forensics have got a pretty full list of urgent jobs on, so I doubt they'll get round to that handwriting analysis until at least the middle of next week.'

'What? You can't be bloody serious?'

She ignores me. 'And I intend to push ahead with a charge of theft and possession of a controlled substance.'

'For God's sake, Grace ...'

'Think about it, Al.'

She reaches for my arm, but I jerk away. I am thinking about it – about my Rosie sitting in a remand cell, watching her life go down the pan and not having a clue why.

'I'm sorry,' she goes on, 'but suppose we present that new evidence at the hearing on Monday – we give the killer a clear message that their attempt to set up your daughter hasn't worked, and that results in one of two things. Either they disappear and we never catch them, or they worry Rosie might work it out and give us a name, so they try to kill her before they disappear. You and I both know that the safest place for her right now is the inside of a cell where we can make sure she doesn't get any unwanted visitors. Dodds knows it too – you've already had that conversation with her, so don't fight me on this, Al. We both want her safe and sound and back with her husband and child, right?'

'Right.' I've got nothing more to say, and lean back against the wall, defeated.

'Good. Let's get to it, then.' She raises her voice. 'Sergeant? Get your arse out of that chair – you're with me.'

While we're waiting for George to mobilise himself, she asks, 'Have you told Larson about ... you know ...'

I shake my head. 'No. What business is it of his, anyway?'

'None, except I think maybe you should. The poor sod deserves to know what he's up against. You'll have to break the news to him about Rosie, too – it would be better coming from you; you're family, after all.'

Before I can object, George lumbers into the hall, and Helston shoos him to the door. 'Come on, Sergeant, you can drop me off at the station on your way home.' She turns and pats me on the shoulder. 'Get to it, Inspector – I'll be in touch.'


FIVE MINUTES later I'm still in the hallway, discovering how hard it is to regulate my breathing and curse at the same time. On top of that, my knees seem to have locked, and my right hand is doing a tap dance against my thigh. I haven't taken my pills for a couple of days, so I've only myself to blame – not that that stops me from throwing a few choice expressions in my DCI's direction of the sort that would breach both equal opportunities and harassment regulations if anyone was in earshot.

A door opens quietly, and Larson sticks his head out. He looks me up and down, opens his mouth, presumably to ask if I'm okay, but thinks better of it and pads off upstairs. A couple of minutes later he comes back down with my bottles of tablets and a glass of water. He unscrews the caps. 'How many?'

With a supreme effort I get my breathing under control. 'One of each.'

He shakes them out and hands them to me. Thankfully the jitters have subsided enough for me to get them to my mouth without dropping them. He hands me the glass, and I swallow, trying, not very successfully, to push down the surge of fury that he's seen me like this. 'Jesus, shit!' I manage to say.

'I take it things didn't go too well?' He's on his way back into the living room, and I follow, reclaiming my armchair.

'They're not going to let Rosie go,' I tell him. There's no point beating around the bush.

He gives a slow nod. 'I figured as much. She called while you were out there, and I did my best to explain, but ...'

'Oh, God!'

We sit in silence for a while, and then Larson says, avoiding my eye, 'Look, I don't want to pry, but ...'

'That's good,' I snap before I can stop myself, 'because if there's one thing I hate, it's a nosey bastard.'

He doesn't back off. Instead, he looks me in the eye and says, a little too calmly, 'Believe me, Inspector Crow, this is as difficult for me as it is for you, but we're both here, tolerating each other because we both love Rosie, right?'

I don't say anything.

'Right,' he goes on, 'and I don't know about you, but I love my mother-in-law and my son, and I don't want anything to happen to them either. We have to watch each other's backs, and if there's a likelihood you're going to flip out on me, I think that gives me the right to be a nosey bastard.'

The insult that was bubbling into my damaged cortex

doesn't quite make it to my mouth. He does have the right, and however irritating he is, like the DCI says, he's family now. So I make the decision, and before I can change my mind, I tell him. Early on in my recovery, Rogers had told me the story of a railroad quarryman in the first half of the nine-teenth century by the name of Phineas Gage. Victim of a rock-blasting accident, the explosion sent a tamping iron – a three-foot metal rod – through his lower jaw and right out through the top of his head, destroying a large portion of the brain's frontal lobe on the way. Miraculously, Gage not only survived, but managed to get back to his lodgings a mile away sitting in the back of a cart, after which he sat outside chat-ting to friends as he waited for the doctor to arrive. Despite the relative crudity of medical procedures in those days, Gage eventually made a good recovery, although not without some changes to his personality and social skills.

'He was an intelligent, mild-mannered sort of chap,' Rogers had said, 'but after the accident, according to his doctor, he developed a very short fuse – if you'll pardon the pun – and his behaviour, at times, was so unlike his former self that family and friends weren't sure how to react towards him.'

I see Larson's mouth twitch into a grin, probably at the idea that I might ever have been 'mild mannered'.

'Back then,' I continue, 'there was very little knowledge of what was physical and what was psychological. Even now, nobody is entirely sure.' I end with the bottom line. 'So, aside from the hole my brain is trying to rewire itself to get around, I have, according to the friendly neighbourhood shrink, OCD, PTSD, various mood disorders and God knows what else. The drugs help with the OCD, and they join some of the dots between one synapse and another, and the beta blockers are for the tremors, but as far as a cure goes, it's a bit like having your leg amputated and trying to stop the bleeding with a packet of sticking plasters.'

I trail to a halt, and there's another long silence while I wait for him to say how sorry he is, how awful it must be for me and all the rest of the crap I've come to expect. 'Do Rosie and Christine know?' he asks finally.

I shake my head. 'Only that I got shot and the bullet lodged in my brain.'

He gives me a sidelong look, a lopsided grin. 'Well, Ollie, another fine mess you've got me into.'

'You're showing your age, son,' I tell him. 'That's my line.'

## 13

Since I've been on sick leave, Sunday mornings have had two distinct advantages. One is that I won't be bothered by anyone official trying to get me on the phone. The other is that since I'm no longer on call, I don't need to worry about making myself presentable in case one of my colleagues tries to batter the door down and haul me out of bed to attend some emergency or other. Last night, it didn't take me long to realise that I was in no fit state to make any progress, and neither, unsurprisingly, was Larson. Within a couple of hours of DCI Helston leaving, we were both tucked up like a couple of exhausted kids after an overexciting party. Now, at just past 8am, I'm suffering from another common childhood affliction – too much sleep. I'm still checking to make sure all my body parts are connecting to my brain when someone bashes my front door with enough force to rattle the bedroom window. The shock nearly makes me fall out of bed, and my heart is still hammering as I struggle to untangle the sleeves of my dressing gown and negotiate the stairs. Larson gets there first and throws the door wide before I can stop him. I freeze halfway down the staircase, wishing I had a heavy implement to hand, just in case. There's a mumble of voices, I hear the door close, and Larson comes through from the porch, loaded down with carrier bags.

'What the hell do you think you're doing?'

He offers me a bright smile over the mountain of groceries. 'Morning. You said we didn't have any food – I ordered some online last night. That's okay, isn't it?'

Online shopping? Jesus bloody Christ! If he's going to be staying here, I really do need to sit him down and set out the ground rules. I don't have many – actually just two. When it comes to deciding who comes to the house, it's easy – nobody except the postman, which is unavoidable. The second, and possibly more important, rule is that any person of a naturally sunny disposition first thing in the morning can sodding well keep it to themselves until I've had my second cup of coffee. It used to be just the one, but my tolerance levels have dropped a bit over the last year. I feel my nails dig into the palms of my clenched fists and decide it would be better for all concerned if I took a short timeout, so I backtrack to the bathroom and the one activity I can rely on to force the demons back into the box.

It was Rogers – making himself useful this time – who came up with the idea. Everyone, he told me, needs a 'procedure'. That was his word, not mine. It's different for everyone. One man, he said, took up the violin and aimed to perform Vaughn Williams' 'Lark Ascending' note perfect. When I asked Rogers if the guy made it, his answer was that succeeding wasn't really the important thing. Another took up yoga, and for someone else it was writing an autobiography. What was important, he said, was being in control – taking an activity and turning it into a ritual that shuts out everything else, gives all those thoughts that are scouring mental ruts a chance to stop whirring away, spraying clods of crap everywhere. Choose something, he said, that works for you. So the day after I left hospital, I drove to St Nicholas Market and bought myself an ivory-handled cutthroat razor. Shaving takes a long time – but it works for me.

What works even better is the smell rising from the kitchen when I open the bathroom door. I'd almost resigned myself to being presented with the kind of green sludge that seems to be all the rage these days and would probably double up as an efficient toilet cleaner. The scent that wafts to my nostrils, though, is the heavenly mixture of fresh coffee and, unbelievably, bacon. Somewhere deep down, in a place I don't normally connect with these days, I feel a fleeting warmth towards the world. It fades before I have the chance to grasp it, and I make my way down to the kitchen, where Larson is cracking eggs into a pan. He looks up as I walk in. 'Beans, fried tomatoes or both?' he asks, plunging the lever down on the toaster.

'I don't suppose you've got any black pudding to go with that?' I should have simply said 'thank you', I suppose, but why break the habit of a lifetime? I try to calculate how many breakfasts Chrissie must have cooked to see me out on early morning shifts, how many dinners left in the oven for those times I didn't get home 'til God knows what time. It's not that I expected her to do it – I might not be a 'new man', but I never wanted her to give up anything on my account, chain herself to the kind of drudgery I'd seen written on the faces of so many unfulfilled women in the course of decades of policing. That, I remember thinking, would never happen to my wife. And it didn't – not until Terence the tosser took a dive from the upstairs landing and my Chrissie became a full-time wheelchair pusher and shit shoveller. Even so, if I'd shown a bit more appreciation back then, maybe things would have been different. Or maybe not.

'What's the matter? Is something wrong?'

I realise my fork has been hovering halfway between my plate and my mouth for the last two minutes. I shake my head. 'No, son, nothing's wrong. Nothing at all.' I look up at his anxious face on the other side of the table and manage to force the words out. 'Thanks. It's good. It's all good.'

HE WASHES AND I DRY. I'm stacking the last plate when my letter box flap goes off again like a firecracker, and I nearly tip the whole pile of crockery off the table. I give Larson a questioning glare, and he drops his gaze to his feet like a guilty schoolboy. 'What the fuck is it now?' I ask. 'Hasn't anybody heard of the Lord's day being a day of rest, for God's sake?'

He shrugs. 'I don't think the Lord reckoned with next-day delivery services.' He gets the door while I recover myself, and comes back with a hefty box plastered all over with 'Jungle Express' logos. 'That's great,' he says, beaming like a seven-year-old. 'I thought I might have to wait all day for this.'

'And what might "this" be, exactly?'

'A new laptop, of course. I can't do much without one, can I? I could use yours, but if we're going to get anywhere, we both need to be working on the stuff at the same time.'

'So you ordered one up – just like that?' I suddenly feel very old and out of touch.

'Yep – just like that. It should only take half an hour to set up, and I'll be back in business. Look, sorry about the disruption. I know you're not comfortable with all this ...'

'It doesn't matter whether I'm comfortable or not,' I butt in, 'as long as Rosie gets home, and none of us ends up headless or drowned. Go and get started – I'll make more coffee. Unless you'd rather have that fancy green stuff?'

He grabs the box and heads for the living room. 'Coffee's fine. I suppose I'll have to dispense with the morning run?'

I have to grip the edge of the sink. 'You've got to be bloody well ...' I stop, catching an uncertain twitch at the corner of his mouth.

'Yeah,' he says, breaking into a grin. 'I was.'

While I'm waiting for the kettle, I grab the notepad and pencil I use for reminders from the top of the fridge and make a list. Some things are pretty obvious, such as checking CVs and employment dates of staff at the various mental hospitals, doing background checks on the female victims and so on. The relevant police forces will have done this already, which makes our job easier. What they won't have done is set the three cases – if there are only three – side by side and joined the dots. If, of course, there are any dots to join. There have to be, and I'm starting to have faith in the boy wonder's ability to root them out. I suck the end of the pencil for a minute and add a few more musings.

1. Why decapitation?
2. Who visited the nurses?
3. A legless tosser climbs stairs?
4. Who is the Pratt in the Hat?

I pause again and then add at the bottom, in capital letters 'WHERE THE FUCK IS MARKHAM?' and draw two lines underneath. Satisfied, I pour water onto the granules in two mugs, add three sugars to one and stir. I hover over the other, undecided, with a milk carton, swear under my breath and fill a small jug, wondering when exactly I last made coffee for a visitor. I might as well go the whole hog, so I empty some sugar into a bowl, put the lot on a tray and take it through to where Larson is busy pecking away at his new machine, fingers moving so fast they are almost a blur.

'Okay,' he says, jamming a flash drive into one of the slots, 'ready to go.'

Now I get it – all the information was on a memory stick, and that's why he wasn't too bothered about the laptop going missing. That, though, brings another thought bubbling to the surface – a not very pleasant one. 'You had that on you when ...'

'Yes – it was in my pocket – got bloody soaked. God knows how it's still working. Lucky fluke, I guess.'

'Right. And your wallet?'

'Same. Lost twenty quid, but the plastic was fine. Why are you asking?'

I point at his phone – not the fancy smartphone he left on my sofa when he was out being mugged, but the one he's just taken out of his pocket – Rosie's phone. 'Because whoever did this might have missed the memory stick, but I'll bet whatever you like they had a good look through that.'

'How ...' I see the bulb go on, and he hesitates before saying, 'They couldn't have – our phones are passworded, like everything else.'

There's something about his tone that isn't convincing though. 'What password?'

He doesn't answer, just rubs his forehead, mouth set in a thin line. I grab the phone and start to fiddle with the keypad that appears when I switch it on. It takes me three tries. I drop the thing on the coffee table, under his nose. 'There's an old saying,' I tell him, 'and I've just demonstrated that it's not a myth.'

'Go on,' he says, 'amaze me.'

'I think it goes something like, "anyone with half a brain could work it out". Our murderer, son, might be crazy, but they are clever enough, so if I can guess the password in less than ten seconds, how long do you think it took them?'

'I was going to change it,' he mumbles, fiddling with the milk jug. 'It's quite a new phone – Rosie put my name in as a sort of joke. So she wouldn't forget who I was, she said.' He's not looking at me.

'Why would Rosie think she might forget who you are?'

Now he does look up. 'What the hell do you mean by that?'

I spread my arms. 'I'm a policeman. I ask questions. It's what I do.'

'How about you ask something sensible, then – like why some bastard's out there trying to kill us all?' He lets out a long sigh. 'I told you – it was a joke, sort of. Rosie works shifts, and the last six months I've been working on a big contract. We hardly saw each other ...' With a suddenness that makes me jump, he brings a fist down on the table, making the mugs rattle, slopping coffee over the tray. 'Damn it! If I hadn't been so busy, maybe I'd have seen something was wrong – anything ...'

'Yeah, maybe,' I tell him, 'but maybe not. Rosie herself didn't think anything was wrong until she was arrested, so there's no chance you would have picked anything up. It's not your fault, son. I wish she'd changed that password, though.'

'So do I ... oh, shit!' He grabs the phone and fiddles, then holds it up at me.

I peer at the screen and feel a cold sheen of dread start to creep across my skin. Not only is Chrissie's address and phone number on the list but, just below it, her mother's details. 'Call Chris,' I tell Larson. 'Now! I'll get hold of Grace.' Before I can think about it, I grab the house phone and ring through to the Sinkhole. George Saint isn't on the desk, but the duty sergeant catches the urgency in my voice and puts me straight through to the CID office. It doesn't surprise me that Grace answers in two rings – I've often suspected that she doesn't actually have a home to go to, and I know for a fact that while most coppers keep a bottle of Scotch in the filing cabinet, Grace Helston's entire bottom drawer is taken up by an inflatable mattress. I'm halfway through explaining when Larson flaps his hand at me. 'Hang on, Grace,' I say. 'What is it, son?'

'Christine – she says she and Ben are fine. So's her mother. There's a Detective Constable MacDonald in the kitchen, helping with the washing up, she says.'

I interrupt the DCI's flow of curses and the usual mutterings about expense, manpower and overtime and pass the information on, gesturing for Larson to keep Chrissie on the line.

Grace puts on her reassuring tone. 'I'll give MacDonald a call and tell him to keep things tight down there, make sure he doesn't miss his check-ins. There's no way I can spare another body at this stage – we don't even know if there is an imminent threat to Christine or to Ben. Meanwhile, tell them to stay inside, make sure the doors and windows are locked – you know the drill, Al.' She pauses and then adds, 'Don't get any ideas about going over there either. I don't want our meagre resources wasted dragging your son-in-law out of the harbour twice in twenty-four hours – he might not be so lucky next time. Just stay put and find me some evidence I can use, okay?' When I don't answer, she says, 'I mean it, Al. If you want to stay in the loop, you play by my rules. Fuck up, and I'll make sure your sick leave is exactly that, you understand?'

'Isn't there some sort of law against workplace bullying these days?' I ask her, adding, 'Not to say gender discrimination ... ma'am?'

A snort of laughter comes down the line. 'Let me know the minute you find anything,' she says, and hangs up.

As soon as I'm finished with the DCI and the message has been passed on to Chrissie, I show Larson my list, half expecting him to laugh. He doesn't though. He considers it for a while, frowning, and then nods. 'I agree, the method used to kill the women is a bit … flamboyant?'

I remind myself that the kid's a bit lacking in the police vocabulary department. 'If that's what you call "bloody weird", then yes, it is. I don't know much about mental patients, but I can't see three completely different psychos going for the same obscure – and pretty precise method, can you?'

'Of course not.' He gives me the kind of look that suggests I might be losing my marbles a bit sooner than I thought. 'We've already established they were being instructed by someone else – the question is, why so elaborate? What's the meaning behind it? We probably won't know that until we know who, so it's a question for further down the line.'

I have to smile. 'You want to watch it, son. You're in danger of sounding like a detective.'

'Be careful, Inspector. That was very close to a compliment.' He half-grins and examines the list again. 'Is the record of prison visits available via the police computers?'

'No, but I can get the information from Grace.'

'Okay. If you deal with that and see if you can dig up any witness statements about the murder victim's mysterious visitor, I'll concentrate on the overseas stuff, see if we can find any patterns. There must be some somewhere – aside from the obvious, of course.'

Now he really *is* sounding like a policeman. It occurs to me that perhaps his job and mine have some fundamental parallels. Hacking into other people's computer systems must take quite a bit of detective work. The fact he also seems to have taken charge jabs at my 'unreasonable' switch, but doesn't quite trip it. When it comes to technology, he's the expert, after all. 'Right,' I say, and hunch myself in front of my own laptop.

For the next two hours the only sound in my living room is the pattering of Larson's fingers over his new keyboard, punctuated by the far less fluid stabs of my index fingers as I pick my way through the dozens of documents that have already accumulated on the Sinkhole murder. The dead woman – name Alison Crawley, age twenty-three, originally from Brighton, wasn't a typical Cabot Rise tenant, but then, the recent property boom in Bristol has pushed a lot of young professionals into the more down-at-heel areas like St Wilfred's, St John's and West Hill, where rents are more affordable. In a few years' time I suspect the twenty-four-hour laundromat on the high street will have transformed into a free-trade, eco-friendly coffee bar, and the drugs will be of the designer variety. Right now though, the traditional community is still hanging on by the skin of its teeth, and the laundromat is the regular shop window for prostitutes and drug dealers alike.

Crawley, a graduate in business studies from the University of Sussex, had been living in the area just six months, subletting from a friend, a Bristol University languages student who was in China for a year on a foreign exchange. The tenancy wasn't exactly legal, but commonplace among Bristol's large population of students. She had no job as yet, but according to her parents hadn't been drawing on the bank of Mum and Dad, so where she was getting the six hundred or so a month rent from is the first question that pops into my mind. I'm sure it will have crossed the DCI's as well, and given where she was living, there is an obvious answer. Somehow, though, I don't buy it. As I read through the character statements from parents and, via Skype, from the friend in China, it becomes clear that prostitution wasn't in Alison's line. So where the hell did the money come from? I have a strong suspicion, but I'm trying not to let my personal feelings cloud my judgement. Still, I can't help noting that Alison was less than half Terry Markham's age, and that if the bastard was screwing her, he might have been doing it while he was still with Chrissie.

Moving on, I open the statements from the neighbours. The descriptions of the mystery visitor read like a character in a penny dreadful. Two women, independently interviewed, described a man, approximately six feet tall, smartly dressed, wearing a dark, expensive-looking long coat and a hat, which one witness thought might be a trilby, and which the other described as 'one of those wide-brimmed gangster hats with a kink in the top'. A fedora, I decide after a minute's thought. Great – either the guy was on his way to a fancy dress party or we're looking for Humphrey bloody Bogart. Neither got a good look at his face, as they only saw him once, at night, but each on a different date, so he might have visited Alison more often than that without being seen.

I lean back to get the crick out of my neck and realise Larson's fingers are still. He's staring at his screen, frowning. 'What you got, son?'

He doesn't answer straight away, so I give him a minute to work out whatever it is he's got in his head. Eventually he turns to me. 'Rosie's new boss, Dr Lynch – did you say she went on holiday not long after the murder?'

I nod. 'That's what Jenny Pugh said. She was interviewed first though, probably by Grace, and if there were any suspicions, I'm pretty sure she wouldn't have been allowed to leave the country.'

'She would have been asked to leave an address, though, in case the police needed to contact her?'

'Hang on.' I scroll through the list of statements from the hospital staff. Sure enough, there's one titled 'Lynch, M.' I open it and skim through, noting that the statement was taken, not by the DCI at the police station, but a sergeant at the hospital, presumably in Lynch's office. Then I see what he's getting at, and my heart rate goes up a notch. 'A hotel in a place called Vinuela, southern Spain, which is …'

'Less than fifty kilometres from Malaga,' he finishes for me. 'And look at this.'

He twists his laptop so I can see the screen. It's her work record prior to taking the post at Coombe Hill – three years as a psychiatrist with the Royal United Hospital, Bath, followed by a two-year temporary management post at a specialist unit in Malaga.'

'Shit!' I glance at Larson, who gives me a humourless smile.

'Okay,' he says, 'now look at this.' He brings up another document. 'During her stint at the unit, she stood in on a number of occasions for the chief consultant at the San Sebastian hospital.'

'And the timeframe fits with the Malaga decapitation. Dear God! Why the hell didn't Grace pick up on this and stop the woman leaving the country? It's unbelievable!'

Larson shrugs. 'Like you say, your DCI didn't take the statement, and at the time neither she nor the Spanish police were aware of a connection between the two cases.' He pauses before adding, 'There's something else.'

'What else?' He doesn't answer, just brings up a third document on the screen. I can hardly believe what I'm reading. I glance at him and see that he's just as shaken as I am. Lynch visited the nurse, Gloria Marinez, in prison – less than twenty-four hours before her death. 'Jesus bloody Christ, son – I think we've got her!'

# 14

'What do you mean, nothing? There's got to be something somewhere, for Christ's sake! If you haven't found it, you're not looking hard enough.' As soon as the words are out of my mouth, I regret them. The kid's still in pretty bad shape after what he went through yesterday, yet he's been glued, uncomplaining, to the screen of his new laptop for well over three hours since I called Grace with the information about Margaret Lynch. He shoots me a look, and I realise he's probably too exhausted to read what's in front of him. 'I know,' I tell him, 'I'm an arse, and I'm not helping. Why don't you take a turn round the garden, and I'll make some tea?' It's finally stopped raining, and there's even a sliver of weak afternoon sunlight poking through, highlighting the tangle of brambles crawling over what used to be a patio.

He glances through my French windows, then back at me, and bursts out laughing. 'Sure – whatever else you think of me, even I'm not *that* much of a masochist!' He's got a point. 'Tea would be good, though,' he adds, and pushes himself unsteadily to his feet. He badly needs rest, but I won't insult him by telling him so. I just nod and make for the kitchen, trying to keep the lid on my unpredictable temper.

It just can't be possible that there's no evidence of Margaret Lynch ever living or working in Scotland. According to all the records Larson has managed to dig up, she's never even been there on holiday. There are no academic conferences, no research collaborations, no family or friends, not even an old college boyfriend. There are, of course, some sources that he hasn't managed to hack into, but right now, there's no way we can link her to all three murders. What started as a shot of elation has slowly degenerated into frustration and, as my lack of mood control kicks in, infuriation.

When I get back with the tea, he's leaning against the open door, mobile glued to his ear. 'Hang on,' he says into the phone, and turns to me. 'It's Ben. He wants to talk to you.'

I suppress the tremor in my fingers and take it from him. 'Hello, Ben. How's it going?'

'We're having cake. It's got green icing because Granny said I could choose the colour, but it doesn't taste green.' He stutters over the word 'because', and I remember how Rosie used to have the same trouble with long words. With barely a pause he goes on, 'Granny says you're my grandad.'

I can't quite work out whether it's a question or a statement. 'Yes, that's right, I am.' Silence. 'You okay with that, Ben?'

'Yeah, I guess so. You can go swimming with me and Mummy if you like.' I'm grappling with 'Mummy's' probable reaction to that idea when he says, 'Granny's here,' and Chrissie's on the line.

'Al? Sorry about that. Ben was supposed to have a swimming lesson this morning. Are you and John okay?'

'We're fine,' I tell her. 'Don't worry about us. Just make

sure you and Ben stay safe – and your mother. Is that policeman still with you?'

'Yes, he's been playing with Ben. He's a nice lad – is he one of your "babies"?'

'If he's that nice, probably not. But don't let him get carried away – he's supposed to be making regular checks, not reliving his childhood.'

'Al ...' I recognise the note of exasperation.

'Sorry. I'm sure he's doing a fine job – and thanks – for telling Ben. About me, I mean ...'

'I thought it was time. Listen, Al, we can talk about that later. There's something I need to tell you.'

There's a reticence in her voice now. 'What? What is it, Chris? Has something happened?'

'No – well, yes, but ... look, I'd rather not talk on the phone. Can you come over? Is that allowed?'

It isn't. Grace has made herself quite clear about that. 'No problem. I'll square it with the DCI. We could both do with a break anyway. We'll be there in an hour, okay?'

I ring off and hand the phone back to Larson, who gives me a dubious look. 'Didn't the chief inspector say ...'

'Sod the bloody chief inspector,' I tell him, and grab my jacket. 'Come on, son – and bring your fancy machine with you. You don't want that one getting nicked as well.'


DC MacDonald, judging by the way his stubble is competing with his acne, spent most of last spring taking his A levels. As soon as he sees me, he stands to attention and gives me a crisp, 'Sir!' as I walk past him into my mother-in-law's hallway.

I lean in close to his ear. 'Relax, son. This isn't the SAS.'

'No, sir.' He stands at ease. 'I'm sorry, sir, but I'll have to inform DCI Helston that you're here.'

'Inform who you bloody well like,' I counter, and he gives me a confused nod and wanders off to commune with his police radio.

Ben comes bounding through from the lounge and collides with his father's knees, shouting, 'Daddy, Daddy,' and after a breathless moment of hoisting and hugging, he points at me. 'Look, Daddy, I've got a grandad!'

The simple enthusiasm of Ben's delivery gets me like a kick in the shin. All of a sudden my legs are threatening to give under me, and I'm having to swallow down the lump in my throat. Then I realise Chrissie's been watching from the lounge doorway. I meet her eye, and she smiles, comes over and takes my arm. 'Come on, Al, let's go through. Ben's with Mother in the kitchen, making biscuits. John – you can give them a hand.'

'Tall bread,' Ben informs me. 'But it's not tall, and it's not bread.'

'Shortbread,' comes a cheerful voice from the kitchen. 'Make yourself at home, Al. I'll bring some in as soon as they come out of the oven.'

'Thanks, Joyce,' I call back, remembering how much I've missed Chrissie's mother, too.

Ben grabs his father's hand and drags him off to the kitchen, while Chrissie guides me to an armchair in the lounge and pushes me into it. She sits on the sofa opposite and draws in a breath, but doesn't speak, just stares past me through the lounge window, hands clasped tightly together in her lap. It's a pose she always used to adopt when she knew she was about to say something that would challenge my fragile grasp on the concept of family 'status quo'. I want to take her in my arms, but past experience has taught me that under these circumstances, it's not a good idea. 'It's okay, Chris.'

Her gaze jerks to my face. 'No, Al. No, it's not.' She hesitates, then digs into the pocket of her oversized cardigan and pulls out an envelope. Without a word she hands it over, then gets up and paces across to the fireplace, keeping her back to me.

The envelope is stamped with a company name – Cowley Finance. I steel myself and pull out the single sheet. It's a demand for ... 'Oh, Christ all fucking mighty!' I look up and see her shoulders shaking as she desperately tries to hold back tears. I abandon caution and get up, take a tentative step and brush her arm. She shrugs me off. 'Come on, Chris.' I have to fight to keep my voice from mirroring the tremor in my hands. 'Chrissie, it's all right, I promise. We can fix this.'

She whips round to face me, her expression almost contemptuous. 'Is that all you've got to say? It's all right? We can fix it? For God's sake, Al, did you read that letter? We're talking about a hundred and fifty thousand pounds! I'm going to have to sell the house – *our* house, the one where Rosie grew up, the one that's still half yours, and you stand there and say it's all right? Christ, you're unbelievable! You could at least shout or stamp your foot or something!'

'Would it help?'

For a moment she just blinks at me, bemused, then suddenly she's in my arms, sobbing quietly against my shoulder, and I'm holding her, stroking her hair, and hating the part of me that's thanking God for the disaster pushing us back together, even if only temporarily. There's a movement behind me, and I'm vaguely aware of Joyce setting a tray down on the coffee table, the rising scent of freshly baked shortbread. I twist my head and meet her eye, and she gives me an understanding nod. I catch sight of DC MacDonald hovering in the doorway, eager, no doubt, to pass on the wrath of DCI Helston. He doesn't get the chance, though, as my ex-mother-in-law steams back out into the hall, forcing him to take a step back, and closes the door firmly behind her. I try to forget about the trouble I'm in with my boss – right now I've got more important things to worry about. Chrissie has calmed down a bit, so I steer her to the sofa and sit down next to her, afraid to say or do anything else in case it sets her off again. I feel utterly useless – I don't even have a clean handkerchief to give her, for Christ's sake. Chrissie, however, always resourceful, pulls a pack of tissues out of her pocket and dabs her eyes.

'Al – I'm so sorry. This is all my fault ...'

'Look, Chris, maybe if I knew what "this" was – I mean, you didn't haul me over here just to tell me you owe money, right?'

'Right.' She reaches out and grasps my hand. 'I wouldn't have told you. I would have sorted it somehow, but then, with what's happened to Rosie, and that woman, the one who got killed, and ...' She squeezes my hand even tighter.

'Chris ...' She's starting to scare me. 'Chrissie, what are you trying to say? You're telling me that the money's got something to do with Rosie – with what's happened to her?'

'Yes – no ...' She shrugs. 'I don't know. Maybe. That's why I brought the letter with me. I've just got a feeling it's important, that money has something to do with it all somehow.'

To give myself time to get my thoughts into line, I grab the mugs of tea from the coffee table and hand one to Chrissie. Why, I ask myself, would Chrissie need to borrow a hundred and fifty grand? Both of us have always been what a bank manager would call 'cautious' with debt. I can clearly remember the week-long conversation we had over a credit card application when things got tight after Rosie was born. Plus, as far as I know, there's nothing she needs so desperately she would risk the house – unless maybe it was for Rosie, but Rosie's hooked up with a guy who, whatever else I think about him, is more than capable of keeping her in pretty good style. I'm missing something – something I get the feeling I'd be right on top of if my brain was working as it should. I'm on my second sip of cold tea when the tumblers click, and I'm left with two possibilities, neither very pleasant. I discount the first. Chrissie's not the type to give in to a black-mailer, and she lived with me long enough to know that with that sort of crime, silence isn't a good option. That leaves just one other explanation.

'You lent Terry the money, and he didn't give it back, right?'

She manages a nod, but presses her lips together as if too frightened to say any more. After a moment, though, I realise that it's not fear of how I might react – she's simply too furious at what the bastard has done to speak. Even with my blunted sensibilities, I know the best thing I can do right now is nothing, so I just sit, feeling her tight grip on my hand, listening to the sounds of clanking pots and conversation drifting from the kitchen. Ben gives a little squeal of excite-ment, presumably at a new batch of biscuits emerging from the oven. At least, I think bitterly, someone is enjoying them-selves in the midst of all this mess. I wonder if Helston has told Chrissie yet about Markham's DNA in the dead woman's flat – if not, it would probably be a good idea to keep quiet about it for now. I wait until the pressure of her fingers on my hand starts to slacken, and say, about as gently as I can manage, 'Tell me everything, from the beginning.'

For a moment she looks as if she's going to slap me, but then breaks into a smile and says, 'You mean, pretend you're a policeman?'

I have to smile back, if only with relief to see some of her spark returning. 'That's about it – you think you can manage that?'

'Not sure – maybe if you had your little black notebook and pencil ...'

'Bugger the notebook – anyway, we don't have them in

CID.' She's got a point, though, and an idea occurs to me. 'Have you got a smartphone?'

She narrows her eyes for a minute, but then she gets it, pushes herself up and goes across to a little writing desk by the window. She rifles in a drawer, pulls out a tiny silver machine and clicks it on and off, checking the battery. 'Mum's Dictaphone,' she says, bringing it across to show me. 'I bought it for her last Christmas, for shopping lists and so on. Her arthritis hasn't been so good the last couple of years. Will it do?'

'It'll do fine – great work, Chris!' As we've been talking, the atmosphere has taken on a subtle chill. She doesn't sit next to me, but takes the armchair opposite, back straight, hands in her lap. She's become a witness, and I'm about to take her official statement. Whatever it is she wants to tell me, it's important, and she knows it. Judging by the unsteadiness in my hand as I place the little Dictaphone on the arm of her chair, so do I. 'Are you ready?'

She clears her throat and nods, and I press the switch. A little red light shows that it's working, so I lean back and say, 'From the beginning, Chris. Try not to leave anything out – you never know what might be significant.'

And so, she tells me the story.

'It was just over six years ago – a year before Terry's accident ...'

I nod. 'Never mind that, Chris. Go on.'

'Terry came home one night, really excited. He and Mick – that's Michael Swann, his business partner, had come across the opportunity of a lifetime, he said. It would change our lives, we'd be able to retire within eighteen months, set Rosie up with her own place, get a holiday home somewhere, maybe Spain or the Caribbean. Our troubles would be over, he said.'

'What kind of business, Chris? Last I heard, Terry was some kind of glorified insurance salesman.'

She bristles. 'You mean you checked him out? What kind of bastard does that, Al? Did you have one of your DCs staking the place out in case he went for a pee in the middle of the night as well?'

The truth is, she's damned right I checked him out, right down to the last parking ticket. I'd have done the same with any man who was going to be living in the same house as my daughter. No criminal convictions, no alarm bells – apart from being a complete tosser, Terence Markham brushed up as spotless as the chief constable's underwear. At least, that's what the police computer said. I push the idea that I might have missed something, let Chrissie and Rosie down, to the back of my mind. 'Don't be daft, Chris,' I say. 'What somebody does for a living is hardly a state secret.'

She gives me a weak smile. 'Sorry. You're right – about his business I mean, sort of. He was always very close-mouthed about it – "very complicated and difficult to explain" he used to say. The little I did manage to glean was that he and Mick advised people on investments – property mostly, and land, and anything else they thought would give investors a good profit.' She sighs, grabs her empty tea mug tightly in both hands and stares into it.

I flick the switch on the Dictaphone and go across the lounge to the cupboard where Joyce used to keep her evening tipple. She still does, so I pour a generous slug of brandy for Chrissie and, after a slight hesitation, a much smaller one in another glass. I have no intention of drinking it, but decide it might make her feel less self-conscious. I needn't have bothered – she ditches the mug, takes the glass and empties it in a single gulp. 'You want some more?'

'You're damned right I do, but I don't think it would be a good idea. God, Al, when I think of how stupid I was ...' She shakes her head. 'I was such a bloody idiot. I suppose I just didn't want to believe it, and whenever I asked him about anything, he either changed the subject or got angry, and ... I suppose I was scared.'

'Of him?' I force down the image of my fingers round Markham's throat and hope my expression is still calm.

'No, not that so much – scared of what I might find out if I dug too deep. Scared of finding out I'd made a terrible mistake – you know what I mean?'

'Yes, I know.' I want to tell her she could have come to me, that I could have helped, but deep down I know it's probably not true, and now isn't the time to risk her clamming up on me. 'Do you want to carry on?'

'Yes. You need to know all this. It might be important.' She reaches over and switches the machine back on. 'The signs were all there, but I suppose I chose not to see them. He never actually had any money – oh, he took me out to dinner, to classy London hotels for the weekend, shows, concerts and so on. He'd come home some nights with bags and boxes full of designer clothes for Rosie, or tickets for rock concerts – even a pair of tickets for Glastonbury Festival one year. She loved it. As far as she was concerned, Terry could do no wrong.' She gives another deep sigh. 'The longer it went on, the closer she got to him and the further away she got from me. If there was an argument over where she went or what time she came home, he always took her side, and looking back, I can see how he was deliberately marginalising me, using Rosie as a lever if you like, to get what he wanted.'

'And what *did* he want, Chris?' It's only with a super-human effort that I manage to keep my tone even. Inside I'm desperately trying to keep my footing on what seems like a frozen lake in thick fog. Everything is tilting wildly, and I've trapped my hands tightly between my knees so that Chrissie won't see them shaking.

'He wanted money,' she says simply. 'Yes, he was lavish with the gifts, the trips away and so on, but when it came to paying the bills, there was always something – clients hadn't paid on time, the business was in the middle of some deal or other and the payoff wouldn't be until the next month. There was always some plausible reason, and I fell for it every time. Then he started asking for loans. A few hundred at first, to tide the business over until the next big deal came through, and ...'

'Don't tell me,' I say. 'The loans got bigger, and he told you the only way to get your money back was to throw more in, right?'

She nods. 'And meanwhile, like an idiot, I was paying for everything – sometimes even for the presents he gave to Rosie. I couldn't bring myself to tell her what was happening, and anyway, she wouldn't have listened. He could have said anything and she'd have believed it, taken his side. Then I woke up one morning and realised I had hardly anything left. That's when he came up with the big deal – the chance of a lifetime, the one that would get me all my money back plus enough of a bonus to give us a comfortable nest egg. All I had to do was take out a loan secured on the house, and within five years we'd be rolling in it.'

'But you had to move quickly; otherwise the chance would be lost and wouldn't come again.'

'That's about it. And I fell for it, Al. Oh, God, I'm so sorry ...'

'Not your fault, Chris. Conmen like Markham are clever bastards. They count on people being honest, and the thing about honest people is they take things at face value.' I try to smile. 'You can't blame yourself for being a good person – you did nothing wrong.'

She looks unconvinced. 'You haven't heard the end of the story yet. I did what he asked, and took out a loan for two hundred thousand pounds on condition he helped with the repayments. He agreed, and for a year he kept his word and paid half. The investment was starting to pay off, he said. The money had gone into a development of student flats somewhere near Glasgow, and it was all set to bring in millions. We were going to be rich. And then ... and then he ...'

'And then he fell off the balcony and broke his spine. Oh, shit, Chris.' She opens her mouth, but I hold up a hand. 'Don't tell me, he stopped paying, you gave up work to look after him, and ...'

'It gets worse than that. Al, you have to understand, I didn't realise, not at the time. With hindsight I can see how he set it all up, but back then I was in so deep I didn't know what was going on, not until it was too late. I need you to believe that; otherwise ...'

I brace myself. 'Just tell me, Chris. Whatever it is, it's okay.'

She gives a grim laugh. 'No it isn't. It's a long way from okay. I've already said he'd got Rosie in his pocket by then, and after the accident it just got worse and worse. All of a sudden the so-called investment in Scotland wasn't mentioned anymore. If I asked him about it, he'd just lose his temper, tell me to mind my own business, and then his mood would switch, and he'd say everything would be all right, there was just a delay in completing the building, or problems had been found and needed to be rectified before the rental income came back on stream. In the meantime, he said, we could make up the shortfall by suing you for compensation for personal injury or something like that. I refused to have anything to do with it, but he worked on Rosie, tried to get her to back him up. By this time, though, she was seeing John, and even though she was still under Terry's influence, she couldn't bring herself to go up against you, and John was able to persuade her not to go along with it. Of course, Terry hated John – he was too much of a threat. You know yourself that John's no fool. He could see right through Terry from the moment they met. I was so relieved when he proposed and Rosie said yes. But it meant I was left alone in the house with Terry in a wheelchair, all my savings gone and no way of earning a living.

'It all came to a head when Rosie announced she was pregnant. There was an argument, Terry told me the building project had failed and there was no money. That's when he told me the truth about the accident too. The next day he was gone. The loan was taken out in my name of course. John offered to help out, but he and Rosie were happy and settled, about to have their first child. I couldn't possibly accept his offer. I felt bad enough about what had happened and couldn't burden them with a problem I'd brought on myself.'

'You could have come to me,' I say before I can stop myself.

She gives me an almost pitying look and carries on as if I hadn't spoken. 'After Terry had gone, I decided to do a little digging. I suppose I knew what I'd find. I just hadn't been able to admit to myself that I'd been taken in for so long. There was no building project – there never had been. Everything he'd ever told me had been a lie, an elaborate series of scams to part me from my money. That was the real business he and Swann were in. They were fraudsters, con artists. I was just a convenient piece of window dressing – a front he could hide behind, a ready-made family to put the victims at their ease, make them think he was respectable. I'm sure that if it hadn't been for the accident he would have left sooner – the minute the money ran out.'

'Do you have proof of all this?' I ask, and then add quickly when I see her start to bridle, 'I just mean that if we had evidence, names of any of his other so-called clients, or of the non-existent investments he was offering, it would make a stronger case.'

She reaches into her shoulder bag and pulls out an envelope. 'It's not much, but there are a few names here. They were on a list I found in his study a couple of months before he left. I don't even know if they were clients or business contacts or just potential targets, but if you could trace any of them, maybe you'd find out more.'

I give the list a quick glance. There are a dozen or so names, but none I recognise. I put it back in the envelope and slip it into my jacket. 'I'll get people on it, Chris – and I promise you, one way or another, I'll get every last penny back. You have my word.'

She nods. 'There's one more thing, Al. I know this sounds crazy, but ...'

'Go on, tell me.'

'Well, I was over in Clifton Village a few weeks ago, looking around the vintage clothes shops for Rosie – you know how she likes that sort of thing – and I was in a shop in the arcade when this man walked past the window. Al, I would swear it was Terry. I know it's impossible, but if it wasn't him, it was his twin brother. It wasn't just his face – in fact, I didn't see his whole face because he was wearing this hat, an old-fashioned thing with a brim ...'

'A fedora?'

'Yes, that's it. It was on an angle, so I only caught a glimpse, but I know Terry, the way he walks, his build, everything about him, and I'm pretty sure I didn't make a mistake.'

I turn off the Dictaphone and lean forward, grasp both her hands in mine. 'I'm pretty sure you didn't, too,' I tell her. 'Thanks, Chris. You've been more help than you know.'

Her reply is cut off by a loud knock at the door, and without waiting for permission, DC MacDonald stamps in clutching a mobile phone. He thrusts it out to me. 'I'm sorry to disturb you, sir, but DCI Helston says she wants to speak to you right away.'

I take it from him. 'Ma'am?'

Grace is clearly not in the mood for niceties. 'DI Crow, I hope you've got a very good reason for being out in Long Ashton.'

'Yes, ma'am,' I reply, trying to sound non-committal.

'Good. I look forward to hearing it. I want you at the station at eleven in the morning, and bring Larson with you. In the meantime, you can both get your bloody arses back to where they're supposed to be, do you understand?'

'Perfectly, ma'am.'

She hangs up, and Chrissie gives me a knowing look. 'I thought you said your boss was fine about you coming over?'

'She will be,' I say, and get up. 'Try not to worry, Chris. I'll get this sorted, I promise.'

As I make my way to the kitchen to grab Larson, I try to count up the number of times I've said that over the last four days, very aware that with each repetition, the chances of my making good on the promise seem to fade a little more.

## 15

DCI Helston reaches across her desk and switches off the Dictaphone. 'Okay, Al. So what you're saying is that your ex-wife's former boyfriend has miraculously regained the use of his legs and is wandering around the city dressed in a gangster outfit when he's not having sex with the local prostitutes in West Hill? You're sure Christine wasn't mistaken?'

'Chrissie doesn't make mistakes – not about things like that,' I tell her. 'Plus, I don't believe the dead woman, Alison Crawley, was working as a prostitute. What if Markham had set her up there, was paying her rent, using her for some scam or other?'

Grace waves a dismissive hand. 'A bloody expensive way to set up a con – and who would have been the target? She didn't have any money and neither, from what we've managed to find out, did her family. Sorry, I don't buy it. But I agree, something doesn't add up. Until we've found Markham though, we're not likely to find out. What concerns me far more than his shady financial life is any connection he might have with the murder. It may be none, but he needs to be eliminated. The sooner we can do that, the better – I don't have the manpower to go dashing up blind alleys.'

'And the fact he's been conning people out of their life savings, probably for years?'

'Not our case, Al. I'll alert the fraud squad, and they can look for him and his partner, Michael Swann. When they find either of them, we'll be informed. I'll send them through a copy of that list Christine gave you, and one of their people will go round and interview her.'

So far Larson, hunched beside me, has kept his mouth shut. Now, he looks from me to Grace, horrified. 'That's all you're going to do? After what he's done to Christine and probably dozens of others?'

I clear my throat, and Grace sighs. 'Believe me, Mr Larson, the fraud squad takes this sort of thing very seriously. They'll catch him, you can be sure of that. There's also the question of possible benefit fraud if he's been faking his disability, and once those people are on the case, they don't let go. Meanwhile, I didn't call you both in here to talk about Terry Markham.'

'So why are we here, Grace? You do realise Rosie's due in court in less than an hour's time?'

'And that's one reason for keeping the pair of you here,' she shoots back. I feel Larson stiffen next to me, but he doesn't get the chance to protest. 'In the first place,' she goes on, 'I want to avoid any repetition of last week's performance at the magistrates' court, and in the second place it's too dangerous. There's already been one attempt on your life, Mr Larson, and I'm not about to risk another.' Her expression softens. 'Believe me, I understand how difficult this is for both of you. Carol Dodds has had a long conversation with Rosie, so she understands the situation, and I've arranged an escorted visit for you this afternoon. An officer will take you to the prison and return you to Inspector Crow. Meanwhile' –

the sympathetic look fades as she turns to me – 'you stay the hell away from Long Ashton, Al. We don't know who's at risk and who isn't, and I don't want all my potential victims herded into one pen like a bunch of sacrificial goats. If you want to talk to your ex-wife, you can pick up the phone like everybody else, okay?'

'You're the boss, Grace.'

'You're dead bloody right I am – ignore my instructions one more time and your sick leave will consist of cocoa, a tartan rug and a pile of jigsaws.'

'You said "one reason", Grace,' I prompt.

She snorts out a breath and sits back in her chair. 'I'm bending the rules, but I thought it might be useful if you listened in to an interview I'll be conducting shortly. I'm afraid I can't extend the invitation to you, Mr Larson, but I give Inspector Crow my consent to pass on any information he sees fit.' At this point her phone rings, and Larson and I exchange frustrated glances. There's a pause while she listens, and then, 'Good. Interview room 2, ten minutes.' She hangs up and pushes herself to her feet. 'Right. You're with me, Inspector. Mr Larson, you stay here – I'll get one of my DCs to bring you in some tea. If you need anything else, just ask.'

'For Christ's sake, Grace!' My irritation quotient is fast approaching its trigger level, and I just manage to stop my fist making a dent in the DCI's pristine hardwood desk.

'Oh, didn't I say?' There's a very slight twitch at the corner of her mouth. 'Your daughter's boss, Margaret Lynch, landed at Bristol Airport an hour ago. We sent a car to pick her up, and she's just arrived at the station.' If my expression is as ridiculous as my son-in-law's, it's no wonder the DCI finally cracks a brief smile. 'Well, Inspector – are you coming or not?'

. . .

'YOU'RE TELLING me she agreed to come in voluntarily? Why? What the bloody hell is she playing at?'

'At this point, my guess is as good as yours,' Helston replies as we make our way to the interview rooms on the other side of the station. 'The local Spanish police sent an officer round to her hotel, and whatever they said to her, it was enough to make her book a flight back first thing this morning.' She gives me a sidelong glance. 'Maybe she wants to confess – now wouldn't that be convenient?'

We've arrived at the interview suite, and Grace ushers me into a side room equipped with a one-way mirror and a monitor picking up sound and video from the cameras installed next door. Someone else has got there before me. A balding, overweight middle-aged man in a maroon sweater and matching corduroys unfolds himself from his chair and sticks out a hand. I take it warily – he looks as if he's just got back from Glastonbury Festival and hasn't had time to shave or take a shower. In other words ... 'Don't tell me,' I say, 'you're the profiler, right?'

He gives me a watery smile to go along with the Play-Doh handshake. 'Don Burke,' he says, in a pseudo-transatlantic drawl that doesn't quite cover an accent from somewhere west of Birmingham. 'I'm a psychologist. DCI Helston thought my insight might prove useful.'

Luckily for both of us, Grace's voice, relayed via the video system, prevents me from blurting out the string of choice comments that swoops into my head. We both turn to the mirror, and while Grace introduces herself 'for the benefit of the tape', I get my first look at the stiff, unsmiling figure of Margaret Lynch, perched on the edge of her chair on the opposite side of the table. Next to Grace, a young female DC, most likely a trainee doing her stint in the Sinkhole, is trying her best not to look like a spare part. Lynch, greying hair scraped back into an untidy ponytail, looks tired, on edge, but not, as far as I can tell, intimidated – at least not yet. Grace doesn't waste any time getting to the interesting questions. Didn't Dr Lynch think, in view of the role of her department in the escape of Harold Shaw, running off to the Costa del Sol might give the wrong impression?

Lynch straightens up and sniffs. 'I'm not in the least bit interested in impressions, Chief Inspector.'

'Really?' Grace gives one of her sweetest smiles. 'An odd thing for a psychiatrist to say.' Lynch takes in a breath, but Grace doesn't give her time to respond. 'And yet you cut your holiday short to come back and speak to us – forgive me for saying so, but that doesn't seem like the action of someone who doesn't care what other people think.'

Lynch gives what looks like a superior smirk. 'That's hardly the same thing. Naturally, when the Spanish police told me you wished to contact me, I returned as soon as possible. However, I did not cut anything short. I had no particular plans – I simply had a few days leave arranged, and I believe I explained this to the officer who interviewed me before I left. It was at no time suggested that I should not take that leave, nor that I shouldn't use it as I saw fit.'

I see Grace's lips tighten at this, but whether it's at Lynch's apparent lack of concern for her staff or the almighty cock-up some idiot constable made letting her leave the country is hard to say – probably both. I glance across at the aptly named Burke, who is sitting back in his chair with his arms folded, chin on his chest, squinting at the mirror and looking slightly bored. That suits me fine – I have to contend with enough intimate chats with mental health services as it is, and my opinion of their contribution to police work generally ranks just below that of a trainee in their first week on the beat.

Grace has regained her non-committal smile. 'Quite so, Dr Lynch, and we are very grateful for your cooperation, even at this late stage.' There's an emphasis on the 'late'. 'I wonder if you would mind very much just going through the timeline of your arrangements with us, just to make things clear. According to our records, you were interviewed on Wednesday last following the arrest of your nurse manager, Rosemary Larson?'

Lynch nods, but says nothing.

'And the day before that – the day Harold Shaw absconded from Coombe Hill secure unit and murdered a woman in West Hill, you were in Wiltshire on a staff development exercise for senior managers. Correct?'

'That's right. It was a one-day event with a meal in the evening. I got home just after eleven. I did go through all this at the time.'

Grace looks down at a small stack of papers in front of her, presumably a copy of Lynch's statement, and then back up at Lynch. 'I'm sure you did. I just want to make sure we have everything straight, for our records. So when, precisely, did you hear about Shaw's disappearance and about the murder?'

'Not until Wednesday morning. There was a voicemail from a colleague on my mobile concerning the unauthorised absence of the patient from the secure unit. It was left the night before, but I didn't notice I had a message until early on Wednesday. I'd switched my phone off while I was engaged in the development meetings and had forgotten to switch it back on – I was very tired when I got home.'

'And the murder?'

'Not long afterwards – perhaps half an hour later – it was on the local breakfast news.'

'I see.' Grace's smile grows a little wider. 'And your hotel room and flight – when did you book those?'

For the first time, Lynch's stony expression gives a slight twitch. 'I can't quite recall exactly ...'

'Really? According to airline records, you booked the flight at 9.17am on Wednesday morning, and the hotel took a call from you approximately fifteen minutes later at around 9.30. Forgive me if I'm jumping to conclusions, but from our point of view it looks very much as though you picked up the message from the hospital, saw the report on the news, and decided to jump ship before the shit hit the fan.'

Lynch gives an outraged snort. 'That is utterly ludicrous. You will know very well from your records that I went straight to my office that morning and made myself available to your officers. It was clear to them, if not to you, that I had nothing to do with the events of the previous day. My presence was not required, and as I have already said, there was no objection to my leaving the country.' She sits back in her chair and folds her arms. 'Perhaps I should call my solicitor just in case you decide to charge me with the murder? After all, you do seem to be floundering, and I'm sure your superiors are quite keen for you to arrest somebody, even if they happen to have been with a dozen other people forty miles away at the time.'

Grace's smile doesn't slip. 'I assure you, Dr Lynch, I have no intention of arresting you on a charge of murder.' She pauses, peruses the papers in front of her for a good minute, and then looks up, meeting Lynch's eye. 'I was thinking conspiracy might be more appropriate, or withholding evidence, maybe even forgery or theft, but definitely not murder.'

Lynch's mouth flaps soundlessly for a moment before she gathers herself, lurches to her feet and hisses, 'You have got to be insane!'

'Not at all. However, I would prefer not to charge you with anything just yet, Doctor. In fact' – Grace stands up and taps her papers into a neat pile – 'I think we'll leave it there for the moment. Thank you for your cooperation, Dr Lynch. I'm sure we'll be in touch shortly, so in the meantime, please don't make any further travel arrangements.'

Grace sweeps out of the room, leaving Lynch open-mouthed with indignation. I glance across at Burke frowning to himself in the corner, and can't help but grin. A minute later the door swings open and the DCI joins us. Burke is on his feet before I can take a breath.

'Chief Inspector, I really think ...'

'Thank you, Professor Burke, I wonder if you would mind giving me a moment? I need to talk to Inspector Crow. Perhaps you could grab yourself a coffee, and I'll join you in a few minutes?'

She holds the door open meaningfully, giving the psychologist little choice but to comply, forcing a smile through gritted teeth. 'Of course. No problem – I'm at your disposal, Chief Inspector.'

As soon as he is safely out of earshot, I give her a raised eyebrow. 'Professor? Seriously?'

She laughs. 'At the university, apparently – teaches forensic psychology. It wasn't my idea, I promise you. The ACC's got a bee in his bonnet at the moment. Violent crime, he tells us, is by and large committed by nutcases, so the input of a mental health professional has to be a good thing.'

'You think Lynch is a nutcase?'

She shakes her head. 'Far from it. She's sane enough to know we can't charge her with anything, but with luck I've given her something to think about. I've no doubt Burke will be falling over himself to explain the finer details of whatever disorder he can shoehorn her into, simply to justify his consultancy fee. How did she strike you?'

'I can understand why she doesn't win any prizes for popularity among her staff,' I remark, 'but unfortunately being unpleasant isn't a crime. Withholding information is, though, and I'm damned sure she's doing that. Whatever she was up to in Spain, it wasn't a bloody holiday.'

'Agreed. I'd like you and Larson to concentrate on that side of it – what the hell *was* she doing? Warning someone off? Meeting an accomplice? Maybe covering her tracks – or someone else's. I need to know, Al – if you're up to it, that is.' I give her a look, and she shakes her head. 'I'm not blind, Al. You're not physically fit yet, but that's not my main worry. This is putting you under a lot of stress, and according to the record, you're ignoring your appointments with the psychiatric services ...'

'Oh, for God's sake, Grace ...'

'No, Al – you listen to me. Can you put your hand on your heart and tell me you're not suffering post-traumatic stress? That all those attacks of the shakes aren't connected with the shooting?'

I take a breath, but before I can speak, she goes on, a little more sharply, 'Think carefully before you say anything, Al. Because from where I'm standing, I'm looking at a good man who's going to let the rest of his life go to hell because he refuses to accept help – and it's not just work I'm talking about, it's Chrissie and Rosie and ... damn it, you've got a grandson to think about. That's more than a lot of us have ...' She trails off, half turns away, and says very quietly, 'What I mean is, I'm not just your boss, Al. I'm your friend, and I don't want to pull rank on you – but I will if I have to. If you want to stay a part of this, you get yourself sorted. I'm not asking – you understand?'

Again, I'm about to answer, and again I'm interrupted, this time by the trill of my mobile in my jacket pocket. I fumble for it, but the twitch gets me first, and it jumps out of my hand, clatters to the floor between us. 'Jesus fucking shit!'

Grace stoops and scoops it up before I can regain my coordination. She glances at the screen, presses 'answer' and puts it to her ear. 'This is DCI Helston.' She listens for a moment, then, 'That's fine. We're done here for the moment. I'll send him straight up.' She hangs up and hands me the phone. 'That was your son-in-law. The car has arrived to take him across to the prison. You need to go with him.'

'Why? He's got an escort, hasn't he? He doesn't need me to hold his hand all the time.'

'That's true,' she replies with a smile, 'but if you want to see Rosie, it might be a good idea.'

'Rosie?' I blink at her stupidly.

'You know – your daughter – the one all this is about? She's asked to see you. I suppose I'd better go and humour Burke before he complains to the ACC that I'm ignoring him.' At the door she turns and gives me a nod. 'Remember what I said, Al – and good luck. I'll be in touch.'

# 16

We spend most of the journey across town in silence, hunched together in the back of an unmarked police car. We're several miles up the motorway by the time I manage to get the tremor in my hand under control. Larson has considerately kept his gaze on the scenery, waiting for me to speak first. The car is pulling in outside the main prison gate when I finally manage it.

'What did she say?' I ask him, not sure if I want to know the answer. 'What's changed her mind – about seeing me, I mean?'

'I don't know.' He pulls his attention from the walls towering over the narrow street in front of the prison and looks at me. 'I didn't speak to her.'

'What do you mean, you didn't –'

'I spoke to Carol Dodds,' he interrupts. 'She gave me the message and asked me to pass it on. That's all – I don't know any more than you.' He pauses and gives me an uncertain smile. 'It's good though – isn't it?'

I don't know how to respond to that, and am still thinking about it when the young DC at the wheel pipes up, without turning his head, 'Sorry, sir, you'll have to walk from here. When you're ready to leave, the officer at the lodge will let me know, and I'll pick you both up.'

'For Christ's sake,' I can't help muttering, 'haven't you got anything better to do? It's not as if the West of England has run out of crimes to investigate.'

'DCI's orders,' he replies, and adds another, 'Sorry.'

It's not until we're out on the pavement that I realise Grace has us under surveillance – or maybe not 'us', exactly. She wants to know if we're being followed. That conclusion leads me to thoughts of being stalked by a fake cripple in a fedora who wants to kill my daughter, and I stop dead. 'Fuck it!'

Larson, misinterpreting me, blinks and says, 'Look, Inspector, are you sure you want to go in?'

'Of course I'm bloody sure!' I need to get myself under control. The last thing Rosie needs is to see the father she hasn't spoken to for five years dissolve into a quivering wreck in front of her. I take a couple of deep breaths. 'I'm fine, son. Let's just get on with it, shall we?'

DODDS AND A PRISON officer are waiting for us at the far end of the long corridor that separates the blocks for convicted prisoners from those on remand. Somehow, she's managed to persuade the authorities to place us in one of the small rooms usually reserved for meetings between prisoners and their solicitors, or for police interviews. At least our meeting isn't going to be in full view of any other prisoners in the main visiting hall. I'm willing to bet that half the inmates here know me, at least by sight, and it won't make Rosie's life any easier to be labelled as the daughter of the man who put some of them inside. I'm sweating with the effort of control- ling my nerves when we reach Dodds, who shakes Larson's hand and gives me a token nod. The officer, whom I know by sight, offers a smile of recognition, and I force myself to return it.

'We've got a few minutes before they bring Rosie down,' Dodds says. 'John, I know it's difficult, but it would be good if Rosie saw Inspector Crow alone – we won't be too long, I promise you.' She waves a hand at the officer. 'This gentleman will take you to get a cup of coffee, and he'll come and fetch you when we're ready.'

I'm not sure whether the look Larson shoots me is sympathy, envy or annoyance – probably all three. He does as he's told, though, and allows himself to be led away through a side door.

'So,' I say, as I follow Dodds into the room, which is quite well furnished with four armchairs and a small coffee table, 'are you going to tell me what's going on here?'

Dodds sniffs. 'Would you like to sit down, Inspector?'

'Oh, for God's sake!' The conflict between my aching desire to see my daughter and the panic at how she might react when she sees me is making me dizzy. My thoughts go back to the day Rosie was arrested, and George Saint leaning across the desk in the front office ... *You can tell anybody you like, as long as it's not my rotten bastard father* ... I make a decision and start towards the door, but too late. It's blocked by a female prison officer. The woman stands aside, and there she is – my Rosie, dressed in jeans and an oversized Aran sweater – one of Larson's by the look of it – hands clasped in front of her, head lowered, long, dark hair hiding her face, the way it always did when she was a teenager. At least she's not wearing that ghastly suit from the courtroom. I stand there like an idiot, frozen, while, without a word, she squeezes past me and sits down in one of the chairs – the one furthest from where I'm standing.

I stay where I am, locked into position, until the woman

in the doorway shuffles back a step. 'I'll have to leave the door open, I'm afraid.' Her voice is firm, but not unkind. 'I'll be just outside. You have around fifteen minutes.' She moves away, although I can still see her shadow just beyond the door. The interruption jolts my body back under control, and I sit down. Dodds has moved her chair a little to one side – as close as we're going to get to privacy.

I can feel Rosie's eyes on me from under the curtain of hair and make a supreme effort to move my mouth. 'Are you okay, love?' is the best I can come up with.

For a long moment there is silence, and then Rosie lets out a breath, lifts her head and tosses back her hair in a familiar, defiant gesture that almost reduces me to tears of relief – my baby's in there after all – in there and still fighting. She hesitates and then throws me an unexpected question. 'Does it still hurt? I mean ...' She points to her head and twiddles a finger.

Taken by surprise, I have to fumble for an answer. 'No – no, not really. Sometimes, a headache now and then. It's not important ...' I trail off, thinking of all the other stuff – the stuff that does hurt.

She nods slowly, as if considering, and then jerks her gaze from the floor to my face, her whole body rigid, determined. 'I want you to promise me,' she says, almost spitting the words, 'that you'll tell me the truth – just the truth, nothing else. Do you promise?'

'Yes,' I tell her, trying to keep my expression steady, praying I can keep my word, 'I promise.'

'Did you do it?'

She makes the question sound like an accusation, and I can't help thinking if she hadn't gone into nursing, she'd have made a damned good lawyer. I look her straight in the eye. 'No.'

There's a pause, and she drops her gaze. 'What's the matter with your hand?'

I realise a jitter has started up, and it's too late for me to hide it. 'Nothing – it just happens sometimes ...' And suddenly, I can't remember how, we're both on our feet and she's wrapped herself around me, sobbing on my shoulder, trying to tell me something, but the words aren't making any sense, they're spilling out too fast for me to catch. I glance across at Dodds, who's diplomatically turned away to give us as much privacy as we're going to get. 'It's all right,' I tell Rosie, stroking her hair and rubbing her back as if she's a three-year-old, because it's all I can think of to do. 'It's all right, sweetheart. Just slow down, okay? Take your time, and tell me what's happened. It will all get sorted out, I promise ...' I carry on, saying whatever comes into my head, until eventually she sinks into a chair, the one next to me this time, taking in shuddering gulps of air. I grab a handful of tissues from a box on the coffee table and push them into her hand. She wipes her eyes, blows her nose, and lets me hold her hand while she calms herself down. I force myself to at least appear in control. I'm not quite sure whether she's hanging on to me or I'm hanging on to her, but at least the jitters have stopped for now. 'Okay, love,' I say when her breathing is almost back to normal, 'tell me all about it.'

That brings a tiny, but spontaneous smile. It flits away, and she says, eyes on her hands, 'I got a phone call last night. From Terry.'

I frown across at Dodds, who nods. Rosie goes on, 'I was relieved, at first. I mean, I'd been wondering why he hadn't come to the police station or tried to get in touch before.'

'You were in contact with him a lot, then?' I can't help asking, thinking that the bastard probably took every opportunity to drip poison into my daughter's ears.

She nods. 'He'd call or email several times a week, asking

how I was, how Ben was getting on, all of that. Always at work though. John doesn't know we kept in touch – you won't tell him, will you? They didn't get on, especially after Terry walked out on Mum, and whenever Terry rang the house, there'd be a row. In the end I just told Terry to ring me at work.'

Larson shoots up yet another notch in my estimation. 'It's okay, love. He'll have to know, you realise that, and sooner rather than later, but he won't hear it from me, I promise.' I have a feeling he probably knows already. My son-in-law is a lot of things, but I've learned over the last few days that stupid isn't one of them.

'I know. I'll tell him myself – I just need to ...' There's a tear in her eye again, but she pulls herself together. 'Anyway, when I heard Terry wanted to talk to me, I was sure every-thing would be all right. He always used to say he had a trick up his sleeve for everything, and I figured if he hadn't called before, it was because he was working out what to do.'

'Right.' Knowing what I know about Markham's 'tricks', he probably wasn't exaggerating. 'So what did he say?'

Rosie shakes her head, brows drawn together as if she's still trying to make sense of it. 'I was so pleased to hear his voice – I thought, now he knows where I am, he'll do some-thing, get me out of here, find out who let Harry out of the unit, and everything will be back to normal ... I was so stupid – completely and utterly stupid ...'

She trails off, and I squeeze her hand, thinking of how her mother said the exact same thing to me less than twenty-four hours ago. 'It's all right, Rosie. So he didn't offer to help?'

'He said ...' She closes her eyes, searching for the words, 'he said, "I just rang to say goodbye," or something like that. He said he didn't want to disappear without hearing my voice one last time.' Her eyes snap open, wide and still full of disbelief, but her voice is flat, business-like, a witness wanting to give an accurate recollection. 'I asked him where he was going, but he wouldn't tell me. So then I said I needed his help, and he just laughed. He said, "I'm sorry, my dear, but it's either you or me, and it's really no contest, is it?"'

'He said that? Exactly? "It's either you or me"?'

She nods. 'That's exactly what he said. I couldn't believe it. I asked him what he meant, and he laughed again, and then he said, "You should talk to your father. You never know, now that he's only got half a brain, he might forgive you for all those lies you've been telling about him." She gives me a nervous glance, then looks down at her lap. 'I said, "What lies?" He laughed again and said something like, "Surely you didn't believe all that crap about him pushing me off the balcony? You're as gullible as your mother. But then, that's why I chose you, after all." I can't remember the exact words, but that was the gist of it. Then he said, "Don't worry, wherever I am, I'll be thinking of you. It will be nice, knowing I can picture exactly where you are, for the next twenty years or so at least." Then he hung up.'

'Sweet fucking Jesus!' I look across at Dodds, and suddenly it's obvious that she's already heard the story, and it's because of her powers of persuasion that I'm here. I nod my gratitude, and she acknowledges it with a twitch of an eyebrow. I turn back to Rosie, who is still struggling to hold back tears.

'Dad, I'm so sorry ...'

'You've got nothing to be sorry for,' I cut in, trying, unsuccessfully, to get the image of what I feel like doing to Terry Markham out of my head. 'Terry was a very clever, manipulating bastard, and both you and your mother were way out of your depth. That's the thing with criminals like him – they always target the most honest, most trusting people they can find. Like he said, that's why he chose you. Damn it, he even had me fooled for a while. But one thing I can tell you for certain, there's no way you're going to be in here for a minute longer than is necessary, and when we find that man, we're going to make sure we put him away for a very long time – the rest of his natural life if I have anything to do with it.'

She wipes her eyes and looks up at me. 'Will you find him?' She doesn't sound convinced.

'Believe it, sweetheart,' I tell her. 'We'll find him.'

There's a short silence, and then she says, 'Carol says you've spoken to Mum – and you've seen Ben, too.'

'Yes, I have.' I fall back on my new mantra. 'Ben's a great kid.'

Rosie inexplicably breaks into a giggle, and for a brief moment she's the daughter I last saw five years ago. 'Of course he is, Dad. He's mine, isn't he?' She reaches out and grasps my hand, serious again. 'It *will* be all right – won't it?'

I reach out and gently lift her chin with a finger so I can look right into her eyes. 'It will be all right,' I tell her. '*Everything* will be all right. I'm going to damn well make sure of it.'

I hear a shuffle behind me, and a polite cough. My time's up. 'Hang in there, Rosie. If you need anything, just tell Carol, and she'll get a message to me, okay?'

I get to my feet, and she follows, pulls me into a hug. 'Just one thing, Dad. Look after John for me? Don't let him do anything stupid, get into any trouble. I couldn't bear it if anything happened to him.'

I catch Dodds's frown. Clearly nobody has told Rosie about the attack at the harbour. 'Don't worry,' I tell her, 'he'll be safe with me. I give you my word.'


I FOLLOW the prison officer back down the corridor in silence. At the door we have to stop while she sorts out the right key, and it's then that a wave of nausea hits, and I suddenly want to rip the reinforced steel off its hinges with my bare hands, get out into the fresh air and scream at nobody in particular.

'Is everything all right, Inspector?'

Her expression tells me I must look like shit. I manage a nod. 'I will be, as soon as I get out of here.'

She gives me a twisted grin. 'That's just about how we feel at the end of every shift.' We bypass the waiting room, and she leads me straight back to the main gate. As I wait at the hatch for my wallet and house keys to be returned, she leans towards me and says, 'Don't worry, Inspector Crow. We're keeping a close eye on your Rosie, me and a couple of the other officers. Nothing's going to happen to her, not if we've got anything to do with it. We'll get her back to you in one piece, I'll guarantee it.'

She turns and heads briskly back towards the main building. Then, before I realise it, I'm out on the street, and the main gate slams shut behind me. That's when I finally lose it and sink into a crouch, back against the wall, vainly batting at the tears that won't stop coming.

## 17

From the kitchen doorway, I watch my son-in-law flex his fingers as he hunches over the laptop, waiting for it to power up. We haven't spoken a word to each other since leaving the prison a couple of hours ago. I can't get the look in Rosie's eyes out of my head – the one I saw every time she mentioned Larson. I can't forget the promise I made to her either, that I'd look after him, make sure he was safe. The old saying about horses and stable doors springs to mind. One thing is clear to me, though, as I study his hollowed cheeks, the feverish intensity in his eyes as he bashes away at the keyboard – he's not the same man he was just a few days ago. The one I'm looking at now is a world away from the fidgeting bag of nerves who met me over at West Hill the day Rosie got arrested. Come to think of it, I'm not the same man either. A week ago I wouldn't have been standing in the kitchen dabbing at a camomile teabag, wondering what precise shade of green the final brew was supposed to be. A week ago, my brain had trouble stringing two coherent thoughts together, and my only problem was how to avoid attending my next counselling session with Rogers.

Larson glances round and catches my eye. 'Are you okay?'

'No.' I push myself upright, join him in the living room and hand him his mug. 'You?'

'Not really.' He shrugs and opens his mouth as if to elaborate, but thinks better of it. After all, what is there to say? His eyes switch back to the screen, and he types away frantically for another minute, then suddenly stops and brings a fist down on the coffee table hard enough to slop half his tea onto my long-suffering carpet. 'Damn and sod it!' It's such a sedate curse my mouth has twisted into a grin before I can stop myself, and he glares at me, furious. 'You really think this is some sort of bloody joke?'

'No, son.' I shake my head and flop down in my armchair, trying my best to rearrange my expression. 'It's no joke – at least, not unless we're part of some divine comedy. There are way too many things that don't make any sense, and maybe a year ago I could have seen how it all fit together, but now ...' I know I ought to be showing a bit of backbone, chivvying him along, but coming face to face with Rosie has thrown all my inadequacies into sharp relief, and I'm starting to wonder if I ever was as good a copper as I made myself out to be.

It's his turn to offer a humourless smile. 'Tell me about it.' He straightens up. 'Look, maybe we need to look at this from a different angle? I mean, maybe there *is* a link, but it's somewhere else – like three-legged cows and nuclear power stations, or ...'

'What?' Now I think he really has lost it.

'Sorry – it's something Rosie used to say, from her psychology classes. According to a fictional example in her statistics manual, cows that graze close to a nuclear power station give birth to more calves with only three legs, so people automatically assume the number of legs is connected to pollution from the power station. In reality, though, it's caused by a genetic defect resulting from inbreeding the cows to produce a greater milk yield – a third factor that hasn't been taken into account. There's no fault in the statistics, but without knowing the other factors, the conclusion will always be unreliable. A "faulty causal connection" she called it.'

'And that helps us how, exactly?'

He shrugs. 'Maybe not at all, but ...' His brow furrows, and I give him time for the wheels to turn. After a minute or so he lets out a long breath and raises his eyes. 'Okay. Terry walked out on Christine three and a half years ago, yes?'

I nod. 'Once he realised the gravy train had dried up. He'd most likely been faking, or at least exaggerating his injuries for a while, so he was probably worried Chris would find out about that, too.'

'Yes, but he wasn't running scared – he made no attempt to disappear and even kept up the benefit scam over in a new flat barely a couple of miles away. It was only after the murder and Rosie's arrest that he dived for cover. So what if he found something out – something we don't know yet? Maybe he disappeared, not because he's afraid of the law, but because he knows he's next on the list.'

I open my mouth to say that he's not telling me anything I haven't already worked out, but he holds up a hand. 'The point is, *how* does he know, and how much does he know? Your DCI said she hadn't been able to trace Terry's business partner. So maybe we should focus on finding out where Michael Swann is, and what he has to say about it.'

He pauses again, and I know we're both thinking the same thing. I have to try to get over this damned phobia sometime. 'Okay,' I tell him, 'I'll give Chrissie a call.'

·  ·  ·

THERE'S a silence on the line as Chris tries to cast her mind back. I can feel Larson's eyes on me and on my hand, which is shaking so badly I can hardly keep the phone to my ear. I know there's no point hiding it anymore, but the fact I can't control it still makes me furious.

'I'm sorry, Al,' Chrissie says finally. 'I only met Mick a couple of times – the last was around four years ago. I remember him sitting with Terry, drinking whisky and mouthing off about how he was going to make his pile and retire one day to a villa on the Costa del Sol and dodge the taxman, you know the sort of thing. He didn't stay long, and I can't say I was sorry when he left. I never saw him again ...'

'Whoa, Chris, back up a step.' I curse myself for not asking the question sooner. 'Those were his words? Exactly? He was going to retire to the Costa del Sol?'

'For God's sake, Al! It was four years ago, and I honestly didn't take that much notice. I didn't like him, and whenever he came round, I left them to it. You can hardly expect me to remember exactly what he said. Surely it's not that important, is it?'

'It is if he actually did it,' I snap, and then, realising I'm not being very fair, try to modify my tone a bit. 'Sorry. It's probably nothing, and you're right, it was a long time ago. You're really helping, Chris – there is just one more thing though. How was Terry after Swann's visit? I mean, did his mood or his behaviour change? I know it's difficult, but if you can remember anything – it might be really important, so please, Chrissie, try to think.'

There's another silence, and I note, with some satisfaction, that my tremor has started to die down. 'I suppose,' Chrissie says, 'it was close to the beginning of the end for us. Whether Mick had anything to do with it, I can't say for sure. Terry's moods were pretty bad by then anyway and getting worse by the day. It wasn't until a few months later he finally

snapped and walked out on me. I'm sorry, Al, but the best I
can say is that Mick's visit didn't help.' There's another long
pause, and then she says, 'One thing though – several times
after that I caught Terry trying to get through to Mick, and
once I heard him shouting down the phone, making all kinds
of threats, obviously to voicemail. When he noticed me, he
hung up and accused me of spying on him. I didn't think
anything of it, and if I'm honest, I was relieved in an odd sort
of way. It meant I wasn't the only person he was treating
badly, and his moods weren't all my fault. Does that make
sense?'

'It makes perfect sense, Chris,' I tell her, 'and you've been
a huge help, really. You want to talk to John?'

I pass him the phone and let my brain sift the information while he's discussing fine art and ice cream with Ben. By
the time he hangs up, I've managed to piece a story together,
and hope I can sound convincing enough to get him on
board.

'Well?' he asks, and I catch a fleeting return to the old
nervy edge in his voice.

'Okay.' I clear my throat and launch in, pretty certain I'm
heading in the right direction, but also damned sure I haven't
got a shred of evidence to back it up. 'Just do me a favour, son,
and don't butt in 'til I've finished, all right?'

'Scout's honour,' he says solemnly, holding up two crossed
fingers.

I don't trust myself to respond to that, so I just give him a
stiff nod. 'Right. So we've got two old buddies, Mick Swann
and Terry Markham, who probably started their crime partnership in the playground cheating the other kids out of their
dinner money, and worked their way up the scam ladder
until they were big players in property fraud. By the time
Terry latched onto Chrissie, they'd made themselves quite a
pile, but also made a fair few enemies along the way. I don't

mean victims who'd lost a few thousand here or a pension pot there. Once you get close to the big league, you tend to start pissing off some very powerful people if you look like you're going to tread on their toes. It's a whole different society out there that normal people hardly ever see, with its own pecking order, its own rules, you get me?'

Larson nods, but keeps his mouth shut. 'So, around six or so years ago, Mick and Terry made a wrong move, bit off more than they could chew, or maybe tried to con the wrong person – who knows? The bottom line was they ended up owing money – a lot of it. Terry tried to get out of it by persuading Chris to borrow on the house, saying he was going to invest in a fake property deal. He probably handed the money straight over to whoever he'd got on the wrong side of to buy himself some time. A year later he got drunk and fell off the balcony. Maybe at this point Mick decided the partnership was over, and it was every man for himself. So he grabbed whatever was left and jumped ship to Spain. He tried to cover his tracks, but not well enough, and whoever it is caught up with him. Terry, meanwhile, was slowly recovering, but kept up the pretence to give himself time to work a few more scams – a fake disability can be a distinct advantage in the con business. It's clear from what Chris said that Terry and Mick weren't on each other's Christmas lists, so it's only when Alison Crawley was murdered and Rosie arrested that he realised Mick might already be dead, and went into hiding.'

Larson's eyebrows have knotted, and he's tapping his lip with a finger. 'Well?' I ask him, and when he doesn't answer, 'Come on, son, you must have something to say?'

His brow finally smooths, and he nods. 'I think you've got something, but ...'

'But I've got no evidence, right?'

He gives me a snort of frustration and sits back in his

chair. 'That's not what I was going to say. I agree that all this seems to be pointing to Terry, his business partner and their dodgy dealings, and I know you're more of an expert at this than I am, but surely, if these were mob-style killings, they would be a bit more obvious – you know, less complicated? Isn't the idea to send out a message, a deterrent to others who might try the same scam? If Terry didn't even twig that something was wrong until two years after the killing in Spain, and the object was partly to spook him, then they didn't do a very good job of it.'

The kid's got a point, damn it. 'Okay,' I concede, 'anything else?'

'Only one thing for now,' he says. 'We don't know for sure that Michael Swann is dead.'

There's no answer to that one. It's more than likely Swann changed his name somewhere along the line, maybe more than once. While I'm pondering on this, Larson has turned back to his laptop.

He pecks away for a minute or so and then says, still frowning at the screen, 'Do we have a photo?'

'If you mean the police, we've never managed to arrest him for anything, so the answer is no. I could ask Grace to get onto DVLA, see if he took out a photo driving licence, or the passport office, but that would take time. I suppose it's possible Chrissie has one somewhere, but from what she said, it's unlikely. You want me to ask her?'

'Worth a try,' he agrees, 'but as you say ...' He stops, squints at the laptop, then grins. 'Gotcha!'

He twists it so I can see the screen. It's an old – very old, by the look of it – grainy, black-and-white newspaper photo of a smiling group of men, mostly in their mid-twenties, all in formal dinner dress. A headline above the image reads:

*Coombe Down Sweeps the Board*

And underneath:

*Last night, the FSA presented its prestigious customer
service award to small, Somerset financial services agency
Coombe Finance. The company, only founded two years
ago, beat off hundreds of established firms from all over the
country.*

I peer closer to read the caption under the photo:

*From left to right, Robert Vale, John Maitland, Craig
Arnott, Michael Swann.*

The slightly blurred figure at the end of the line is young,
skinny, and showing off the kind of tousled, shoulder-length
hairstyle that was all the rage in the '70s and early '80s. It
looks blond, but it's hard to tell whether that's just the
newsprint. There's no mistaking the glassy stare though, or
the self-satisfied set of the mouth. Unlike the other three,
whose broad smiles reflect the pride in their achievement,
Swann has the look of exactly what he turned out to be – a
fledgling crook who has made his first kill and is revelling in
the knowledge that, as yet, nobody is any the wiser. Of course,
my perception might be coloured by what Grace would call
'being too close to the problem'. Somehow, though, I don't
think so.

'Well, at least we know what he used to look like,' I say,
and can't help adding, 'Nasty little bugger by the look of it.' I
glance at Larson. 'This must be – what – thirty years old at
least? He might have looked like that back then, but that
doesn't help us now. Three decades ago I could have been a
marathon runner, for Christ's sake!'

He nods agreement. 'True, but there are ways around that.
The facial features change on the surface, but the underlying

bone structure remains the same. Haven't you seen any of those TV cop shows – the ones where they make a clay head out of a skull? There's a bit of dramatic license of course, but the principle is sound, and there's some pretty good computer software out there, so I should be able to get a fair idea. Once I've done that, I can set up an automatic search for any matching images in a given area or timeframe. It probably won't throw up any hits, but it's worth a try.'

He lost me after the second sentence, but I figure if it keeps him busy for an hour or so, it will give me time to think. That idea is short lived though, as a minute later my phone rings. He gives me an enquiring look, but I shake my head and reach for it, take a deep breath and put it to my ear. The voice of Rosie's friend Jenny Pugh drifts through the earpiece, and for a second my heart gives a hopeful leap. There's no great revelation, though. She just wants to ask after Rosie. She tried to get to see her, but the request was turned down – she's left some relaxation CDs from the hospital and asks if I can make sure Rosie gets them okay. And how are John and Ben and Rosie's mother? I try to answer as politely as I can, very aware that small talk is something I've never seen the need to practise, but at the same time knowing I need to keep her onside. I give her a gentle reminder to keep her eyes open and let me know if she comes across anything even remotely out of the ordinary at Coombe Hill, and ring off, feeling frustrated and, worse, utterly useless. At least, I think bitterly, the twitch I get every time the phone rings seem to be fading – just a little.

# 18

The breakthrough doesn't come until midway through the following morning. Larson appears not to have slept at all. When I take him a coffee, I have to wedge it between two empty, unwashed mugs. He looks terrible, hair messed where he has been constantly running his fingers through it, five o'clock shadow, dark circles round his eyes – I must have looked much the same back in the day, pulling all-nighters to get the jump on fast-track graduates with more qualifications than enthusiasm for the job. Remembering how sharp I used to be does nothing for my temper, nor my growing sense of uselessness as I watch my son-in-law wrestle with technology I haven't got a hope in hell of ever understanding. I leave him to it and retreat to the kitchen, where I can nurse my resentment without distracting him.

Around an hour later I'm still wallowing in my own feelings of inadequacy when a shout from the living room jolts me back into action.

'Got him!' Larson announces as I put my head round the

door, and gives me a bleary but grim smile. 'Come and look at this.'

I lean on the back of the sofa and peer over his shoulder at the screen. It's a blurred reproduction of what looks like a page from a Spanish newspaper.

'Okay,' I tell him, 'I give up. What's it about?'

'It's a report of a boating accident off the coast of Malaga, dated a month after the discovery of the murdered woman's body. Tragic, you might think, but not relevant – until we get to the last part of the article. Listen to this.' He clears his throat and translates – without, I note, having to consult his language program – '*The yacht's owner, local resident Martin Scott, sadly died. He was the only person on board. Señor Scott was already known to the police, having been questioned in connection with the gruesome beheading four weeks ago of Conchita Esteban, a market trader in the El Perchel district.*'

'And you think Scott and Swann are the same person? Why?'

He grins. 'Easy – look at this.' He clicks away for a few seconds, and another newspaper article fills the screen. 'I did a search for other reports of the same event, and luckily for us, this one came up.' He scrolls down, and there it is – a small but clear photo of Martin Scott.

The face is some thirty years older, but the smile is the same knowing smirk as the one in the old picture we saw yesterday. There's no doubt about it – Scott and Swann are one and the same. At least, they *were*. All I can think of to say is, 'Shit!'

Larson nods. 'Looks like that's it, then,' he says. 'Terry and Mick Swann pissed somebody off enough to make them want to wipe them off the face of the planet, together with everyone who meant something to them.'

'And that someone,' I add, 'is clever enough to make those deaths look completely unconnected, not to say accidental.'

'I wouldn't say,' Larson points out, 'that a beheading is "accidental".'

'Don't get clever with me, son,' I snap, but get interrupted before I can offload the rest of my frustration by a short, firm rap at my front door.

'Coffee, black, two sugars,' Grace orders as she pushes past me into the hallway, pulling off her raincoat and shoving it into my hands before I can object.

There's something in the tone of her voice that stops me pointing out that the local greasy spoon is three doors down. 'Right,' I manage, hang her coat in the hall and do as I'm told.

Walking back into the living room with the tray is a bit like stepping into a dentist's waiting room. Grace is perched on the edge of my armchair, hands clasped tightly in her lap. Larson's eyes are on his laptop screen, but his fingers are still. I feel the hairs on the back of my neck start to prickle, and a slight tremor in my wrist reminds me to put the tray down before asking a question I won't like the answer to.

'What is it, Grace?'

Her grip tightens just a little. 'Sit down, Al.'

'Jesus, Grace, what the hell ...'

'I said sit down.'

Her tone has dropped a notch – just a little too quiet. It's the one she uses when she's visiting a murder victim's nearest and dearest and wants to leave no doubt as to what the next sentence is going to be. I press my lips together and lower myself onto the sofa next to Larson, who has caught the atmosphere all right, but doesn't know the DCI as well as I do.

'Chrissie?' I ask, in almost a whisper.

Grace shakes her head. 'Nobody's died, Al. It's all right. Rosie's okay – I need you to know that before I say any more ...'

'Rosie? What do you mean, Rosie? So help me, Grace, if anything's happened to her, I'll ...'

I'm on my feet, but my legs refuse to hold me up and I topple back onto the sofa. My vision starts to blur, and my right hand is doing a little St Vitus dance on the cushion beside my knee. I take a couple of deep breaths and feel a hand on my shoulder. Larson, his face tinged a ghastly green – or maybe that's just me – is staring at me with an expression halfway between concern and terror. I try to pull myself together.

'Don't fuss, son. I'll live.' He whips his hand away as if it had been caught in the till, and I turn back to Grace, give her a nod. 'Sorry. I'm okay.'

She lets out a breath and switches her attention to Larson, rigid and silent beside me. 'I'm afraid there was an incident in the early hours of this morning. We don't know the full details as yet, but it appears your wife attempted to take her own life. Luckily she didn't succeed – a prison officer was able to raise the alarm in time. She was taken straight to the infirmary, and I'm told she should make a full recovery. I've managed to obtain permission for you to see her later on this afternoon.' She flicks me a glance. 'You too, Al. She's under sedation and hasn't said much except to ask about her son. We're hoping one or both of you can get her talking, find out what happened, particularly in the light of ...'

It's Larson who recovers first and snatches the words as my brain is trying to transmit them to my mouth. 'Rosie? You're telling us Rosie tried to kill herself? I mean, weren't you people supposed to be keeping an eye on her? Isn't that why she's still in prison? So where the fucking hell were you? In a back room with a takeaway and a movie? Jesus Christ, she should have been at home, with me, where I could look after her, keep her safe ...'

He stutters to a halt, and in the thick silence that follows, I hear myself say, 'How?'

Grace shifts in her chair. 'One of the blankets. She managed to tear it somehow, and ...'

'She tried to hang herself? Dear God!' The only way I can deal with this is to cling onto the floating plank of procedure like the proverbial drowning man in a shipwreck. 'So what happened, Grace? I mean, between our leaving the prison and last night? Visitors, letters, phone calls? There has to be something – something that happened within the last twenty-four hours. When we left her, she was fine. Well,' I correct myself, 'not fine, but ...'

Grace shakes her head. 'We don't know, Al. There were no calls and no visits, not even from her solicitor. A friend of hers from the hospital dropped off some CDs at the main gate, but didn't go into the prison.'

'CDs?' I suddenly remember the call I had yesterday. 'Of course – Jenny Pugh. She rang me. There was nothing else?'

'Nothing. And the CDs were vetted before they were passed on. Just those waterfall and whale song things, you know, relaxation therapy. Nothing sinister. I'm really sorry, Al.' She gets to her feet and smooths her skirt with a single, slick sweep of a hand. 'I have to go. The ACC's been chasing for an update, and I don't want it coming from anyone else. Meanwhile ...' She gives my shoulder a squeeze as she moves past, 'you and Mr Larson won't be allowed to see Rosie until at least three this afternoon, so there's no point either of you dashing over there until then. I'll arrange for her mother to meet you both at the infirmary, and that gives you' – she looks at her watch – 'a good five hours to try to make some bloody sense of all this. I've managed to keep the ACC onside so far, but it's not going to last unless I can give him something concrete. At the moment I've got bugger all except for two suspiciously related attempted suicides. So do what you used to be so good at, Al, and join me some dots before someone else dies, okay?'

The silence that follows Grace's departure is stifling enough to make my head ache. I know my hand must be shaking, but I can't feel it. I glance across at Larson crumpled on the sofa next to me, head in hands, looking totally defeated, and realise I need to do something, but paralysis has set in, and I can't even force my mouth open to utter the curse that is on the tip of my tongue. The soft trill of a mobile rips the air like a gunshot and has a dual effect, setting off a major tremor in my right arm, and jerking Larson out of his daze. He looks questioningly across at me, then reaches down and scoops my phone off the coffee table.

'Christine? It's John.' His voice is surprisingly calm. He keeps her talking while I make a supreme effort and pull myself together. After a few deep breaths, I manage to get the twitch under control and give him a nod. 'He's fine, Chris,' I hear him say. 'I'll hand you over now, okay?'

He offers me the phone, and I manage not to drop it. 'Hi, Chrissie, it's me. No, don't worry, we're both okay, really.'

There's a quiver in her voice, but Chrissie is a tough cookie, and she's holding it together, just about. 'The police said ... they said that Rosie ...'

'She'll be okay too, Chris. She's in hospital, and there's someone with her every minute. Nothing can happen to her in there, believe me.'

'That's what they said about prison, Al,' she says, echoing my thought exactly. 'I mean, why would she want to do something like that? It's not like her, Al – so what the hell happened?'

'That's what I'm going to find out,' I tell her. 'Just sit tight and wait for an officer to come and pick you up this afternoon. We can meet up at the infirmary and find out more then.'

I'm about to hand her back to Larson, who is flapping his hands, presumably because he wants to talk to Ben, when she says, 'Al, wait – there's something else. I went through the back bedroom yesterday, you know, the spare one that we used to use for Rosie's friends when they stayed over.'

'I know. And?'

'I remembered Terry used it to store some of his stuff from the study – overflow from his filing cabinet, mostly. He took everything with him when he left, of course, but I thought I'd root around just once more, and there was a folder wedged behind the wardrobe. It looks as if it slipped down there years ago, well before his accident, so he probably doesn't even realise he left it here. I'll bring it with me later, but there's one document I think you might want right away – a list of names, looks like people who were investing in one of his projects. If you like, I can scan it and send it over by email?'

Thankfully, I manage not to ask why the hell she didn't find it before now. Instead, I stumble out a few grateful words and ask her to send it straight across to Larson before handing over the phone and fidgeting impatiently while he communes with Ben on the subject of some cartoon or other. Eventually he ends his call, and I tell him to check his email. True to her word, Chrissie has sent through a scan of the document, and I have to wait another couple of minutes while Larson hooks up my ancient printer and coaxes it into churning out two copies. He hands one to me, and I can't suppress a small whoop of excitement. It's a list, three pages long, of names and, unbelievably, contact details, part of what looks to be a spreadsheet. The final four columns are headed 'Date', 'Unit Price', 'Total Units' and 'Total Paid'. The entries are in alphabetical order, and at a rough glance the dates seem to cover the first half of 2008. Like Chrissie said, it's an old document, left behind when Markham moved out, and because of its age, probably not missed. I glance across at Larson. He's slumped forward on the sofa, elbows on his knees, head propped in trembling hands. It takes me a few seconds to realise he's actually crying.

Over the years, the idea of my life falling apart has become so familiar it's like falling into an icy river and automatically remembering how to swim. For this poor devil, though, the nearest he's probably come to real trauma up to now is having to watch Rosie giving birth to Ben. A lifetime in the job has given me the resilience to cope, even with the near-fatal effects of a drug dealer's bullet. For the kid next to me, the last few days have pushed him so close to the cliff edge his toes are hovering over thin air. I reach out and put a hand on his shoulder.

'Take it easy, son.' He doesn't answer, but his hands stop shaking, and I feel his body stiffen. 'Listen, John, I know how you're feeling ...'

His head whips up, he glares at me and says, with emphasis, 'No – no, you bloody well don't.'

I hold his gaze and say, very slowly and distinctly, 'Yes – yes, I bloody well do.'

He thinks for a second and then nods. 'Yes, you do. Sorry.'

'Then listen to me. You've been drugged, almost drowned, and chances are you haven't eaten properly or slept since the paramedics pulled you out of the harbour. You look like shit, and you don't want to be turning up at the hospital letting Rosie see you like this.' He gears himself up to protest, but I cut him off. 'Yeah, I know – I look like shit too, but I'm a policeman, and I'm used to it. It doesn't take two of us to look through a list of names, so if you want to have any chance of seeing Rosie this afternoon, you'd better go and get your head down for a couple of hours. Besides, I need you sharp, son, and right now you're as much use as an ashtray on a motorbike.'

To my surprise, he doesn't argue, but just nods and forces himself onto his feet with all the alacrity of a pensioner with rheumatism.

'Thanks,' he mumbles, shuffling to the door. 'Just need to be alone for a while – an hour, that's all.'

I wait until I hear the door to the spare bedroom close, and settle down with the list. It doesn't take me long to find what I'm looking for. Halfway down the second page a name jumps out at me:

*Lynch, Margaret H.*

The address is somewhere in Devon, with a Plymouth postcode, and most importantly, it tells me that in April 2008, Rosie's boss paid Terry Markham one hundred thousand pounds in exchange for a share in what most likely turned out to be a very expensive chunk of thin air. For once, it's excitement that makes my fingers tremble as I scoop up my phone and dial Grace's direct line.

## 19

In the event, I have to shake Larson awake some four hours later, following a call from Grace asking us to meet her at the infirmary before going in to see Rosie. As we make our way to the family room on the fifth floor, there's tightness in the jaw, a hardness in the eyes that I haven't seen before, and for all my talk of wanting to see him show some backbone, I know that if we all get through this, neither he nor Rosie will ever be the people they were. If they are really lucky, they might claw back some of the innocence this nightmare has taken away from them – the kind of naïveté I lost less than a week after I became a policeman. Deep down, though, I know I might as well be an atheist praying for a miracle.

Grace intercepts us as we get out of the lift. She hardly breaks stride as she beckons for us to follow her down the corridor, and shoos us into a side room like a couple of stray chickens. She flops into a chair with a long sigh and massages her forehead with a hand that seems to have picked up my twitch. The bad feeling in my bones takes another nosedive.

Larson opens his mouth, but I bat his arm before he can speak, and point to a chair. He sits.

'Rosie?' I ask for both of us, and sink into the remaining seat before my legs forget their primary function.

She blinks at us, realises the impression she's making and pulls herself together. 'Oh God, no – she's fine. Carol Dodds is with her, and she's talking. You'll be able to see her as soon as she's done with her brief. I didn't mean to …' She gives Larson an apologetic look. 'Sorry.'

I give the relief a moment to flush through, and then ask, 'So, what? Something's rattled your cage, Grace. What do we need to know?'

She shakes her head. 'You want the truth, Al? The more we find out, the more impossible this case seems to get. There's something I want you both to hear, if we can find …'

A knock at the door interrupts her, and a young PC comes in, clutching a machine that looks as if it should have been scrapped in the early '90s. I know, because I've got one very similar in my back bedroom. It's one of those portable radio CD players that were all the rage back in the day.

'Is this what you wanted, ma'am?' he asks, dumping it on the small coffee table, where it puffs up a little shower of brown dust. 'One of the nurses found it in the basement. I've put some batteries in it, and it's working okay.' He stands to attention, looking pleased with himself.

'Thank you, Constable,' Grace concedes, and when he doesn't move, 'That will be all.' His face falls, and as he makes for the door, she adds, 'And get yourself cleaned up – the public don't want to see officers with dust all over their uniforms.'

'You don't think that was a little harsh?' I ask as the hapless PC retreats down the corridor.

Grace shrugs. 'He'll get over it.' Another sign, I think, of how stressed out she is, which does nothing for my sense of equilibrium. She grabs a tissue from the box thoughtfully provided for the use of distressed relatives, and wipes down the surface of the player before jabbing the power button. 'Right. Bear with me.'

She pulls a CD from the pocket of her jacket, and I notice that there's a slot on the machine for it. Before she slips it into the player though, she hands it to me. Larson leans across to examine it with me. The disc is a copy. Even I can see that. The cover has been badly printed on an inkjet printer that was running out of ink, leaving faded stripes across the washy image of what looks like a mermaid sitting on a rock. The title is *Driftwood: Ultimate sounds for total relaxation*. Inside, the label stamped on the disc is slightly askew and has no text, just another blurred picture, this time of a whale, or perhaps a dolphin – it's hard to make out which. I glance at Larson, and he nods that he's seen enough, so I hand it back to Grace. She puts it in the machine and presses 'play'.

The track starts with what I assume is a recording of waves on a shingle beach somewhere, mingled with some sort of Asian instrument twanging away in the background – a sitar, maybe? The effect on my brain is more like the sound of fingernails scraping down a blackboard than the promised 'aura of tranquillity' boasted on the rear cover. It must be showing on my face, because when I glance across at Larson, he manages a small grin despite the situation.

'They *are* very popular these days,' he murmurs, giving me a half shrug.

'Christ all bloody mighty,' is all I can think of to respond, wondering what happened to the days when 'stress relief' amounted to a decent beer and good dose of the Rolling Stones.

'Never mind that,' Grace snaps, and fiddles with the machine's controls, skipping through the tracks until she reaches the section she's looking for. 'This is it,' she says finally. 'Listen.'

We both lean forward instinctively as a track starts with an unearthly wailing that I guess is a whale noise. She holds up a restraining hand, mostly for my benefit, and it carries on for perhaps a minute, then fades a notch. Beneath the whale song, almost, but not quite inaudible, there is a voice. The machine is already at full volume, but I still have to strain to hear it. I catch the words 'life', 'enough' and then, jumping out of the little speaker and landing like a grenade in front of us, 'Ben'.

Larson has stiffened, and I realise so have I. Grace switches off the machine and takes a sheet of paper out of her pocket.

'I got our IT boys to make a transcript,' she says, unfolding the sheet. 'Do you want me to read it?'

Larson glances at me, and we both nod, unable to speak.

Grace takes a breath and reads.

*'Your life is over. You must realise this. Isn't it time you did the right thing? If not for your husband, your mother and father, then for your son? Do you think Ben should be made to suffer for your father's mistakes? He will, I promise you, unless his mother does the right thing. Your family has been through enough. You have the chance to put things right. A life for a life. You know what you have to do.'*

Grace refolds the paper and stows it back in her jacket. Larson has gone white. I look down and see that my hand has started to shake. I force myself to breathe, and try to keep my voice even.

'Who the fuck let this through?'

'I asked the security section the same thing, believe me,' Grace replies, and the look on her face leaves me in no doubt as to the fate of whoever it was. 'They told me they can't go through every single CD in its entirety – they just skip through the start of each track and look at the content of the folders. Whoever is responsible for this knew damned well that if they embedded a message halfway through a track, it would most likely be missed. At least that tells us the person who did this is probably familiar with prison procedures.'

'So it's because of me?' I say, feeling faintly sick at the thought. '"Suffer for your father's mistakes,"' they said. You think someone inside has found out she's my daughter? Someone with enough of a grudge to tell her to hang herself?'

'It's possible,' Grace says, without so much as a pause to consider, 'but I think it's unlikely.' She takes on a softer tone. 'Think about it, Al. All of this seems to revolve around your ex-wife's former partner, Terry Markham. When whoever this is talks about Rosie's "father", my guess is he – or she – means Markham. It makes more sense, don't you think?'

I nod, grateful for her logic, and pray she's right.

'And Ben? What are you doing about my son?' Larson's voice is flat, as if the horror of it all has drained every ounce of emotion from him.

Grace turns to him, her expression melting, chameleon-like, into one of reassurance. It's a trick I was never able to master, which is probably part of the reason I never made it past DI. 'Don't worry, Mr Larson,' she says, her tone a perfect match with her face, 'I've already sent one of our most experienced officers down to join DC MacDonald.' She glances at me. 'Roz Billingham – you remember her, from witness protection?'

I take my cue. 'Yes, I know her – one of the best, and she's had firearms training. There's no need to worry, son; she'll look after them, you can be sure of that.'

Larson doesn't respond and for a long moment stays locked in his chair like a museum waxwork. Then, with a suddenness that makes me flinch, he shoots to his feet and heads for the door, pre-empting any objection. 'I'm going to see Rosie.' The door slams behind him, and Grace and I wait in silence until his footsteps have faded back along the corridor.

'He'll be all right,' I tell her as she reaches for her radio to warn the PC outside Rosie's room.

'It's not Larson I'm worried about, Al,' she says, giving me a meaningful look and pointing at my hand, which has taken on a life of its own and looks as if it's conducting an invisible string quartet.

'No need,' I say, returning her stare. 'My brain is still here.' I tap my forehead. 'At least, most of it is. If that changes, I'll let you know.'

'That's good to hear.' She smiles. 'Do you want to go and see your daughter?'

'Yes, but not now. She needs some time with her husband, even if there is a prison officer peering at them from the end of the bed.'

'There isn't,' she assures me. 'She's given her word she won't try to jump out the window – she can't, anyway – it's locked. I've told everyone except the medical staff to stay outside.' She sits back. 'So, tell me, what do you think of the woman who brought in the CD?'

'Jenny Pugh? I'd stake my pension on her being straight as a die. She was eager enough to support Rosie when I spoke to her, and was quick to deny any rumours of a relationship between Rosie and Harry Shaw. She wouldn't have known what was on that CD, I'd guarantee it.'

'So you did go poking around the hospital, then?' Grace shakes her head. 'For goodness' sake, Al ...' She decides, sensibly, that complaining about it now is a waste of breath. 'I agree with you,' she says finally. 'We've had her in for interview, and her reaction to hearing that recording was something that couldn't be faked, not even by a Hollywood A-lister. Also, we asked her where the CD had come from, and she said she assumed it had come from the hospital stock. When I asked what she meant by "assumed", she told me the CD had been given to her by ...'

'Margaret Lynch,' I finish for her.

Grace nods. 'Margaret Lynch. I've sent a car to pick her up. After what you told me about her involvement with Markham's investment scam, I think we've got enough to hang on to her this time, at least overnight, and give her a good scare. Unless she slips up, we won't be able to charge her with anything though. It's still all circumstantial, damn it.'

There's not a lot I can add to that, so I get to my feet. 'I'm going to meet Chrissie.'

As I get to the door, though, something occurs to me, and I turn back, to see the same look on Grace's face that must be on mine.

'I know,' she says. 'We're missing something – something important, and I'm damned if I know what it is.'

'Me neither,' I tell her, 'at least, not yet. But you can be sure Margaret Lynch does. Keep at it, Grace. Try to get Lynch to let something slip. I'll go through Chrissie's list again – there must be something else there, and I'll find it if I have to chase up every single name. Meanwhile, about Rosie ...' I pause, trying to find the right way to put the question, but Grace is ahead of me.

'As far as her condition is concerned, the word is she's in a coma, not expected to recover. No harm making our killer a little overconfident, yes?'

When my sick leave runs out and they finally kick me off the force, there aren't many people I'll miss. Suddenly, I realise that Grace Helston will likely be at the top of that very short list. I give her a curt nod and head off down the corridor towards the lifts.

# 20

For an hour or so, Chrissie and I sit together in silence, listening to the soft beep of monitors, watching our daughter sleep. Larson, complete with police escort, has taken Ben to the coffee shop to get milk-shakes and biscuits. At some point I become aware that Chrissie has slipped her hand into mine, and we are clinging to each other like children in an unfamiliar house where some joker has killed the lights and left us in pitch dark. Eventually, an apologetic nurse shoos us out, and we make our way slowly towards the lifts, still holding hands. As we step out into the lobby, Chrissie tugs me to a halt, and I turn to look at her.

For a long moment we stare at each other like awkward teenagers, until finally I say, 'What is it, Chris?'

She hesitates, lets go of my hand and looks away. 'Al, do you think ...' She stops, takes a breath and tries again. 'Do you think, when all this is over, we could ... we could maybe ...'

It takes a second to realise what she's asking me. When I finally open my mouth, the words come from a part of my brain that doesn't seem connected to the rest of me. 'One step at a time, eh, Chrissie? Let's take it one step at a time.'

She looks hurt, but nods, and says, with just the hint of a nervous smile, 'Well – at least you didn't say no.'

Before I can stop myself, I've pulled her into a hug, and she's wrapped her arms around me, holding on for dear life. Of course I didn't say no, I want to say, but I can't – not now, when she isn't thinking straight and will probably hate herself for suggesting it once everything is back to normal – if it ever can be.

A shout of, 'Look, Daddy, there's Granny and Grandad,' jerks us apart in time to stop Ben barrelling into our knees and knocking us both over. Chrissie scoops him up and hoists him into a hug, and to my surprise he leans towards me, arms outstretched. Awkwardly I allow my neck to be caught in a stranglehold until Chrissie prises him away and sets him back on the ground. The police escort – young PC MacDonald, and reinforcements in the shape of the female liaison officer in plain clothes – herd them away to the exit, leaving me and Larson standing there like a pair of forgotten suitcases. I shoot him a glance – there's the beginning of a grin on his face.

'And what the hell are you laughing at?' I snap.

At once the grin disappears. 'I suppose we'd better get back to work. Come on ...' He pauses for effect and then adds, very quietly, 'Grandad.'


THERE ARE forty-two names on the list Chrissie found behind the wardrobe. It starts with 'Arnold' and ends with 'Wellington', the names listed in alphabetical order. With luck, that means the list is complete and contains all the victims of this particular scam. It's a long shot, but if Lynch isn't working alone, it's possible she met her accomplice through the fallout from the same dodgy deal.

'That's if she's involved in the first place,' Larson comments as, back in my lounge, we trawl methodically through Google and Facebook on our respective laptops, looking for information on any of the names. It's seven in the morning, and aside from a few hours of restless sleep, we've been at it since we got back from the hospital the previous evening. I have *A* to *L*, and he is going through *M* to *W*. 'Innocent until proven guilty – isn't that how it works?'

'Oh, she's guilty all right,' I tell him. 'The only question is, of what? I've got enough instinct left to know she's either a murderer or an accessory. All we have to do is work out which.'

He nods thoughtfully. 'Okay.' Then, after a pause, 'You do realise the connection – if there is one – could be anything? An old school friend, a colleague, even a former patient? I mean, even if it's here somewhere, how the hell do we know what we might be looking at? We could be here for weeks and get nowhere, or miss something vital without realising it.'

He's right, of course. In the old days, I'd have had at least half a dozen officers superglued to their desks, the ones with the best talent at picking up on the smallest hair out of place. Even then, we'd be looking at a minimum of two or three days' work, and follow-ups on foot. I take in a breath and glance across at him, but he hasn't even bothered to look up, just carries on scrolling down his screen, a look of dogged determination firmly painted onto his exhausted face. For once, I manage to keep my mouth shut, get up, and shuffle out to the kitchen to put the kettle on.

I'm rooting through the cupboards for the packet of chocolate digestives I'm sure was there yesterday when I hear a movement, and Larson appears in the doorway, one hand gripping the jamb as if for support.

'I think you should come and look at this,' he says and, without waiting for a response, heads back to the lounge. I grab the mugs and follow.

'What have you got?' I peer over his shoulder at what looks like a page from Amazon displaying a book.

'Maybe nothing,' he says, 'but there's a person on our list, a Paul G Radcliffe, and when I did a search on the name, this came up.'

I come round the sofa, deposit the mugs on the coffee table next to his laptop and sit down. 'It may not be the same guy, but this is quite a weighty textbook on psychology, one of several by the same author, see?' He twists the screen to give me a better look at an expensive doorstop with the title *Behavioural Techniques in Clinical Practice*. 'It's not "pop" psychology either,' he goes on. 'This is quite specialist under-graduate stuff, the sort of thing that would be on students' reading lists, published by the Oxford University Press.' He scrolls down and points at the lower section of the screen. 'And look – there's an author biography. Studied at St George's, London, graduated in psychology in 1991 and specialised in clinical practice. He stayed at St George's for two years as a lecturer, then set up a private practice in York. The last book published was a reprint in 2007.'

'And after that?'

Larson shakes his head. 'Nothing here, and nothing immediately obvious on Google either, just a list of academic publications – but a blank beyond that date. I'll keep looking.'

'Yes, do that.' Then I have a thought. 'No – wait. Can you look up when and where Margaret Lynch went to university?'

He raises an eyebrow at me, taps away for a couple of minutes, and laughs. 'Inspector, you're a genius!'

'Tell me something I don't know,' I say, inwardly thanking the Gods that I'm still capable of some kind of analytical thought. 'From the look on your face, can I assume that she was at St George's as well?'

'Not only that,' he says, flexing his fingers and reaching for his tea, 'they graduated in the same year. Lynch was a medical student, but they may well have known each other, probably took some of the same classes.'

We sit for a moment in silence, letting this revelation sink in. 'Do we know what he looks like?' I ask eventually.

'Not yet,' Larson replies. 'There's nothing on his Amazon page. Give me a few minutes, will you?'

He starts tapping again, and while he's busy, I grab the list off the coffee table and run my finger down to his name. The entry almost makes me choke on my tea.

'Jesus bloody Christ! Three hundred grand? Where the hell did he get that kind of money?'

Larson doesn't seem fazed. 'Inheritance? Pension pot? I agree, though, it's a lot. Damn!' He sits back and rubs a hand across his face. 'There's no website for his supposed private clinic. That's a shame.'

'Which means one of several things. Either it isn't there anymore, it never was there, or he doesn't want it advertised.'

'Maybe. If I knew what he used as a domain name, I could probably trace it – if he had one, of course.' He folds his arms and glares at the screen like a teacher confronting an uncooperative pupil. 'There must be something ...' With a sudden jerk upright, he attacks the keyboard again with one hand, adding a flurry of mouse clicks with the other.

'What?' I snap, with a flash of unjustified irritation.

'Maybe something, maybe nothing,' he mutters, ignoring my tone. 'Hang on.'

I dig my nails into my palms and try to be patient as he clicks through one website after another, the kaleidoscope of words and images making me feel dizzy. I close my eyes to regain my sense of balance, and it is a minute before I realise that the noise has stopped, and all I can hear is Larson's rapid breathing. Cautiously, I squint at the screen and then open my eyes fully as I realise what's on it.

'Jesus!' I say, and look at Larson, who is staring at the web page, open mouthed. I pat him on the back. 'Son,' I tell him, 'you're a genius.'

## 21

For once, George Saint is on his feet at the front desk, ready to wave us through.

'I don't know what you've been up to, Al,' he says, mustering his daily quota of energy to raise an eyebrow, 'but the DCI's jumping around as if someone's dropped a firework down her trousers.'

'Well,' I reply as we wait for him to press the security button on the electronic lock, 'when she's finished with it, I'll ask her to come across and shove it down yours – might keep you out of your armchair 'til the end of the shift.'

'Take more than that,' he mumbles, without so much as a flicker in his expression, and triggers the lock.

George wasn't far off the truth. When we get to Grace's office, she's glaring out the window, arms folded, fingers drumming a lively rhythm on her elbows. She whirls round when she hears us, lets out a long and very eloquent sigh and heads back to her desk. 'Come on in, both of you, and shut the door.'

'What's the story, Grace?' I ask as we flop into the two chairs that she has thoughtfully set out for us.

'Your guess is as good as mine,' she replies under her breath. 'Lynch is downstairs, but we haven't interviewed her yet. We were about to when your message came through.' She twists the monitor on her desk so that we can all see the screen. The web page Larson dug up is displayed there – an archive of officials of the St Georges Hospital Student Psychology Society, and there, under the listing for 1990:

*Secretary: P.G. Radcliffe (psychology)* and *Events Organ-iser: M. Lynch (medicine).*

Grace turns to Larson. 'That was good work. If you ever want a change of career, maybe you should consider the police force, Mr Larson.'

'Don't listen to her, son,' I put in before Larson has a chance to take her up on it. 'The last thing you want is to end up like me, and Rosie would probably divorce you.'

He gives me a wry smile, but still colours at the DCI's compliment and says, with a deprecating shrug, 'Just a bit of good luck. Not all universities keep records that far back, and she's never married, which made things a bit easier.'

Grace dismisses his response with a wave of the hand. 'Nevertheless, it gives us something to work on. It's still not enough though.' This time she's looking at me. 'All it does is prove they knew each other twenty-five-plus years ago, and that they fell for the same scam.'

'Stretching coincidence though, wouldn't you say?' I reply, even though I know she's right. The DPP wouldn't give it more than a minute's consideration, and even a trainee duty solicitor would have Lynch back on the street before teatime.

Grace and I exchange a look. 'Agreed,' she says, 'but we both know the score.' She massages her temples with thumb and forefinger while Larson glances from one to the other of us, clueless. 'Okay,' she says finally, 'right now, Lynch is not under arrest, she is "helping with enquiries". That gives us a bit of leeway. If she declines to have a solicitor present, we can hit her with this before she has a chance to take advice, and we've got a shot. If she puts a foot wrong, we can have her for obstruction if nothing else. That will give us more time. What's puzzling me, though, is why there is no record of Radcliffe after Terry Markham's scam. I've contacted North Yorkshire, and they're making enquiries, but God knows how long that will take – usual story, overworked and under-staffed. I've flagged it as urgent, for all the good that will do.'

Beside me, Larson lets out a groan. We both look at him. 'What?' I ask.

He gives us an apologetic shrug. 'Well, there's one pretty obvious reason why there's no record after 2009, isn't there?' My face must be as blank as Grace's, because he shakes his head. 'I didn't think – but before we do anything else, maybe we should check births, marriages and deaths?'

'Shit!' Grace slams her hand on the desk, scrapes her chair back, stomps across to the window and rests her fore-head on the glass. The printout of the pathologist's report in front of us sets out the stark facts: Date of death, 24 December 2007; cause, rupture of the vertebral and carotid arteries leading to cerebral ischaemia. In other words, death by hanging. At the same time, her phone rings and, of course, that triggers the inevitable twitch in my right hand. I slide it under my thigh, but not before Larson notices and raises an eyebrow. I nod that I'm okay as Grace comes back and jabs the speaker button. 'Yes?'

'A Sergeant Henshaw from North Yorks for you, ma'am,' a woman on the switchboard announces, 'says you asked for some urgent information?'

'Put him through.'

The voice that floats out of the speaker has that rich, comforting quality peculiar to the softer Yorkshire accent – a deep, *Come on, love, put the kettle on and let's get this sorted* tone, but at the same time not putting up with any nonsense. I reckon he's mid-fifties, a solid, career copper on his way to a decent retirement of fishing, football and fortnights in Benidorm.

'Ma'am,' he says, 'my inspector asked me to give you a ring. He says you want some information about the Radcliffe case. It's a while back now, but I was one of the attending officers, and he thought I might be able to help? I'll do my best, but it's a good ten years or more, and some of the details might be a bit rusty by now.'

'Don't worry, Sergeant,' Grace replies, injecting a healthy dose of charm into her voice, 'we're just grateful you have agreed to talk to us. I'm sure anything you can remember will be really useful.'

'Right, ma'am, I'll do my best.' There's a pause while Henshaw gets his thoughts together. 'It was a sad case all right,' he says eventually. 'Not that it isn't always sad when someone decides to top themselves around Christmastime, but this was a particularly bad one. He'd left his wife, you see, just walked out without a word, and left her on her own with their daughter – a lovely kid, I remember, around sixteen, maybe a bit older – Lucy, her name was, same as my girl, except mine was only two back then. The wife had reported him missing, but nobody took any notice.' I visualise his apologetic shrug. 'You know how it is, ma'am, not enough time or manpower to go running after a grown man who's probably gone off with a younger model or whatever.'

'Except that wasn't what happened in this case,' Grace prompts.

'No, ma'am. We got the call close to midnight on Christmas Eve, around two weeks after the missing persons report. His wife couldn't sleep – natural enough, I suppose – and according to her statement, she was in the kitchen making a drink when she saw a movement down by his office. He had a home office, ma'am, in an outbuilding at the end of the garden, to see private clients without them having to come in the house. He was some kind of therapist, you see, mental health, wellness or something like that. Anyway, she said she didn't go out straight away to investigate in case it was a burglar, and was in two minds whether to call the police or not, when she saw the lights go on in the building. She figured a burglar wouldn't be daft enough to do that, so it must be her husband, and rushed out to see.'

He pauses, and I can hear him click his tongue. Grace holds onto her patience, giving him time to marshal his thoughts. At last, he goes on, 'When she got there, he was swinging from one of the beams in the ceiling. He was still alive though, and she tried to lift him up, relieve the pressure, but couldn't manage it. There was a phone extension down there, so she called 999, but of course it was too late by then. The paramedics were treating Mrs Radcliffe for shock when we arrived on the scene. We'd told them to leave him where he was until SOCO had had the chance to root around. It was pretty clear it was suicide, though, and that was the verdict at the inquest.'

'Any idea why?' Grace asks.

'Why suicide?' Henshaw gives a knowing grunt. 'That wasn't too hard to work out, ma'am. If there's no history of depression, it's usually either love or money. In this case it was money. His practice wasn't doing too well, and he'd remortgaged the house. There were other loans too, almost half a million in total. Most of it went into some dodgy property deal that promised miraculous returns. That fell through of course, and then he couldn't afford the repayments, and the house was about to be repossessed. He hadn't told his wife, so until his death, she was in blissful ignorance. It must have been pretty tough – first she lost her husband, then her

home, poor woman. He'd even gambled his pension, and
there was no way she could keep going on just the one
income. No payout from any insurance, of course, on account
of it being suicide.'

'I see,' Grace says. 'Thank you, Sergeant Henshaw, you've
been a great help. I don't suppose you know what happened
to the wife or the daughter?'

'I'm afraid not, ma'am. As soon as the inquest was over, it
was case closed. I do remember driving past the house a
couple of months later and seeing a "Sold" sign outside, but I
don't know where they went. Sorry.'

Grace thanks him again for his time and ends the call.
'Well?'

Larson speaks first. 'If I can use your computer, it
shouldn't take me long to get a marriage certificate – if they
were legally married, that is.'

A horrified look passes across Grace's face, and she
glances at me. I realise I'm grinning, and shrug. 'Now you
know what I have to put up with.'

With a shake of the head she pushes her chair back and
gestures for Larson to come round the desk. 'You do know it
is against every rule in the book to allow a civilian access to a
police computer? I want your word you are not going to use it
for anything illegal.'

He holds up a hand and says solemnly, 'Absolutely not –
just a quick visit to ancestorsonline.com should do it.'

'And while we're waiting,' I add, 'you could get a DC to do
a search for Lucy Radcliffe – you never know, might have got
a parking ticket or a speeding fine some time in the last ten
years?'

Grace snorts. 'You'll be lucky – we can't even keep a
handle on traffic offences from last week!' Nevertheless, she
rings down to the squad room, adding a request for coffee,
'and not from that damned machine. Get someone to trot

along to the bakery – three Americanos and a bag of chocolate croissants if they've got any left. If not, whatever looks as if it hasn't been sitting on the counter for a week.'

I check my watch – it's just after nine, and by the look of it, Grace, who has taken to pacing up and down at the window again, has had as little sleep as the two of us. For the next ten minutes the only sounds are the DCI's muffled footsteps on the office carpet and Larson's now familiar tapping and clicking as he searches his ancestry site. A young DC who must have joined the team since my enforced leave brings coffee on a cardboard tray, together with a bag of assorted pastries and, to my relief, a handful of packets of sugar. He's on his way back down the corridor when Larson surfaces from the computer screen.

'Got it. Paul Gerard Radcliffe, married Anna Jane Croft at a registry office in Hampstead on 21 July 1990.'

'Which means,' Grace says, 'that he was still a student at the time, at St Georges with Margaret Lynch, so it's possible she knew the wife as well. Maybe they were all students together?'

'Hopefully, when we question Lynch, we'll find out ...' I start, but don't get to finish the sentence, as there's a flurry of activity outside and the same DC who brought the coffee bursts in, this time brandishing a file and looking excited.

'Ma'am, you need to see this right away!' He thrusts the file into her hands and turns to me. 'Inspector Crow, sir, it's a pleasure to meet you. The others talk about you all the time, sir. I'm Darren – Darren Jackson. I joined a month ago.' He holds out a hand, and I shake it, lost for words and wondering precisely what the 'others' say about me behind my back.

Grace gives him one of her dismissive smiles. 'Thank you, Darren, that will be all for the moment.'

'Yes, ma'am. Sorry.' He shuffles to the door, but can't resist waving to me on his way out. 'A pleasure, sir. Hope to see you again.' And he's gone.

I glance at Grace, and to my surprise, she's grinning. 'He's right,' she says. 'They do talk about you. They all miss you, Al, especially the young ones like Darren. He'll be a good officer – if he survives without you watching his back.' Before I have a chance to comment, she sighs and drops the folder on the blotter. 'Right. Let's get back to business.'

Larson politely vacates her chair and comes back to my side of the desk. Grace sits and flips open the cover, pulls out a fairly thick wad of paper. She flicks through the first half dozen pages and then comes suddenly to a stop, one hand hovering in mid-air. Her lips move silently for a moment, and then the hand makes it to her forehead, and she whispers, 'Dear God!'

Larson and I exchange glances. 'Grace?' I prompt when nothing else is forthcoming. She seems, to my mind, to have gone slightly pale. It takes her a full thirty seconds to come round and focus on me.

'We've got it, Al,' she says, shaking her head as if she doesn't believe what she has just read. 'The connection – we've got it. The case in Spain and the one here both involve Markham and Swann and their property scam, right?'

I nod. 'We know that already, Grace.'

'Yes, but we haven't been able to link either of them with the one in Inverness, have we?' She gestures to the file on the desk and smiles. 'We have now. The nurse – the one who let the killer loose and hanged herself in prison – it was Lucy Radcliffe.'

## 22

Grace has put young DC Jackson in charge of my son-in-law, with instructions to supervise and facilitate a search for any information on Anna Croft/Radcliffe, while we make our way down to the interview suite. Grace's step is slow, thoughtful, as she mentally goes through her strategy, wanting to anticipate every reaction her suspect might make, every possible twist in the interview's direction. In all my years in the force, I've never seen anyone better at it than my DCI. She has an uncanny ability to lead her quarry right to the cliff edge before they've even realised they've opened their front door. It's a rare skill, and one, even when my brain was at its peak, I was never able to master. She stops suddenly and turns to me.

'Markham's partner, Michael Swann – he died in a yachting accident, yes?'

'Yes. Just off the coast of Malaga. Why?'

'Do we know how, exactly? I mean, did he fall overboard and drown, was he whacked on the head by the boom – what?'

I force my mind back to the newspaper report. 'I don't

think it was made clear in the article Larson found. All it said was that a man – Swann – died, and that he was the only person on board. Why?'

'Because the first assumption most people would make is that the death of a sailor in a small boat at sea is from drowning, especially if there is no other information. But what if it wasn't? What if he died some other way?'

'You've got something in mind, Grace?'

She nods. 'Perhaps. Can you get Larson to find out? Call up to him as soon as you get to the observation room, would you? I'll be wearing an earpiece, so if anything comes through, you can let me know.'

We carry on down in silence, and when we reach the interview suite, I open the door to the observation room to find George Saint already camped on one of the stools, tea and ham sandwiches set out on the shelf in front of the one-way mirror. He points to a second mug. 'Thought you'd like a cuppa while we're here, Al,' he says through a mouthful of sandwich. 'The DCI said you'd rather have me down here as the "official" observer than a uniformed PC, and it means I get a longer lunch break.'

'At least you're not a bloody psychologist, George,' I tell him, thinking back to the last interview with Margaret Lynch. 'Who's riding shotgun, do you know?'

'Polly Sillitoe,' he replies as I ease myself onto a stool. 'She's a new DS, up from Exeter, been here around six months now. The boss asked for her especially. She's sharp as a tack, and I wouldn't be surprised if she nabs your job once they pension you off. Bit of a looker, too, but picky with it, if you know what I mean.'

'You mean she politely declined your offer of a drink after work? Hats off to her, George, that's all I can say.' I suddenly feel so far behind the game that maybe I should have taken early retirement five years ago, before any of this nightmare started. 'Besides,' I add, 'nobody worth their salt stays here long, unless they're complete idiots like you or me.'

'True enough,' he agrees, helping himself to another sandwich.

I send a text to Larson, asking him to look into the precise manner of Swann's death as a matter of urgency, and then give my full attention to the other side of the mirror. Margaret Lynch is seated at the table, looking relaxed, if slightly bored, hands folded neatly in her lap, an untouched plastic glass of water in front of her. She might, I think, be waiting for a bus. She's been there for perhaps an hour, but there's no sign of anxiety or impatience. It's the kind of attitude common in hardened criminals used to being questioned by the police – that, or someone skilled in psychological techniques. The PC standing guard just inside the door is completely still, eyes fixed on an imaginary spot on the opposite wall, giving Lynch nothing to break the monotony. He straightens a fraction as the door opens, and Grace breezes in, followed by DS Sillitoe, tall, blonde and stylishly dressed in a pinstripe trouser suit. George is right – every male officer in the squad is probably queuing up to make an impression. I get the feeling though, that Polly Sillitoe is not one to be easily impressed. Even through the observation mirror there's a glint in her eye that could spear a mosquito at a hundred paces.

Grace drops a file onto the table and sits, putting on her most apologetic smile. 'Dr Lynch, I'm so sorry to have kept you so long. I'm afraid something came up. This is Detective Sergeant Sillitoe.' The DS takes her cue, nods and sits. 'Would you like tea or coffee?' Grace goes on. 'I'm sure we could rustle up some biscuits too if you're hungry.'

'Thank you, no, Chief Inspector.' There's a slight edge of frustration in Lynch's voice. 'I'd appreciate it if we could simply get on with it. I do have a unit to run, and my time is very valuable.'

'And we very much appreciate you offering some of it to help us, Doctor.' Grace's smile widens. 'I hope you don't mind if we do, though.' She turns to the PC. 'A couple of coffees, please, Sam, black, no sugar, and some biscuits if you can find some.' She waits until the PC has closed the door behind him before continuing, 'I would like to stress, Doctor, that you are not under arrest. However, you are entitled to legal representation, and if you would like a solicitor to be present, I would be happy to wait.'

Lynch lets out a long sigh. 'I don't need a solicitor, Chief Inspector, as I have nothing to hide. What I need is to get back to work. Please, can we get on? You said there had been an incident at the prison – that you wanted more information about nurse Larson?'

'That's right, Dr Lynch. Oh – I assume it's okay with you if we record the interview? Just for our records you understand.'

Lynch opens her mouth to reply, but at the same moment the door opens, and the PC comes back with a tray on which is set a large cafetiere, three cups and saucers, a jug of milk, a bowl of sugar and a plate of chocolate digestives. DS Sillitoe beams up at him as he sets it on the table. 'Oh, Sam, how thoughtful. You're quite right – Dr Lynch might change her mind later on – and you remembered my favourite biscuits, too. How's the little one? She must be, what, a month old now.'

'Three and a half weeks, Sarge,' Sam replies, and the banter continues, uninterrupted by Grace, whose eyes haven't left the increasingly agitated figure on the other side of the table. Lynch's irritation is now plain in her thunderous expression, and the hands in her lap that have now curled into fists, her nails digging into the palms.

George lets out a rumbling chuckle. 'Told you young Polly was sharp, Al. Another minute and we'll be able to do Lynch for assault!'

At last, Lynch cracks. 'Oh, for God's sake!'

She half rises and is immediately cut off by Grace, who gives a placating smile. 'Quite right, Doctor – I do apologise.' She turns to her DS. 'Where do you think you are, Detective Sergeant, a coffee morning? Constable, that will be quite enough. I'll let you know if we need anything further.'

'Yes, ma'am.' The PC sidles out, and Sillitoe clears her throat and mutters, 'Sorry ma'am.' It's an Oscar-winning performance from all three of them.

'Right,' Grace says. 'Sorry about that, Doctor. As I was saying ...'

'Yes, it's fine if you record the interview, and no, I don't want coffee and biscuits,' Lynch grates through clenched teeth. 'If we could just get on with it – please?'

'As you wish.' Grace starts the recording and goes through the regular procedures, but in her preamble she clearly states that Lynch has declined representation and is happy for the interview to be recorded without a solicitor present. The first part of the mission has been deftly accomplished without Lynch even noticing the danger. 'I believe you have already been informed of a serious incident involving Rosemary Larson yesterday evening, Dr Lynch?'

'Yes,' Lynch replies, 'although not the details, only that she had been injured and was in hospital. I trust she was not too badly hurt.'

Grace flips open the folder in front of her, studies the contents for a moment, then says, without looking up, 'She tried to hang herself, Doctor. She almost succeeded, but thankfully a prison officer got to her in time, and we expect her to make a full recovery – physically, at least.'

'I see.' Lynch's expression is glacial – no concern, no emotion whatever. 'I'm glad to hear it, but I don't see what it has to do with me, unless you wish me to make some sort of diagnosis. The girl is clearly unstable – recent events have demonstrated that beyond doubt, I should think.'

'That's your professional opinion, Doctor?' Sillitoe pipes up.

Lynch gives her a withering stare. 'I have no *professional* opinion, since I haven't examined her.'

Grace has neatly slipped a plastic bag from the folder and slides it across the table. 'Do you recognise this, Dr Lynch?'

It's the CD we listened to at the hospital. Lynch hesitates, but at a nod from Grace picks it up and examines it briefly, then shrugs. 'It's a CD. Am I supposed to recognise it?'

Grace flashes an understanding smile. 'They do look all the same, I agree. This particular CD, though, is the one you gave to Jenny Pugh, a member of your staff, to take into the prison for Rosemary Larson, to help her relax. Is that right?'

Lynch frowns. 'I may have done – if Ms Pugh says so, I'm sure she's right. I can't remember every little thing I do in a day. It can't be that important, surely?'

'I'm afraid it is,' Grace says, extracting a sheet of paper and twisting it so that Lynch can read the contents. 'This is a transcript of the message that was embedded in the middle of it.'

She gives time for Lynch to read it through before placing it back in the folder. 'If I were you, I would try very hard to remember where this CD came from, and why you chose to give this particular one to Jenny Pugh.'

For the first time a look of concern crosses Lynch's face. 'I can't ... I mean ... I had absolutely nothing to do with this. It's ridiculous. I don't even know what it means.'

Sillitoe takes up the reins. 'Nobody is accusing you of anything, Doctor. However, you have to admit it does look a little' – she pauses before finishing, articulating each syllable with deliberation – 'unfortunate?'

There's a long silence, in which Lynch rubs her forehead,

closes her eyes and shakes her head, as if the gesture could make it all go away. When she opens them, though, Grace and her DS are still looking at her expectantly. She takes in a breath and says, 'I was in the storeroom when Pugh came in, I remember that.'

'Why?' Sillitoe asks. 'Is it usual for the head of the unit to be rummaging around in a storeroom?'

Lynch stiffens. 'I am the manager. Contrary to popular belief, I don't sit in an office all day. I believe in hands-on management. I wasn't "rummaging", I was checking that the store was being properly organised. I make it my business to keep an eye on every aspect of my department and visit each section at least once a month.'

'So you were checking the store, and Jenny Pugh came in. What happened next?'

'Yes. I'd just got there, I remember, and she said she'd come down to get a stress-relief CD. She certainly didn't tell me she was going to take it out of the unit. If she had, I wouldn't have allowed it. All the cupboards are kept locked, and each item has to be signed out and back in again.'

'So you unlocked the cupboard and gave her the CD? What made you choose that particular one?'

Lynch hesitates again. 'I must have ... no, wait – there was one already on the counter. I didn't open the cupboard at all. I gave it to her and told her to make a note of which one it was so that I could enter it in the book. I must have assumed someone had left it there and forgotten their cupboard key or something.'

Grace raises an eyebrow. 'I see. Not that organised, then, Dr Lynch.' Before Lynch can reply, she goes on, 'So *you* entered the details in the book after Nurse Pugh had left, is that right?'

'I must have ... yes – no ... I can't remember. Is it really so ...'

'Important?' Grace waves a hand at Sillitoe, who hands over a red plastic ring binder. She opens it and leafs through, selects a page and turns it to face Lynch. 'This is the record of items checked out of the storeroom the day before yesterday. Two board games, several novels and a jigsaw. No CDs.'

'Then I must have forgotten. I ...'

Sillitoe takes over. 'There's something else, too, Doctor. We looked through all the CDs in the store, and every one has a serial number taped to the spine, and the same number written on the CD itself, presumably so that they don't get mixed up. The thing is, this CD' – she holds up the case – 'has no number, not on the case, and not on the CD itself. We can only conclude that it didn't come from your collection at all. That means someone put it there, knowing Jenny Pugh would probably pick it up. As the storeroom is kept locked at all times, and only staff have a key, whoever left it there must be someone working in the unit. The question is, Dr Lynch, do you have any idea who that person might be?'

Lynch looks from one to the other of her interrogators, as if struggling to understand the question. 'No,' she says finally. 'No, of course not. What makes you think I would have any idea?'

Sillitoe smiles. 'Well, Doctor, as you have said yourself, you are in charge of the unit, and you take great pains to make sure it is very well organised, from the staff right down to the storeroom. Clearly, things do escape your notice.' A pause, and then she goes on, 'The thing is, we have an idea that the person who deliberately left this CD for Jenny Pugh to pick up is the same person' – she pauses again for effect – 'is the same person who forged Rosemary Larson's signature on the form authorising Harold Shaw's release from the hospital.'

This time, Lynch's expression is one of complete shock. Her mouth works soundlessly for several seconds until finally she whispers, under her breath, 'Forged? Forged? It's not possible ...'

Before she can say anything else, Grace is on her feet. 'I think we'll take a break there, Dr Lynch. I'll have some fresh coffee brought down – just in case. We can resume in, say, fifteen minutes?'

Lynch is still shaking her head in disbelief as Grace formally stops the recording, and she and DS Sillitoe sweep out of the room.

## 23

There's a spring in Grace's step when she joins us in the observation room. 'I think we've finally rattled her,' she says, coming up beside me to watch Lynch, who is looking distinctly less comfortable than she was half an hour ago.

'She looked genuinely shocked when you mentioned the forged signature,' I comment, and she nods thoughtfully.

'Yes, but whether that's because she didn't know about it, or she didn't think we'd be sharp enough to discover it, it's hard to tell. Has Larson come through with anything yet?' I'm about to tell her no when DC Jackson comes in waving a couple of sheets of paper and looking pleased with himself. Grace smiles at him. 'What have you got, Darren?'

'No luck on Anna Radcliffe yet, ma'am,' he says, 'but Mr Larson's found some more information on that boating accident in Spain.' He hands Grace one of the sheets. 'You were right – Swann didn't drown. According to this report from the Malaga coastguard, he was forward of the main mast, and they think he was trying to secure the dinghy on the deck with the spinnaker halyard when a freak gust of wind caused him to slip, the halyard tangled itself round his neck, and he strangled himself.'

'In other words,' Grace says, raising an eyebrow at me, 'he was hanged. What else have you got there?'

'Mr Larson said this might be useful, ma'am.' He hands over the other printout. Grace grins and hands it to me. It's a copy of a book's dust cover. The book is *Reducing Anxiety: New Approaches to Therapy,* by Paul Radcliffe, and Larson has scrawled a note in the top right-hand corner:

*published June 2005.*

There are three endorsements on the back of the cover. The second one reads:

*One of the most comprehensive guides on the market today:*
*an excellent resource for general psychology practitioners –*
*Dr Margaret Lynch.*

'Darren,' Grace says, patting Jackson's shoulder, 'you've just earned your pay for the week. Get back to Mr Larson, will you, and tell him thank you, this information is really useful. We still need to find out more about Anna Radcliffe though, so if he wouldn't mind, we need him to keep at it.'

'Good work, son,' I mutter to the absent Larson, and then to Grace, 'Well, she can't very well deny she knows Radcliffe now – or rather, knew him.'

'No – she can't.' Grace leans back against the mirror. 'But I don't see how it's going to help us, Al. Radcliffe is dead, so is his daughter, and his widow seems to have disappeared off the face of the earth.'

In a sudden burst of clarity, something that's been niggling at me since Larson's tangle with the bottom of the harbour becomes so obvious I wonder how I didn't see it before. 'The phone call,' I say to Grace, 'Christ, how could I have been so stupid? I was so taken up with …'

'What phone call? Come on, Al, spit it out – if there's something I need to know, I need to know it now.'

'The call Larson got, supposedly from Carol Dodd's secretary,' I explain, 'the one that lured him down to the harbour and nearly got him killed. It was from a woman, Grace. With everything that was going on, it didn't register, but it's starting to make sense now.'

Grace jumps ahead of me. 'And you think that call might have been made by Anna Radcliffe?' She blows out a long breath. 'Why not Margaret Lynch?'

'Partly because of her reaction to the signature, but that's not the only thing. I don't think she knew about Rosie either – at least, not precisely what happened to her.'

'So what's she hiding? Something, that's for sure.'

'I don't know, Grace, but whatever it is, it's scared her. If she is an accomplice, I'd bet she's not a willing one. Maybe she's been threatened, or simply thinks she might be next on the list, especially if she recommended the scam to Radcliffe.'

Grace straightens up and dusts down the front of her jacket. 'Okay, Al. If you're right, and we want to root out Anna Radcliffe, we're just going to have to make sure we scare Lynch more than she does.' She looks at her watch. 'We've had Lynch for around three hours. That gives us another twenty-one before we have to charge or release. I think I've got enough to hold her pending enquiries without any objections from higher up – give her time to think things over.'

'And while she's doing that,' I tell Grace, 'I'm going to have another chat with Jenny Pugh – unofficially, of course.'

THE DRIVER, a uniformed PC Grace has insisted accompany me everywhere – *for your security, Al, and I won't have any arguments* – drops me off outside the Roasting Bean, an expensive coffee lounge where Coombe Hill's nurses spend their lunch breaks and, I suspect, a good portion of their salaries. Luckily, the main road outside has double yellows all the way down, so my minder has to stay at the wheel. It's not quite lunchtime, but the place is pretty crowded, and it takes me a while to catch sight of Jenny, who has laid claim to a table in the gloom right at the back, underneath a sign bearing a big red arrow and the label 'Terrace and WCs'. She sees me, waves, and I gingerly pick my way through the minefield of chairs, handbags and laptop leads, hoping I don't get an attack of the jitters and knock over somebody's table. Thankfully, I make it without causing an incident, and she stands up to take my arm, her face full of anxiety.

'How's Rosie?' she asks as I flop into a chair. 'Is she going to be all right? I can't believe … I mean, Rosie would never …' She pulls a paper serviette out of the holder on the table and dabs at her eyes. 'It's all my fault, isn't it, Inspector Crow? If I hadn't taken her that CD … Oh, God!'

'Of course it's not your fault,' I say as gently as I can, 'and Rosie is going to be fine, don't worry.' There are two drinks on the table – something in a glass that smells of the stuff you dab an aching tooth with and, next to me, a large mug of black coffee. Beside it there is a small jug of milk and a pile of sachets of sugar. 'Did you get that for me?' I ask, hoping to distract her, and she gives me a miserable nod.

'Sorry – it's just plain coffee. I didn't know what you would like, so I thought an Americano was safest.'

'It's perfect.' I reach across and pat her hand. 'Black coffee with lots of sugar – just the job.' I point at her glass. 'What on earth is that? It smells like a chemist's shop!'

'Chai latte.' At last I get a very small smile. 'It's really quite nice when you get used to it.'

I smile back. 'I think I'll stick to coffee. Listen, Jenny, I'm hoping you might be able to help me again if you feel up to it. It's still not official, but my boss knows I'm here this time. She's interviewing Dr Lynch at the moment, trying to work out where that CD came from, so anything you can remember might be really useful.'

She nods. 'Yes, of course. I went down to the store to pick one up after my coffee break. Dr Lynch was there, checking the books.'

'Did that surprise you? I mean, was it out of the ordinary for her to be there?'

'No, I wasn't surprised.' She gives me a sheepish grin. 'I was a bit annoyed, I suppose – strictly speaking we're not allowed to take things off the premises, so I was hoping nobody else would be there. You never know with Dr Lynch though; she's always prowling about, checking up on every-one, you know?'

'Yes, I got that impression. What happened next?'

Jenny frowns, trying to remember. 'She was in a bit of a mood, I could tell that as soon as I walked in. She had all the books spread out on the desk. She asked me what I wanted, and when I told her I wanted to check out a CD, she got quite irritated and said it wasn't really convenient. It's like a bar counter, you see, with a bit at the end that you have to lift up to get to the shelves and cupboards, and Dr Lynch had piles of books and box files all over it. She started to move them though, to let me in, and there was a CD already on the counter under the files. She gave it a quick look and asked me if it would do, and I said yes, fine, so she gave it to me and said she would make a note. I took it and left. I was a bit relieved, to tell you the truth, because it meant I didn't have to explain who it was for. Now that I know what was on it, though, I wish I'd taken more notice, checked that it was part of our stock ...'

'You couldn't have known, Jenny,' I tell her, and then have

a thought. 'You said "piles of books and files". Surely they weren't all for CDs and games and so on. Is anything else kept in that room?'

Jenny nods. 'Oh, yes. All the games, CDs and DVDs are in a cupboard at one end of the store. Then there are a couple of TVs on trolleys, a fold-up table for ping-pong, all old things mainly that nobody's bothered to throw away. All that's on one side of the store, and all the cleaning and maintenance equipment is on the other – mops, buckets, polishers, supplies of bleach and detergent, tools and paint – that sort of thing. It's pretty much full, but pretty well organised. Dr Lynch sees to that.'

'So what are all the books for?'

'There's a book for every section,' Jenny replies. 'There's one for the recreation resources – the things in the cupboard – one for the cleaning machines and tools, others for liquids and detergents, electricals, general tools, audio-visual hardware, decorating – I think that's it. Everyone who takes anything from the store has to sign it out and sign it back. Some of our patients are unstable, you see, and if they got hold of a hammer or a bottle of bleach, they could harm themselves or others. We have to keep a pretty close eye on things.'

'So the room is kept locked, and everybody has to sign for what they need, and sign it back in when they bring it back. That's a lot of traffic, I should think, in the course of a day.'

'Quite a bit, yes,' Jenny agrees. 'The cleaners, electricians, handymen and of course the nurses – but we are very careful to make sure it's always locked.'

'Yes, I can see why. So who has a key? Does a nurse have to go down to open the door every time someone wants to go in?'

She shakes her head. 'No. If that were the case, we'd spend most of our shifts running up and down. All the senior nurses have keys, and the two cleaning supervisors, morning and evening, the chief electrician, the site maintenance manager, and Dr Lynch.'

'Right.' I push myself to my feet. 'I need to be getting back. Thanks, Jenny. You've really been a lot of help. And thanks for the coffee.'

She gives me a weak smile. 'Anything I can do to help Rosie, Inspector Crow. You will – I mean ...' She holds out a hand.

'I'll give her your love,' I say as I shake it. 'And I'll tell her you'll see her very soon.'


BACK IN THE CAR, I tell my minder to get me back to the station as quickly as possible, then grit my teeth, get out my phone and dial Grace's line.

## 24

By the time I make it back to Grace's office, it's starting to look more like a World War II operations room than a cosy DCI's bolthole. Every available surface is covered in record books and box files.

'Anything?' I ask, hunting vainly through the chaos for somewhere to sit.

'Give us a chance,' Grace answers, without looking up. 'We only got the stuff brought up five minutes ago. It would help if we could narrow it down a bit.' She points vaguely towards a pile of papers on one of the chairs. 'Dump those on the floor, Al, and pull up a seat.' She finally raises her eyes and gives me one of her stiff glares. 'I hope you're right about this. If not, we're going to be wasting a lot of time here. I've got the entire squad ploughing through the CCTV records for the last four weeks, and all we can do is try to marry up every movement with a signature to try to find one that doesn't match. We could be here for months!'

'I know I'm right, Grace,' I reply, and for the first time in a year, I feel my detective's brain isn't letting me down. 'Lynch was flustered, in a panic. Why would she be in there, looking through every single book, unless she was looking for something specific? Maybe she was looking for a name, a signature she didn't recognise – or maybe she was looking for one she did.' Suddenly, another thought occurs to me. Not wanting to make a fool of myself, I dig out my mobile and offer it to Larson. 'Can you give Jenny Pugh a ring? There's a question I didn't think to ask, and it might be important.'

He takes it without comment and dials the number. 'What's the question?'

'Ask her if anyone has the keys to all areas – the storeroom, main doors, pharmacy, the whole lot. And ask her how the keys are kept. Are they all on one keyring, or several?'

Thankfully, Jenny picks up. He puts the phone on speaker so we can all hear. Her answer is the one I half expected. Only one person has all the keys, including to the pharmacy – Margaret Lynch. She keeps them on a single ring and carries them all the time. Larson ends the call, and we sit in silence for a moment, staring at each other.

Finally, it's Grace who speaks. 'She gave someone her keys. If I know anything about hospital security, doing that is pretty much as serious as a police officer giving a bank robber their station access card. She could be sacked. If we can prove it, it not only gets Rosie off the hook, it makes Lynch an accessory, even if she wasn't a willing one. No wonder she's trying to wriggle out of it.'

'And it narrows down our search,' Larson puts in. 'Whoever got into the storeroom also had a key to access the pharmacy and lift the pills Rosie is accused of stealing. That means she must have given her keys to someone before I was attacked. Unfortunately, it could have been days or even weeks before. They could have "borrowed" Lynch's keys, maybe claimed they had lost theirs and could they take them for an hour or so. All someone needed to do was dash to the key cutters across the road, get duplicates made and hand them back. Lynch is so busy she probably didn't realise how long they'd been gone. Now she's trying to cover her back to save her job.'

'It's more than that, son,' I put in. 'I think she has an idea of what – or who – she's looking for. If it were me, I'd be looking for one of two things – either a signature that's unusual, or one that should be there and isn't.'

'That's a tall order,' Larson comments. 'We've only just had the results on Rosie's forged signature back from forensics, and they've had two people working on it. I can't see them going through a whole book of names, just on the off chance. Besides, it's possible we're looking for someone who's been working there for some time, so their signature wouldn't be unusual.'

'Then there must be something else,' Grace says. 'Whatever else Margaret Lynch may be, she's not stupid, and it's my bet she had a pretty good idea what she was looking for.' She gets to her feet. 'There's only one way to find out. Come on, Al, let's see if we can't finally get something out of the wretched woman, even if it's only to narrow down the dates.'

As I'm settling myself in front of the observation window, George shuffles in, a mug in each hand, chocolate muffins on plates precariously balanced on top. 'Thought you might fancy a proper brew, Al,' he says, making himself comfortable beside me, 'and these' – he points at the cakes – 'are PC Sanders's mother's speciality. Not to be missed – he brings a tin of them in every week.'

'You know, George,' I tell him, 'if they set up a squad investigating food quality, you'd be a chief superintendent by now.'

'Nah,' he says, with a grin, 'I'd be chief constable,' and makes a start on his muffin.

He's right – it's a great cake, and the tea is good, too. On the other side of the one-way mirror, a PC has guided Margaret Lynch to her chair. A couple of hours in the cells hasn't done much for her confidence. She's starting to look a little ragged now, and even from where I'm sitting, I can see the tension in her hands clasped tightly in her lap. It's five more minutes before Grace and DS Sillitoe make their appearance, during which we sip our tea and watch Lynch's agitation increase.

'You've got her now,' George comments. 'I'll give it ten minutes. You want to put a tenner on it?'

I think about it. 'Probably more like five. You're on.'

Grace doesn't mess about. She goes through the recording procedure and gives Lynch a bright smile, while Sillitoe, acting the perfect sidekick, leans back, arms folded, and pummels Lynch with a glacial stare.

'Before we begin, Dr Lynch,' Grace says, 'I just want to remind you that you are not under arrest, but that if you wish, you are entitled to have a solicitor present.' Her smile widens. 'I'm sure we won't mind waiting another couple of hours if you would like to arrange something.'

Lynch pales visibly. Her reply, when it comes, is more a mutter than a challenge. 'Just get on with it.'

'Thank you, Doctor,' Grace replies. 'We are very grateful for your cooperation.' There is a long pause, during which Sillitoe leans forward and plants her elbows on the desk. 'There are just a couple of things we would like to clarify, and we're hoping you can shed some light.'

'I think I've said everything I –'

'I'd like to talk to you about your trips to Malaga,' Grace interrupts. 'You visit quite frequently, I understand.'

'I've already explained that to your officers and to you,' Lynch replies, still wary, but a little more confident. 'I used to work there. I have friends there, and yes, I visit quite often. That isn't a crime, is it?'

'No, it isn't, and it makes perfect sense. However, there is one "friend" we are particularly interested in – a young lady by the name of Gloria Marinez. Do you remember her?'

At the mention of the name, Lynch's face drains. She opens her mouth, but nothing comes out.

Grace smiles. 'Let me remind you, Doctor. Two years ago, you visited Ms. Marinez in Malaga Penitentiary, where she had been remanded for aiding the escape of a violent psychiatric patient who was later accused of decapitating a woman in Malaga City using a garden spade. Do you remember that, Dr Lynch?'

'I ... she was one of my nurses when I worked there. I went to see if she was all right ...' Lynch shakes her head, her eyes flitting from one corner of the room to the other, avoiding Grace's eye.

'And less than twenty-four hours after your visit, Gloria Marinez hanged herself in her cell. Do you have any idea why she might have killed herself, Doctor?' Lynch opens her mouth to reply, but Grace doesn't give her time. 'And now, Dr Lynch, we find that you allow one of your nurses to take a CD from your store without signing for it – a CD that has been conveniently left on the counter, and that you suggest she take rather than go through the proper procedure. Twenty-four hours later, Rosie Larson is in hospital following an attempted suicide by hanging, which seems to have been instigated by a threatening message on that CD. I'm sure you can see how the similarities between the two cases might seem a little suspicious?'

Lynch wipes a hand across her brow and shakes her head again, but doesn't reply. It's time for Sillitoe to take over. 'Dr Lynch, it would be in your interest and save us a lot of time if you could tell us precisely when, and to whom, you lent your keys to the wards, storeroom and pharmacy. We know you gave them to someone. We also know you lied to us about your relationship with Paul and Anna Radcliffe, and the purpose of your most recent visit to Malaga. As things stand, unless you can give us an alternative explanation, we may have no choice but to charge you with, at the very least, encouraging a suicide, which carries a maximum sentence of fourteen years in prison. Do you understand, Doctor?'

George looks at me and raises an eyebrow. 'Nine minutes, Al. You owe me a tenner.'

'If you weren't such a lazy arse,' I reply, 'you'd probably have been my boss by now.'

'Nah,' he says, picking up the crumbs of his cake with a finger, 'what happened to you and poor old Joe was never worth the pay rise.'

There's no arguing with that, so I just sip my cold tea and turn back to the one-way mirror. Lynch is staring at Sillitoe, dumfounded. For a long moment there's a stand-off, and then, astoundingly, Lynch crumples and says, in a stuttering whisper, 'I didn't ... I mean, she must have ... the night I lost Freddie ...'

'Freddie? What do you mean, Doctor? Who's Freddie?'

Lynch looks close to tears. 'I had a cat – Freddie – a Burmese, nearly fourteen years old. He was beautiful and very valuable, not that it makes any difference, I suppose. But I kept him in the house or in a run in the garden, you know, to keep him safe, from traffic or from being stolen. Around a year ago, I got home late from work and put him in the run for some fresh air. He'd been out for an hour or so, and I heard a dreadful screech, so I went out to see if he'd got himself caught in the netting or something – it had happened once before, that he'd got his paw stuck.' She pauses and runs a hand across her brow as if trying to wipe away a bad memory. 'Someone had taken a length of wire and twisted it round poor Freddie's neck. He was hanging from the netting on top of the run. By the time I managed to get him down, it was too late. I reported it to the police, of course, but nothing was done. I suppose there were far more important things to investigate.'

'Are you saying,' Grace asks, eyebrows narrowing, 'that you think Anna Radcliffe might have been responsible for strangling your cat, Doctor?'

Lynch hesitates and then nods. 'I didn't then, but now ... the thing is, some nights, if I was tired, I would forget I still had my set of master keys in my pocket. If it happened, I would automatically put them on the hall table so that I didn't forget them in the morning. I was so shocked by what happened to Freddie I couldn't remember whether I had brought them home or not, but I didn't see them. They weren't in my office either, so I went back home to double-check, and there they were, on the table. I assumed I'd missed them earlier. I was just relieved I'd found them. I didn't want to be thought of as negligent – taking the master keys off the premises is a serious matter.'

Grace and Sillitoe exchange a glance, and Grace says gently, 'I think that may turn out to be a bit of an understatement, Doctor. We'll check your story, of course. In the meantime, perhaps you could start at the beginning and tell us what you know? If you are being threatened or coerced in any way, we can help, but you must tell us everything. Would you like something to drink? A cup of tea, perhaps?'

Lynch nods miserably, and Grace gestures to the PC inside the door, who noiselessly slips out on the errand. 'Now,' Grace says, 'let's start with your relationship with Paul and Anna Radcliffe and go from there – in your own time – just try to give us as much information as possible.'

'I met them at university,' Lynch begins, hesitant, her fingers gripping the plastic water cup so hard I think she might crack it, 'Paul and Anna. They were both in their second year, studying psychology. I was in the third year of my medical degree and wanted to specialise in psychiatry, so I attended some of their lectures, just out of interest. They were already a couple by then, had been since they met in the first year. We became friends, I suppose because none of us cared for the usual student stuff – pubs and parties and all the general stupidity. We were more concerned with our careers and used to stay up late – all night sometimes, discussing treatments, new research, that sort of thing.'

She sighs, almost smiles as she reminisces. Grace and Sillitoe hardly move, not wanting to break the flow. 'Paul had a sharp mind, full of ideas about new techniques, more reliable forms of diagnosis and so on – it was clear he would go on to become a great psychotherapist. He had the right manner, you see, good with people, intuitive, the kind of person who inspired trust in his patients.' For a moment there's a hint of bitterness, almost of envy in her expression, but she recovers and carries on. 'Anna, though ...' She shakes her head. 'Anna wasn't just sharp, she was brilliant. She had the most incisive, analytical mind I'd ever seen, and I got the feeling she could have been, done, anything she put that mind to. She left the rest of us way behind, and I can't think of a single instance where either of us won an argument against her. But ...' She stumbles to a halt and puts her head in her hands. 'Oh, God ...'

At that moment, the PC makes a timely entrance with, not the usual plastic cup of cat pee from the machine, but a tray with a pot of tea, milk, sugar and a small plate of biscuits. The timing is perfect and Grace, from the quiet smile that flits across her face, agrees. She plays mother and pushes a cup towards Lynch, who takes it in shaking hands and sips gratefully.

'You were saying,' Grace prompts, 'about Anna?'

Lynch nods. 'As I said, Anna was brilliant, but there was something ... I don't quite know how to explain – she was into the more radical theories of mental health, stuff that had been explored in the seventies by therapists like R. D. Laing for instance – he is said to have once proposed an introduction agency for potential suicides and murderers in order to fulfil the wishes of both without disturbing the balance of society. A monstrous idea, of course, but he had quite a following in his day. Anna was into all that sort of thing. Later, when she went on to do postgraduate work, she specialised in the use of combinations of drugs and hypnotherapy to make violent patients more compliant. She even did a stint at Broadmoor in the mid-'90s, in the research department.'

'So what you're saying,' Sillitoe cuts in, 'is that Anna Radcliffe was capable of using her skills to manipulate vulnerable and possibly dangerous patients?'

'Oh, yes. Not just patients, though – she could convince anyone of anything, just about. People were resources to her, things to be used. Looking back, I think she accepted me only because I could get her access to the medical labs. Like a lot of clever people, she was unpredictable, easily upset if anyone disturbed her thoughts, broke into her routines. She could be quite vicious – verbally I mean. I never saw her being physically violent towards anyone, not back then anyway. Even so, people were scared of her – she was quite intimidating. The only exception was Paul. She really loved him, I think. He was quiet, always calm, accepting, everything she was not. She behaved differently when he was around, even deferred to him if he really felt deeply about something. He was her bridge to the social world, her conscience, if you like.'

Lynch pauses, and George turns to me. 'What do you

reckon, Al? Sounds to me like she's spinning a line to get herself off the hook.'

'I don't think so, George. If she'd wanted to do that, she'd have come up with a much better story. Besides, it fits with what we've dug up so far.'

I can see from Grace's expression that she's thinking the same thing, although both she and Sillitoe have taken care not to show any reaction to Lynch's story. Grace tops up Lynch's cup and gives her an encouraging smile. 'Please,' she says, 'go on. Did you stay in touch with the Radcliffes after university?'

'Yes – at least, with Paul, although I didn't see him often after they moved to York. Anna – well, as I said, she wasn't the sociable type. I used to meet up with Paul when he came to London, but Anna was never with him. I saw her once when I was in York for a conference, but after the scandal, not at all.'

Sillitoe's ears prick up. 'Scandal? What scandal?'

Lynch sighs. 'They set up a practice together. It was a good business – Paul was a highly respected cognitive behavioural therapist and grew quite a large client list in a very short time, mostly referrals from the hospital. Anna took a different path though. She set herself up as some sort of troubleshooter for rich, doting parents with problem adolescents. As a psychologist she wasn't able to prescribe the usual medications, so instead she started to experiment with combinations of herbal remedies and hypnosis as a means of behaviour change. It was pretty lucrative, even if the only things most of those kids really needed to change were their parents. Everything was going well until she prescribed St John's Wort for a mild depression in a seventeen-year-old girl. The girl ended up in hospital with acute renal failure. It turns out she'd had a transplant a year or so before, and the mother claimed that the St John's Wort had interfered with her daughter's immunosuppressant drugs. It could have been the case, but impossible to prove. Nevertheless, word got round; it left the reputation of the practice in tatters and the Radcliffes with huge financial problems and no way to recover.'

'And is that when Paul Radcliffe got involved with Markham and Swann?' Grace asks.

Lynch nods. 'We met up in London, and he told me what had happened. They had been struggling for almost a year by then and had no chance of starting up again unless they found the funds to move elsewhere. I had just invested with Markham and Swann. They were promising returns of at least twelve percent within eighteen months, and I thought it was too good a deal to miss.' She pauses, her face screwed up in a grimace. 'Looking back, I can't believe how stupid I was. I wanted to retire to Spain and thought ... but you don't want to know about that. I recommended the investment to Paul, probably the worst thing I could possibly have done. I had no idea he would use every penny of equity he had left to sink into it. I think he even managed to borrow a hundred grand from somewhere. It was around six months after that when I realised the whole thing was a scam. I got in touch with Paul straight away and warned him. I suppose I hoped he'd changed his mind, not gone ahead with it.'

'And what was his reaction?' Sillitoe asks. 'Was he angry? Upset?'

'You know damned well what his reaction was,' Lynch snaps, showing a flash of her old self. 'He killed himself! And if I hadn't mentioned that blasted scam ...'

'You weren't to know, Doctor,' Grace points out, and I catch what seems to be a touch of genuine sympathy in her expression. 'It was a very clever fraud – you were taken in too, after all. Did you stay in touch with Anna after that?'

'No. I tried to call, to ask if I could attend the funeral, but she refused to speak to me. The last I heard from her was a letter not long after Paul's burial. She sent me a copy of the order of service, together with a short and not very pleasant note. She blamed me, partly at least, but most of all she blamed Markham and Swann – well, Markham in particular, as he had been the main contact for both of us. She said she was taking Lucy away to make a new start, somewhere in the north of Scotland, and that if I wanted to do something for her, I should leave both of them alone and not contact her again. She didn't put it quite so politely, though. She wanted to make sure I got the message, and believe me, I did. Without Paul, all her social restraint had gone, although I put it down to grief at the time.'

'Do you still have a copy of this letter?' Grace asks.

'No. It was so upsetting I tore it up and threw it in the wood burner. I suppose, with hindsight ...'

At that moment, DC Jackson bursts into the observation room, looking excited. 'We've got something, sir,' he exclaims, almost bouncing into my lap, 'on the CCTV. Mr Larson said it could be really important, and you and the boss need to see it right away, sir.'

'Right,' I say, flick the switch on the mic in front of me, and relay the message to Grace's earpiece.

She gets to her feet, although I can see a slight irritation in her expression, and halts the interview, indicating with a jerk of the head for Sillitoe to follow her, and leaving Lynch looking both anxious and bemused. A second later, the door to the observation room opens. 'Okay, Al,' she says, through clenched teeth, 'this had better be good.'

## 25

There are five of us crowded round Grace's computer screen – me, Larson, Grace, DC Jackson and Polly Sillitoe. We watch the sequence in silence for the fourth time, all of us knowing that the grainy, monochrome images are giving us our first sight of a dangerous, cold-blooded murderer. The figure is dressed in a nurse's uniform, with a plastic apron and surgical gloves. It is a woman, medium height and build, her back to the camera. She must have called out, because after a few moments another nurse comes into view. It's Rosie. The woman holds something out – a bottle – and Rosie takes it, examines it, says something and hands it back. The exchange is over, and a second later we're looking at an empty space. Larson freezes the video.

'Where did you say this camera was placed?' Grace asks.

'The corridor that runs between the wards on the second floor,' Larson replies. 'We've checked the footage from the ward cameras an hour either side. Rosie was back in ward 8 within twenty seconds, the door on the right of the camera. The other nurse doesn't appear anywhere, before or after. My guess is she took the stairs, because she doesn't turn up near any of the lifts either. It makes sense – there's no CCTV in the stairwells.'

'Damn.' Grace squints at the screen, reading the date. 'This is from two weeks before Rosie was arrested. Is there any way of knowing what those pills are?'

Larson opens another window on the computer screen, and a close-up of the bottle appears. 'Darren – I mean DC Jackson – got in touch with one of your experts,' he says, 'and we've managed to do enhancements on some of the footage.' He clicks on the zoom button until the label is clear. Then he brings up another photo, again of a bottle, this one in a transparent sealed evidence bag. The two are identical.

Sillitoe takes in a breath. 'Christ, boss,' she whispers, almost admiringly, 'she's got a bloody nerve!'

Grace straightens up and stretches her spine. 'So now we know exactly how Mr Larson ended up with a bottle of amitriptyline in his jacket pocket with his wife's fingerprints all over it.' She nods at Jackson. 'I don't know how you managed to get the lab on board without a six-week wait, Darren, but good work.'

He blushes slightly. 'My girlfriend, ma'am – her brother works there.'

Sillitoe grins. 'Come on, Daz – what have I told you about magic tricks? They're only magic if you don't tell people how it's done!'

'Okay, everyone,' Grace cuts in, although she's smiling too, 'back to business. It looks like we're dealing with someone who isn't taking any chances. She's made sure her prints aren't on anything – not difficult in a hospital where surgical gloves are the order of the day. It's my guess she also knows where all the security cameras are, and is being careful not to show her face. Have we got anything else?'

'Oh, yes,' Larson says, and brings up another video sequence. This one is positioned at the end of another corri-

dor, with just one door, around halfway along on the left.
There's a fair bit of traffic here compared with the last recording. A couple of men in overalls walk past carrying metal
toolboxes, heading towards the lift at the end of the corridor.
As they get in, a nurse steps out, stops at the door, unlocks it
and goes inside the room. After a few minutes she emerges
carrying a couple of boxes (Monopoly and Snakes and
Ladders, Larson informs us), relocks the door and heads back
to the lift. Her face is clearly visible – a youngster, around
twenty or so, hair blonde with blue and green streaks and,
importantly, some four or five inches shorter than the figure
from the last video. A few moments later, a group of four
cleaners come out of the lift, three female, one male, and
head towards the door. They don't go in, however, but hang
around, waiting, chatting and laughing among themselves.

'What on earth are they doing?' Sillitoe asks.

In response, Larson holds up a hand, gesturing for us to
wait. The chat goes on for another minute or so, and then
someone else appears, not from the direction of the lift, but
from the other end of the corridor. There is a familiarity in
the build, the gait, and just like before, the figure is careful to
keep their back to the camera. This time though, the woman
is dressed in a cleaner's overall rather than a nurse's uniform.
The others straighten up as she pulls a ring of keys from her
overall pocket, strides up to the door and unlocks it. They all
go inside. Another couple of minutes go by, and they start to
emerge, armed with buckets, mops, vacuum cleaners and
floor polishing machines. Our target is last out, with a bucket
and mop. She locks the door and joins the others at the lift. A
moment later, they are gone. At no time did she let her guard
slip and turn her head. Larson stops the recording. The time
stamp is 5.45am, the day before yesterday – the day Jenny
Pugh picked up the CD for Rosie.

In the silence that follows, Larson fiddles with the mouse

and brings up two stills, one from each video. 'In case anyone has any doubts,' he says, and superimposes a grid of measurements over each faceless figure, 'we may not know what she currently looks like, but we know it's the same person. And that's not all ...' He brings up a third sequence. 'This is from the day Harry Shaw absconded.' It is a shorter video, showing the same corridor as the first extract. The first image we see is of Jenny Pugh, carrying a folder under one arm, moving across from one ward to the other. As she comes alongside the lifts in the middle of the shot, Rosie appears, coming from the other direction. They stop to chat, and the look on Rosie's face suddenly threatens to set off the jitters in my hand. She's smiling, laughing, all the things I haven't seen in her for what seems like a hundred years. I glance across at Larson and realise he's thinking the same thing, his expression a combination of determination and despair. He looks at me, and I give him a nod. We're 'hanging in there', as people say these days, and by Christ, we're going to get Rosie back.

We turn our attention back to the footage. Rosie and Jenny go their separate ways, and Larson, coughing to give himself time to get the evenness back into his voice, says, 'Jenny goes to ward 8, and Rosie to ward 7 – that's Harry Shaw's ward.' We keep watching, and just moments later a woman appears from the direction of the stairs, wearing a dapper trouser suit and a white coat, a pass card of some kind just visible on her lapel. She pauses at the lift and then turns left, towards ward 7. Larson freezes the frame and adds the same measurement grid as for the other two sequences. It's the same woman – the same camera-shy approach, coming into shot from the stairwell with her back to the lens.

'Shit!' Sillitoe says, voicing what we are all thinking. 'We checked the footage when your daughter was arrested, Inspector Crow, and didn't clock this. Damn it!'

'There was no reason for you to think anything was out of

the ordinary, Sergeant,' I tell her, trying, and failing, to sound reassuring.

'Well, I don't think there's much doubt about your Rosie's innocence now,' Grace says, reaching across to give my shoulder a squeeze. Then she straightens up and brushes her jacket. 'Right – let's get on with it. The sooner we get Anna Radcliffe off the streets, the sooner we can get Rosie Larson home. Polly, stop in the squad room on your way down and tell them to round up those cleaners – they saw the woman's face and might be able to give us a description.'

She marches out, Sillitoe at her heels. I try to follow, but only get as far as the door before the room tilts, and I have to hang on to the door handle to stop myself from sliding to the floor. Larson shoots round the table, but I hold up a hand, and he comes to a halt a couple of paces away. I close my eyes and take a few deep breaths. When I open them, he's still motionless, staring at me, his face a mask of anxiety. The world rights itself, and I let go of the door, force a smile. 'It's okay, son,' I tell him. 'I'm okay. I'd better get down there – don't want to miss anything.' He nods, and I step out into the corridor. It's only then I remember what it was I wanted to say and turn back. 'You did a good job there, son – a damned good job.'

As it happens, I manage to get there before the interview resumes. As I reach the bottom of the stairs, DC Jackson catches up with me and hands me three sheets of paper. 'The boss asked for these, sir,' he says, and dashes off again without waiting for a reply. I get the feeling that my performance in Grace's office has spooked him a bit. If he wants to get on, I think to myself, he'll need to toughen up.

Grace is waiting for me in the observation room. 'I hope you told young Larson what a great job he's doing,' she comments, lifting the papers out of my hand and slipping them into her folder. 'If we'd gone through the official labs, we might have been waiting a week for these.'

Larson has printed off three stills from the CCTV footage, showing the person we are now pretty sure is Anna Radcliffe in each of her guises. 'You think those are going to make a difference?' I ask. 'Lynch will know as well as we do that we don't have a positive ID.'

'Maybe. But perhaps Lynch has an old photo we can use as a comparison, and if we can get permission from her to go into her house, it will save us a lot of time getting a warrant. We've hit her with possible charges, so it's my bet she'll want to be of as much assistance as she can from this point on.' She gives me a smile. 'It won't be long now, Al. I promise.'

The interview resumes more or less where it left off. George has replenished the mugs and taken advantage of the break to nip out for a bag of sausage rolls, from which, through a mouthful of pastry, he invites me to help myself. As it turns out, Grace's instinct is spot on, as usual. Lynch seems eager now to get on with her story. As soon as the formalities are over, though, Grace asks the question.

'Dr Lynch, do you have any photographs of Anna Radcliffe?'

'No, I don't think so.' Lynch shakes her head, but then her brow furrows, and she takes in a breath. 'Wait – yes, I might have just one, but very old – a graduation photo, in one of my old albums. Paul and Anna got their degrees on the same day, and I took a picture of the group – the two of them with some of their friends. I would have put it in an album, I'm sure, although I can't remember precisely.'

'Would you mind very much if we sent someone to get it? I think it's important we know exactly what she looks like.'

Lynch hesitates, but finally sighs and says, 'I suppose so, but it's very old – she might have changed a lot since then.'

'Don't worry, Doctor, I'm sure we can deal with that.'

Grace gives her sweetest smile, and to everyone's aston-ishment, Lynch simply says, 'My keys are in my handbag. Help yourself.'

The constable inside the door slips out at a nod from Grace, who rifles through her file for a moment, then turns back to Lynch. 'You were saying, Doctor – you received an unfriendly letter from Anna, which you burned?'

'That's right,' Lynch replies, with a nod. 'After that I had no contact with her at all. I had no idea where she had gone or what she did, until' – she pauses and wipes a hand across her forehead as if trying to erase a painful memory – 'until around three years ago, when a colleague told me about what had happened in Edinburgh, to Anna's daughter, Lucy. It must have been terrible for Anna – I mean, to lose your husband and your daughter in exactly the same way. I'm sure you know about that, of course.'

'Yes, we do,' Grace confirms. 'Did you get back in touch with her at that point?'

Lynch shakes her head. 'No – given her reaction after Paul's death, I thought it better to leave things as they were. I was offered the job in Spain shortly afterwards, and to be honest, I soon forgot about it all – I had other priorities, as you can imagine.'

'So you left for Malaga,' Sillitoe puts in. 'When did you learn that Terence Markham's partner, Michael Swann, had also moved there?'

'What?' There's no mistaking the genuine shock on Lynch's face. 'I had no idea ... I ... Oh, my God! That explains ...' She leans forward, elbows on the desk, head in her hands. Grace and Sillitoe exchange a look and wait. Eventually, Lynch looks up. 'I thought it was me. I mean, I thought she was sending me a message, that she was coming after me. Maybe she was, but I was back in the UK by then, so ...' She pauses, grasping the implications of Sillitoe's question. 'Swann – did she ...? Is he ...?'

'Michael Swann is dead,' Grace says gently. 'He was hanged, on his yacht. He died around the same time as Conchita Esteban, the woman who was beheaded by your escaped patient. We believe Swann and Esteban knew each other – possibly were lovers.' She gives Lynch a few moments to absorb the information, and then says, 'You see, Dr Lynch, the problem this poses for us? I mean, isn't it rather odd that you just happened to get a job in the same area that Michael Swann decided to disappear to, at more or less exactly the same time, and that you just happened to have been working at that particular hospital just prior to the murders of Swann and Esteban? And now, here you are again, in charge of the secure unit at Coombe Hill, and history seems to be repeating itself. I don't know about you, Doctor, but I would say that's stretching coincidence beyond the limit of credibility, wouldn't you?'

In the silence that follows, George and I exchange a look. He jabs a half-eaten sausage roll towards the mirror. 'I'd like to see her get out of that one.'

'We're not there yet, George,' I reply and, when he raises an eyebrow, add, 'She didn't know about Swann. You saw her reaction – I think she was set up, and by the time she realised what was going on, it was too late – she was already in over her head. We just need to know how far in.'

I'm about to say more when there's a knock at the door, and Jackson comes in, flapping a wad of paper. 'Mr Larson's done it, sir,' he says, and thrusts the document at my chest.

'Done what?' I ask, taking it off him and glancing down at a printout of numbers, diagrams and general gobbledegook.

'We got the photo,' he explains, 'from Dr Lynch's house. Mr Larson ran it through a program, and it matches with the

CCTV. It's definitely her, sir – Anna Radcliffe. In the hospital, I mean.'

I rummage in my pockets and, not finding a pen, borrow Jackson's, scrawl 'Positive ID of Radcliffe' at the top of the first sheet, and tell him to take it in to the DCI while Lynch, conveniently, is taking a bathroom break. When he has gone, I unmute the mic and give Grace the news.

'Tell Larson good work,' she says, and then adds, 'We're missing something, Al, but I'm damned if I can put my finger on it.'

I'm about to agree, when George leans across and grabs the mic. 'Ask her how she got the job in Spain, ma'am, and how she ended up back in Bristol. It might not give us anything, but you never know.'

Grace's brow furrows at that, but she doesn't have time to reply, as Jackson breezes in with his wad of papers, Lynch following right behind him. I stare at George, who gives me a grin, and flicks the mute button on the mic. 'Just because I never wanted to be one of the glory boys, Al, it doesn't mean I couldn't have.' He settles back to finish his sausage roll.

Grace gets straight to it. 'I wonder if you could give me a little background, Doctor. How did you come to get the job in Malaga? I mean, did you apply for it, was it some sort of exchange, or were you approached by the institution perhaps?'

'I didn't apply for it,' Lynch answers without hesitation. 'In fact, I had never given it any thought before Professor Davidson called me about it.'

'Professor Davidson?' Sillitoe asks.

Lynch nods. 'Charles Davidson. He was my supervisor at St George's and took over the running of mental health services for the South West around ten years ago. He's always taken an interest in the careers of his best students – he suggested I apply for a post at Bath around five years ago, with the opportunity to head up the unit at Bristol after a time – bigger, with more opportunities for research. I had to wait for the current senior consultant, Dr Kennedy, to retire, though, and as it would have been a big step up, he offered to recommend me for a two-year temporary secondment as deputy director of San Sebastian, to give me the administrative experience to get my application through for Bristol without any fuss. I jumped at it, of course – who wouldn't?'

'I can't imagine,' Grace responds, stopping just short of sarcasm. 'You say he took an interest in his best students. In other words' – she smiles benignly – 'he had favourites.' Lynch bridles, but before she can reply, Grace goes on, 'Who else? I mean, aside from yourself, do you know of any other former students in whose career he took a particular interest?'

Lynch shrugs. 'I've never really thought about it. There were half a dozen or so, I think, in my year, but I didn't know any of them very well, except for Paul and Anna, of course.'

'I see. So Professor Davidson stayed in touch with the Radcliffes after they both graduated? Gave their careers a little push as well, perhaps?'

'I suppose it's possible,' Lynch replies, but uncertainty is starting to creep into her voice. 'You're saying that Charles might have ... that he and Anna ... I can't believe it – not Charles ... Oh, my God!' She hunches forward, head in her hands, defeated.

After a short silence Grace says, 'I think your professor might have been manipulated – just as you were, Doctor.'

Lynch looks up, blinking. 'You believe me, then? That I had nothing to do with these murders?'

'Oh, we wouldn't go that far,' Sillitoe puts in. 'However, it does rather look like you were, as DCI Helston suggests, manipulated, perhaps coerced? At the very least, Dr Lynch, you are guilty of withholding information, and that, I hope you realise, is a very serious offence, especially where murder is concerned.' She pauses for a beat, lets this sink in, then goes on, 'I think it's time you told us everything that happened once you returned from Spain and took up your post at Coombe Hill, don't you?'

## 26

Back in Grace's office, there is a heavy silence as we all grapple with the implications of what we've just heard. Lynch has finally been charged, and requested a solicitor, which means we've got at least a couple of hours to unravel the flood of information in her final statement.

The slap of Grace's palm on her oak veneer desktop jerks us away from our musings. She leans back in her chair and lets out a long sigh. 'Well, at least now we know what we're dealing with.'

Polly Sillitoe gives a loud snort. 'You mean Anna Radcliffe is a complete psychopath? We knew that already!'

'I wouldn't say psychopath,' Larson murmurs, half to himself. 'I mean, don't psychopaths generally go after people they don't know, and ...' He stumbles to a halt, seeing us all glaring at him, and shrugs. 'Sorry.'

'Well, whatever the hell she is,' Grace snaps, 'she's bloody dangerous – and clever. Christ – she must have been planning all this for years!'

'Since her daughter died, certainly,' Sillitoe says, 'and

probably since her husband hanged himself. I feel almost sorry for Lynch, though. Radcliffe played her like a fish.'

Grace's lips quirk into a grim smile. 'Margaret Lynch is a perfect example of the perils of an overinflated ego.' The smile disappears. 'Still, she wasn't the only one being played. As long as our attention was on Lynch, not to mention your Rosie, Al, we weren't looking for Radcliffe.' She gives the intercom button an aggressive jab, dispatches DC Jackson to the deli round the corner with an order for coffees all round and a bag of assorted pastries, and then sits back and stretches. 'Okay, let's go through the story so far. Anna Radcliffe is a brilliant, highly qualified psychologist, extremely manipulative, with both patients and professional contacts, somewhat lacking in the emotion department ...'

'In other words, a psychopath,' Sillitoe puts in, with a glare at Larson, who wisely keeps his mouth shut.

'Possibly,' Grace continues, 'but I think we can leave the diagnoses to the psychiatrists, if we ever manage to bloody well catch her. She did have one weak spot, though – Paul Radcliffe. She needed him to keep her on the right side of normal, and when he killed himself, it sent her over the edge. Agreed?'

There are nods all round. Sillitoe picks it up. 'She might have been setting her sights on the people she blamed for his death right back then,' she says, 'Markham, Swann and Lynch. But then her daughter got mixed up in the Inverness business and ended up dying as well, and ...'

'And as far as Anna was concerned,' Larson pipes up, 'if Paul hadn't died and messed up her life, Lucy would still be alive. She'd lost everything that meant anything to her, and the dodgy deal with Markham and Swann was responsible for it all.'

'Quite so,' Grace agrees, 'not forgetting Lynch, who introduced them in the first place. So she set about making them all suffer – and not just suffer, but suffer in exactly the same way, as precisely as she possibly could. She traced Swann to Malaga, and Markham to Bristol, found out all she could about their private lives, relationships and so on, and set about getting everybody exactly where she wanted them.'

THERE IS a pause while Jackson delivers coffee and Danish pastries, and I mentally go over the phone call with Professor Charles Davidson. Yes, he'd known Anna since her student days, and wasn't it incredible how she'd weathered all the tragedy that had struck her over the years? It was so like Anna to always think of others, when she was going through so much herself…

'What do you mean, "think of others"?' Grace had asked, raising an eyebrow at the rest of us huddled round the desk, listening in.

'When she called me, about the European exchange program she'd set up – that's what you said you wanted to know about, wasn't it?'

I could see Grace counting to five under her breath before responding. 'That's right, Professor – you're saying that Anna Radcliffe was responsible for the whole program?'

'Yes. She'd put in a successful funding application around five years ago, but it had taken a while for a suitable place-ment to come up. By then, she said, she wasn't in a position to go herself, but immediately thought of Maggie – Maggie Lynch, one of her old university friends. I taught Maggie as well, of course, and was still in close touch with her. Anna suggested the project might be a good stepping stone for Maggie, to give her the extra experience she needed to go for the top job at Coombe Hill, and that wouldn't become vacant for another year or so.'

'And you thought that was a good idea?' Grace asked. 'So you told Dr Lynch about Anna's proposal?'

'Oh yes,' Davidson replied, 'it was a perfect idea, but Anna didn't want her name mentioned, and I could understand that – the two of them had lost contact over the years, and Anna had gone through a bad time. She was never the most sociable of people and had become quite reclusive by then. I asked if there was anything I could do to help, but she said it would be enough to know she'd given her old friend a helping hand. She'd be fine, she said, and just needed a little more time. We left it at that. Tell me, nothing else has happened, has it? Perhaps I should get in touch with Anna, make sure everything is all right?'


'INSPECTOR?'

Larson is waving a paper bag in my direction, and I take it, pull out a Danish pastry and pass it on. Grace takes a sip of her coffee and carries on where she left off. 'She set Lynch up perfectly, putting her right on the spot for the murders in Malaga and then engineering her move to Bristol. We've looked into Lynch's story about her cat, and it checks out – she reported the strangling to the local police, who were predictably too busy to follow it up, gave her a crime number and suggested she call the RSPCA. Given the nature of the attack on her precious Freddie, I don't think there's much doubt who was responsible, and it's more than likely how Radcliffe got hold of the keys and was able to take copies. We've got enough to implicate Lynch in the business with the CD, even if she didn't know precisely what was on it.'

'What about Rosie Larson, though?' Sillitoe asks, through a mouthful of chocolate muffin. 'Surely, that was just luck – that Markham's daughter ...' She catches herself and turns to me. 'Sorry, sir – stepdaughter, would be working as a nurse at

Coombe Hill. Isn't that stretching coincidence just a little too far?'

'Not coincidence at all,' Larson says, with a bitter edge in his voice. We all stare at him, and Grace opens her mouth, then catches my slight shake of the head and waits. 'I sent a copy of that photo from Lynch's album to Carol Dodds,' he goes on, 'and asked her to show it to Rosie, get her to think carefully about whether she had seen Radcliffe before.'

'And?' I ask.

'And,' he says, 'Rosie recognised it straight away. She attended a lecture on health psychology in her final year at Plymouth, and a subsequent careers workshop about the opportunities for working in mental health. Both were given by a visiting "expert". No prizes for guessing who that was.'

'Jesus fucking Christ,' I mutter before I can help myself.

'Yeah, right,' Larson agrees, and goes on, 'According to Carol, Rosie remembered it because Radcliffe paid particular attention to her, even took her and a couple of other students out for a pub lunch afterwards. By the end of it, Rosie was hooked on the idea and decided to specialise, particularly after Radcliffe suggested she could pull strings for her at Coombe Hill.' He gives me a sheepish look. 'Rosie and I were just starting to get serious around then, and a placement in Bristol, with good prospects, was just what Rosie was after.' He shakes his head, the pain clear in his expression. 'Damn it, I remember her saying that a chance like that would change our lives. She bloody well got that right, didn't she?'

'You can't blame yourself, son,' I comment, trying for once to sound reassuring.

'I don't!' he snaps back, making it quite clear that the effort is not appreciated.

'All right, that's enough.' Grace's tone is soft, but cuts into the fragile atmosphere with a surgeon's precision. She nods at Larson. 'Good work. Still, it does nothing except confirm what we already know, that Radcliffe spent years setting this up, and that so far we're no closer to catching her than we were before we got Lynch's statement. So unless we can find her, or she makes a mistake ...'

That's when it hits me, with a suddenness that makes my stomach lurch. For a second my vision blurs, and I can feel my balance start to slip, even though I'm sitting down. I reach out and grab the edge of Grace's desk, aware of all eyes in the room swivelling in my direction as I struggle to keep my breathing, and the jitters, under control.

'Al?' There's concern in Grace's voice. 'Al – are you all right?'

I force my breathing to slow and manage a nod. After a minute or so, the world rights itself, and I push myself back into my chair, my embarrassment dwarfed by the realisation of how stupid I've been, how slow to see what this was all, inevitably, leading to. The others give me time to gather myself, get my verbal ducks in a row.

'She did make a mistake,' I manage to say finally. 'Actually, she made two mistakes.'

Grace raises an eyebrow. 'How so?'

'When she started all this, her goal was to make Markham and Swann suffer the same way she did, right? She wanted them to experience the loss of the people closest to them before she murdered them.'

'We've already established that, Al,' Grace points out. 'What's your point?'

'The point is,' I tell her, 'neither Markham nor Swann were close to anybody, not in the way she imagined. They couldn't give a shit about the people around them – wives, girlfriends, even each other – they were all just tools, things to be used, whether for financial or emotional gain. Everyone they came across was a victim, every bit as much as she was. That was her first mistake.'

Everyone is staring at me, and I can see from Larson's expression that he's catching up fast. 'And the second?' Grace asks quietly.

I take a breath and go on, 'When all this started, Chrissie and Markham were still together – Radcliffe might even have been planning it before Markham's accident – who knows? There was no way she could have predicted, at that stage, that they would split up, that Markham would disappear. She might be a psychologist, but she hasn't got any real under-standing of emotions in others – only her own. When Markham went into hiding, she assumed he would still want to protect Rosie, and he'd show himself when Rosie was arrested. It wouldn't occur to her that he has no feelings for my daughter at all – not for her, and not for Chrissie either. What she would think, though ...'

'Is that they are protecting him,' Larson finishes for me. 'She thinks Rosie and Chrissie know where he is. And now that she thinks she's succeeded in getting rid of Rosie ...'

Grace is already calling down to the squad room. There's a long, painful silence as we wait for the reply, and when it comes, it's the one I was dreading. 'No response from PC MacDonald, ma'am. His radio is operating as far as we can tell, but he's not answering.'

'And the AFO we sent with them from the hospital?' Grace asks, almost in a whisper.

'Reassigned this morning, ma'am – tip-off about an arms deal down behind Temple Meads.'

Larson yanks out his mobile, dials, waits, then dials again. 'I can't get Christine – her mobile's switched off, and she isn't answering the house phone – neither is Joyce.' There's near panic in his voice as he adds, 'Ben – what about Ben – what if she's ...'

He's on his feet, blundering to the door, and I grab him, push him back against the wall. It takes all my strength to keep him there until some element of reason returns, and he deflates into a tangled knot of despair. 'Together, son,' I say, trying not to let my own panic drip into my voice. 'We do this together, okay? You, me, Grace, and a load of people who actually know what they're doing. That's how it works. No one's doing a Lone Ranger act, not now. Not if you want Chrissie and Ben to come out of this in one piece, you understand?'

While I'm talking, I'm aware of the flurry around me, Grace barking orders, DC Jackson, who has been hovering quietly in a corner behind Larson, following Polly Sillitoe out of the room at a run. Once they've gone, the room goes eerily quiet apart from Larson's heavy breathing – I realise I've still got him pinned to the wall and very slowly relax my grip and turn to Grace, who, in contrast to the urgency of a minute before, is leaning against the front of her desk, arms folded, like a headmistress waiting patiently for one of her pupils to get over a tantrum.

'Al ...' she starts, but I don't let her get any further.

'Don't even think about it, Grace. I just made the lad here a promise, and there's no way I'm going to break it, not unless you arrest me, so if that's what you're going to do, you'd better get on with it.'

She gives us a long look, weighing things up, and then nods slowly. 'Okay, Al. The pair of you are with me – but you do exactly as I say. Any deviation, and I'll throw the book at you, I swear. You understand? You stay in the car, and you stay well away from the house, whatever happens – both of you. Is that clear?'

'You have my word, Grace,' I say, and give Larson a nudge. He's white as a sheet, the muscles in his jaw doing a fairly good impression of rigor mortis, but he manages a stiff nod.

'Right, then,' she says. 'Let's get on with it.'

## 27

The drive from the Sinkhole to Long Ashton is only around six miles, but the route takes us right through the choked arterial roads south of the river, made worse by the fact that we've hit a combination of the school run, rush hour and the ever-present roadworks blocking both roads leading to the bypass. After what seems an eternity watching the traffic lights on Bath Bridge change from red to green and back again, Grace finally snaps and hits the blues and twos. Sillitoe and Jackson, a couple of cars back in the queue, take the hint and do the same, and our progress moves from stationary to a slow crawl past a line of flustered drivers doing their best to give us room to squeeze past.

She kills the siren as we hit the bypass, lets out a long breath and calls up Sillitoe. 'No lights from here on in, Polly – we don't want to scare the natives – if there are any to scare, that is.' As we turn off onto the road to the village, she glances at me. 'I'll do a drive past, see how things look. You never know, it might just be a line fault, and we don't want to blast our way in to find them all having tea in the garden.'

It's obvious that little statement is purely for Larson's benefit, and equally obvious that he's about as convinced as I am, judging by the muttered curses from the back seat. My ex-mother-in-law's house is a substantial but unassuming 1960s detached halfway along a small, quiet close backing onto the golf course. Grace is about to turn into the street when Larson suddenly jerks into life. 'Stop! Pull in here, and ask your sergeant to do the same.'

She doesn't question, just sticks her arm out the window and gestures to Sillitoe, then draws to a halt, and we both turn to face Larson.

'What is it, son?' I ask.

He hesitates, a hint of the old nerviness creeping back as he says, 'Well, if she – I mean Radcliffe – if she's in there and she's watching out for anything unusual, and if I were her, I would be ...' He trails off, eyes flicking from one to the other of us.

'For fuck's sake, spit it out!' I growl at him through gritted teeth, trying to remember that he's as beside himself with worry as I am, but as I'm about to grab his collar and shake him, Grace claps a hand to her forehead and answers for him.

'She knows him, Al. What's more, if she's been watching the house, she might know you too. If we drive past and she sees us ...' At once, she radios the other car, and Sillitoe pulls out and disappears round the corner.

It must be little more than a minute, but it's long enough to set off the jitters, and I have to grab my right hand with my left to hold it still. The only sound is Larson's rapid, shallow breathing behind me. When Sillitoe finally edges round the bend and pulls back in behind us, the look on her face doesn't need any translation. She joins us, shuffling into the back seat next to Larson.

'The blinds are closed, upstairs and down, at least at the front of the house,' she says. 'Is that normal?'

Larson shakes his head. 'Not at this time of day, no.' His voice is unsteady, and it takes him a minute to add, in a whisper that mirrors my growing panic, 'Do something – please!' I exchange glances with him, remembering that first meeting on the pavement outside West Hill nick, how terrified he was for Rosie, and how easily I'd written him off as a complete waste of space. Now, I have to acknowledge that there isn't that much difference between us, and that right now, my right hand trembling with a palsy I can't control, and my stomach threatening to upend itself all over the footwell of Grace's car, I'm a hell of a lot more useless than he is. Then I remember something.

'John?' His head jerks up, startled, and it's only then I realise I've used his name without thinking about it. 'Did Rosie ever tell you about the Squad Room?' I ask, trying not to get my hopes up.

For a moment his brow furrows, but then his eyes spark as it comes back to him, and he takes in a sharp breath. 'Of course! She told me all about it, how the two of you made it together when she was –'

'Never mind that now,' I cut in. 'Did she ever show you where it is?'

He nods. 'Yes, just after Ben was born. That was only three years ago, and it was still there – Inspector, it's still there …'

'Would the two of you mind telling me what the hell you're talking about?' Grace's patience finally snaps.

'It's a den I made for Rosie when she was little,' I tell her, 'when we lived with Joyce for a while, waiting for an extension to be finished on our house. The golf course backs onto the gardens all along the row, and there's a hundred yards or so of hedging down a steep bank between the gardens and the course. It's bramble mostly and pretty much impenetrable unless you know what you're doing. The den is on the

other side of Joyce's fence, and up the hill a way – we built it
so she could see over the fence from it. It's totally hidden, and
it gives a perfect view through the garden and into the
kitchen and lounge. If the curtains are open and you've got
binoculars ...'

'I've got an app on my phone,' Larson puts in, 'and I can
show you where it is. All we have to do is jump the fence at
the end of the road and work our way round the back.
Nobody would see us, from the road or the house.'

'Grace, please,' I say, forcing calm into my voice, 'you've
got to let him try.'

There's a long silence as Grace massages her temples,
weighing it all up. Then she gives a curt nod. 'Polly, go and fill
Darren in, and you, Mr Larson,' she turns and fixes him with
her 'don't dare to argue' look, 'you do exactly as my DC tells
you, you understand? You guide him to this den of yours, and
you stay quiet and stay put – whatever happens and whatever
you see. You got that?'

'I understand,' Larson says, but he's looking right at me,
and I can see that little glint in his eye.

'Good luck, son,' I tell him.


THE WAIT IS INTERMINABLE. The hidden path down to the
Squad Room – even in this situation, the name Rosie gave the
den makes me smile – will be well overgrown with vicious
brambles by now, although the fact that it was passable three
years ago gives me hope. It was a five-minute scramble way
back when Rosie was eight years old. It's around fifteen
minutes before Grace's radio finally crackles into life.

'We're there, ma'am. It's just as Inspector Crow said – we
can see right over the fence and into the house. Mr Larson's
trying to get the focus right now ...' There's a pause, and then,
'Oh, Christ!'

'Darren? What is it? What's happening?' Another moment of silence and then Jackson's voice, unsteady. 'A body, in the kitchen. I'm pretty sure it's MacDonald, but I can't see if ... he's not moving, ma'am. Radcliffe's in there; I'd stake my pension on it.'

Grace curses under her breath before responding, 'Right. Darren, stay put and keep watching. If you see any movement at all, I want to know. We do nothing until we've got backup, understood?'

Jackson is still muttering in the affirmative as Grace turns to Sillitoe. 'Polly, I need someone watching the front. See if one of the neighbours opposite is in. Make yourself look like a Jehovah's Witness or something.'

'Ma'am.' Sillitoe is out of the car and on her way almost before Grace has finished issuing the instruction. I have to admit she looks the part, in a black business suit, and 'sensible' shoes, the kind that are disguised as courts but are actually high-performance running trainers.

Grace turns to me, takes in the barely controlled tremor in my right hand, the sweat that has broken out on my forehead from the effort of simply sitting still, while a deluded lunatic is doing God knows what to three of the most important people in my life. She puts a hand on my arm, whether in sympathy or as a token gesture of constraint I can't quite tell.

'I'm sorry, Al,' she says quietly. 'I don't have any choice now.'

And she calls in her request for the armed response team.

ANOTHER TEN UNBEARABLE MINUTES LATER, the van pulls up a discreet distance behind us, well out of sight of the house and any nosey neighbours who might start twitching their blinds. Grace is half out of the car, and launching into a dire warning

about what she will do to my pension if I don't stay well out
of the way, when her radio crackles, and Jackson, his
panicked voice raised to a pitch we used to call 'the Sinkhole
Squeak', common in probationers faced by their first drug
dealer with attitude and a large knife, gabbles, 'Ma'am, it's Mr
Larson – he's gone. I'm sorry, ma'am, I couldn't stop him. He
went off in the direction of the back gardens, and I don't
know whether I should go after him ...'

I don't hear Grace's reply as she slams the car door, heads
for the van at a run and disappears inside. It takes less than
two seconds to ditch my last vestige of restraint, and before
my body has time to get in the way of my intentions, I'm on
the pavement, round the corner and out of the DCI's line of
sight. I reckon I've got two minutes, perhaps three, before
Grace finishes her briefing and the squad deploys. It's not
long, but it's enough time to get me to where I want to be, just
as long as my legs don't lock up and I don't lose my balance.
The house next door to Joyce has a narrow side alley to the
back garden. I manage to squeeze through and come face to
face with Larson. His shirt is torn, and he's bleeding from
dozens of scratches from the brambles on the other side of
the fence. Behind him, a blonde woman, who looks to be in
her mid-thirties, is standing at an open patio door. She beckons, and we duck into a kitchen that reminds me of an
autopsy lab – all stainless steel and white tiles.

'John, what the hell's going on? You look terrible! And
who's this?' She points at me, her expression a mixture of
concern, confusion and suspicion.

'Inspector Crow,' I say, and hold out a hand, which under
the circumstances is a bit ridiculous, and add, unnecessarily,
'I'm a policeman'.

'And my father-in-law,' Larson adds. As she's trying to
process this, Larson presses on. 'Fran, there's no time to
explain, but we need to get into Joyce's house without anyone

seeing us. If we can get onto your garage roof, we'll be able to get across to that little window in the side wall and get into the loft.'

'We'll need a roll of cling film, a blanket and a hammer, if you have them,' I add, and exchange a glance with Larson, who has clearly been thinking along the same lines. 'As quickly as you can, please, Fran.'

'Right.' For a couple of seconds she just stands there, stunned, eyes flitting from one to the other of us, and then, taking in a sharp breath, she bustles off, rooting through cupboards and drawers, grabbing what looks like a very expensive throw from the back of her sofa. 'Here,' she says, dumping the bundle on a worktop. 'There's a water butt by the garage wall. My husband uses it to get up there to clean the gutters. It's pretty tough,' she adds, giving me a pointed look.

Larson is already halfway out the door. I grab his arm and pull him back. 'Slowly, son,' I tell him. 'We don't know what's going on in there. If Radcliffe sees us, we don't know what she'll do.' I don't add that by now there will be at least half a dozen AFOs with MP5s trained on the house, and as soon as we are up on the garage roof, we'll be sitting ducks. I push down the nausea that accompanies that thought and turn to Fran. 'Stay inside, and wait for instructions from my colleagues,' I say. 'There are armed officers outside, and it isn't safe. Understand?'

She nods dumbly and retreats to the back of the kitchen.

'Okay,' I say to Larson, 'let's go, and keep well down.'

In less than five seconds my son-in-law is flat on the roof, reaching down to help me up, and I find myself wondering if perhaps I should sign on to that fancy gym of his for a month or two, just until I'm back in the shape I was in a year or so ago. I shrug off my jacket, toss it aside, grab his hand and grit my teeth. A moment later I'm lying next to him, feeling as if my arm has been wrenched out of its socket. 'Stay flat and stay quiet,' I whisper. He nods, and we both wriggle across on elbows and knees until we reach the window, a single glazed pane around two feet square – barely large enough for an adult body to pass through. We end up one on either side, backs against the wall, catching our breath. I gesture for him to stay still, and very carefully poke my head round, trying to squint through the thick layer of grime coating the glass into the darkness of the loft. A second later I jerk back, fighting to get my breathing under control.

'There's someone in there,' I whisper to Larson as soon as I can speak. His eyes widen, but to his credit he doesn't move. Then, before I can take another breath, there's a tap on the window, almost too quiet to hear. A brief pause, and then again, slightly louder. I scrub at the window with my shirt cuff, and Joyce's terrified face appears, staring back at us. At once, I put a finger to my lips, and she nods and then motions the action of opening the window, followed by a shake of the head. It figures – this window has been jammed shut for as long as I can remember. I show her the blanket and the hammer, and she holds up a hand, scuttles off, and returns with an old dust sheet. She somehow manages to stuff it around the inside while we cover the glass on our side with the cling film and blanket, then taps on the window again to indicate she's ready.

It takes just four muffled blows to break the glass. When we take the blanket away and gently peel the film back, a fair number of the smaller fragments come away with it, and thanks to Joyce holding her sheet to catch the remainder, it's easy enough to knock out the rest with my elbow.

'Joyce ...' Larson lunges forward, but Joyce stops him with a look and puts a finger to her lips.

'It's all right, John,' she whispers. 'Ben's here. He's asleep.

Al, you come in and hand him up, quickly, before she realises we're here.'

Joyce's expression is the same one that terrified me when I took Chrissie home for the first time all those years ago. The vision of a lioness protecting her cubs doesn't quite cut it. I do as I'm told, pulling off my shoes and wriggling gingerly through the tiny opening, ignoring the shards of glass tearing my back and palms as I squeeze through. Ben is wrapped in a quilt in a far corner of the loft, thumb in mouth, snoring gently. I pick him up as carefully as I can, and by some miracle he doesn't wake. Larson has meanwhile draped the blanket over the jagged edge of the window and reaches down to take him out of my arms. As he scoops the sleeping child up, I see a helmeted head poke above the garage roof behind him, followed by the ominous sight of a black bullet-proof vest.

'Stall them,' I growl at Larson, and retreat further into the loft, placing Joyce between me and the window. 'No time to explain now,' I tell her. 'Just tell me where you think Chrissie is – upstairs or down?'

'The front room, I think,' she says, and there is a slight quaver in her voice, her resolve slipping as she realises Ben is safe. 'Whoever that woman is, I heard her come up and search all the bedrooms, and then she went down again. She doesn't know we're up here.'

'Good. Try to make a meal of getting out. There's an armed officer up there with John, and the longer you can delay him, the more chance I've got of getting to Chrissie.'

She nods, but before turning back to the window grabs my arm. She doesn't speak – the look in her eyes is enough. 'I'll get her out, Joyce,' I tell her. 'I promise.'

I grab the ring set into the loft hatch and carefully lift it just an inch. The upper landing is quiet, but I can hear muffled voices downstairs – female, more than one. Chrissie is still alive and talking. Painfully slowly, I pull the hatch open, praying there's enough oil in the hinges to stop any tell-tale squeaks. Behind me, I can hear the scuffle as Joyce effectively blocks the window opening, and urgent whispering from the roof. I grit my teeth and lower myself to the landing, praying that muscles that haven't lifted anything more strenuous than a teacup for over a year don't give out on me halfway down. I just about manage it and land noiselessly on the carpet, trying to ignore the pain in my underused biceps. I glance down at my hands, torn and bleeding from the window glass, but, amazingly, rock steady.

As I make my way down the stairs, the voices become clearer. Nobody's shouting. It's almost as if I'm eavesdropping on two friends immersed in conversation over afternoon tea. Almost. I reach the hallway. The sounds are coming from the front room, its door slightly ajar. I can distinguish between them now. The first voice, Radcliffe's, is quiet, but sharp, incisive, matter of fact, completely lacking in emotion. I hear Chrissie respond, her voice instantly recognisable, but not quite right somehow. She sounds tired, distracted, her speech slightly slurred, as if she'd had just a little too much to drink. Drugged, I realise, suppressing a shudder of rage. The kitchen door is open, and through it, I can see the body of PC MacDonald. He might have simply fainted, except for the eyes, wide open, staring blankly down the hall towards me. I turn back to the front room, take a step forward, and gently push open the door.

## 28

I force myself to stand perfectly still, not provoke any
sudden reaction, despite the sickening churning in my
stomach, the almost irresistible urge to launch myself
at the woman who has caused my family so much misery, and
strangle her with my bare hands. Two things stop me. One is
the expression on Radcliffe's face. It's older, a little more
lined, but easily recognisable as the same that a few hours
ago I saw staring out of the faded, grainy, twenty-year-old
group photo from Margaret Lynch's album. She's perched
primly on an arm of Joyce's sofa, watching me calmly, a slight
smile curling the corner of her mouth. That, in itself, is unset-
tling, but what's really chilling is the look in her eyes – not
frenzied, not angry – not even surprised. Her gaze is steady
and utterly blank, as if there is no thought, no emotion there
at all. Beside her, stretched out on the sofa, head resting on a
cushion, is Chrissie, completely still, eyes closed, as if sleeping. The second thing that makes me freeze in the doorway is
the sight of a hypodermic, Radcliffe's thumb on the plunger,
the point of the needle resting a fraction of a millimetre from
Chrissie's throat.

'Please don't come any closer,' she says, her voice calm – too calm, considering the situation we're all in. 'It will take less than two seconds to inject a fatal dose, and I'm sure you are aware that I won't hesitate.'

'I'm sure you won't,' I comment, trying not to let the wave of relief show on my face. Chrissie isn't dead – yet. As I'm speaking, I sense a presence behind me, the hint of a warm breath at my shoulder. I lean against the door jamb and, keeping my eyes on Radcliffe, hold up a hand to the marksman who has silently crept up behind me, hoping the signal is enough to give him the message. 'So what is it this time?' I ask Radcliffe, pointing to the syringe. 'The same stuff you used on John Larson before you shoved him into the harbour?'

Her smile widens. 'Certainly not, Inspector Crow. I wanted to kill Mr Larson. Your ex-wife, however, is another matter altogether. I wanted to talk to her – at first, anyway. This' – she indicates the needle – 'made the conversation a little easier. Unfortunately, even a modest overdose is fatal and, administered intravenously, irreversible.'

'A truth drug?' I manage what I hope is a dismissive shake of the head. 'I'm no psychiatrist, Doctor, but even I know that the idea of a truth serum is just a myth, about as reliable as a lie detector. Besides, as you've been watching my family all this time, you should know by now that Chrissie is just as much a victim as you are. Markham took her money, just as he did your husband's, and she has no idea where he is.'

She gives a slow nod. 'I'm afraid I have come to that conclusion as well, Inspector. As you say, sodium thiopental is a crude tool, but it does reduce inhibitions quite well. I'm quite satisfied she doesn't have the information I need. Even so, I'm sure that Terence Markham, wherever he is, watches the news, accesses the internet. Her death will send a message – however long it takes, I'll find him eventually.'

'Not if you're in a cell,' I tell her. 'You must realise that there are armed officers covering every door and window. Aside from the murder charges you're already facing, there's a dead policeman in the kitchen, and that gives things a whole new meaning.'

'Which is why,' she replies, with another of her icy smiles, 'I'm rather glad I didn't end things for your precious Christine before you arrived. It was touch-and-go, you know.' She frowns, looking me up and down as if I'm a particularly interesting rat in research lab. 'In fact, you're rather interesting yourself, Inspector – or perhaps I should say former Inspector? With an injury like yours and all the side effects – tremors, losing your balance, jumbled thoughts ...' She lifts her shoulders in a half shrug. 'We both know it's never going to get any better, and it will probably get worse as time goes on. You'll have to face it – your career, your marriage, your life – they are all over. Yet, incredibly, you are still trying to protect the woman who betrayed you, went off with another man, turned your own daughter against you. Oh yes,' she says, and I realise my reaction must be showing on my face, 'Christine told me all about it. She blames herself, of course, but it's too late now, isn't it? Even so, here you are, trying to play the hero for her one last time, even though you know you're going to fail.'

I've heard enough psychobabble over the last twelve months to see the game she's playing, and I have to admit she's pretty good at it. But good as she is, she's not perfect, and she's taken one step too far. There's no way I'm going to fail Chrissie, not now, not again. Somehow, the effort of keeping a grip on the poisonous combination of fear for Chrissie and rage at Radcliffe, Markham and not least my own inadequacy is having a magical effect on my body – my hands are perfectly steady, and my legs feel solid under me.

As if on cue, Chrissie stirs and opens her eyes. She looks

straight at me, squinting in confusion. 'Al?' She shuffles and tries to sit upright, but Radcliffe holds her still, the point of the needle still pressed dangerously against her jugular. Chrissie doesn't seem to notice. 'This is Anna,' she says, a slight slur in her voice. 'She's come to visit – it was so nice of her. She wants to help you find Terry, so it's good you're here. Why don't you come in? We can all talk about it, and when Mum gets back, we can have some tea ...' She trails off, brow furrowing, and tries to shake her head, but Radcliffe's grip won't allow it.

I force a smile. 'Hi, Chris. I just popped in – won't be staying long. We can catch up later, okay?' I turn my gaze back to Radcliffe. 'Okay, now what?'

'Now,' Radcliffe says, 'we leave. You're going to walk to the front door, and your ex-wife and I will be right behind you. You're going to explain the situation to your former colleagues outside and ask them politely to keep back.' She rummages in a pocket and throws a set of keys at my feet. 'Then you're going to ask one of them to back my car up to the front door, keep the engine running and move away.'

'And Chrissie?'

'When I'm in the car, I'll let her go.'

I bend and pick up the keys. 'You expect me to believe that?'

She barks a short laugh. 'It doesn't matter whether you believe me or not, does it, Inspector? You really don't have any choice.'

I can see awareness slowly returning to Chrissie's face. She starts to struggle, but she's still too weak, uncoordinated, and it's easy for Radcliffe to push her back as she tries to pull away. 'Al?' Fear is rapidly replacing the confusion in her eyes. 'Al? What's going on? Why are you here? What's happening ...'

Before I can speak, Radcliffe answers for me. 'Don't worry,

Christine. You had a bit of a dizzy spell, that's all. We're going to go for a little walk, get some fresh air. You'd like that, wouldn't you? Al will come with us, to make sure you're all right. Let's see if you can stand up, shall we?'

Radcliffe shoots me a look, and I say, in the calmest tone I can manage, 'That's right, Chris – you need to get some air. Just try to get up, slowly, don't rush it, and keep looking at me. Can you do that?'

She nods and pushes herself unsteadily to her feet. Radcliffe moves with her, one arm tightly around her shoulder, holding her upright. The syringe doesn't move even a fraction of a millimetre from Chrissie's throat. Radcliffe jerks her head at me. 'Move back, away from the door – and I want to see you, every step. Understand, Inspector Crow, my life was over a long time ago. If it stops here for me, it stops for her, too.'

I hold up my hands and step back. 'Whatever you say, Doctor – just be careful with that thing, okay?'

She smiles. 'Don't worry about me. Just do as you're told, and we'll all be fine.' She's reached the lounge door now, manhandling Chrissie in front of her as if trying to guide a drunken friend out of a nightclub, and carefully staying just out of my arm's reach. 'Now, go to the front door and open it – slowly.'

I do as she says, and when I reach the door, I pause, my hand on the Yale, and half turn. There's a silent movement behind her, and a dark figure takes a single step from the kitchen into the hall, weapon raised, trained on the back of Radcliffe's head. 'Ready?' I ask, forcing myself to keep my eyes on Radcliffe. She nods. So does the figure behind her. I turn the lock with a sharp click – one that masks the click of the MP5, and in the next breath several things happen at once. I see Radcliffe fall, hear a high-pitched whine followed by a thud by my left ear as a splatter of hot, sticky liquid hits me in the face. A split second later, the sharp crack of the shot reaches me, and I lunge forward to grab Chrissie, both of us collapsing in a tangled heap. I just have time to register that she's still breathing, still moving – still alive. Then, suddenly, I'm not there anymore.

It takes the rookie three blows with the ram to smash the door open. He stands aside and nods at me. I'm the senior officer, and strictly speaking it's my collar, but I glance across and see the eagerness in Joe's face. I give him a grin. 'Want to go and make some arrests, Sergeant?'

He grins back. 'You bloody bet I do, guv!'

He turns, moves ahead of me, and that's when I see the man at the end of the hall, perfectly still, legs apart, arms out in front of him, hands clasped together, and the gun in those hands, pointed straight at us. I try to shout a warning, but Joe's already falling backwards into my arms. At least, that's what seems to be happening, but the angle is all wrong, and I'm clutching at thin air as the deafening sound of the shot hits me like a punch in the face. What follows is an eerie still-ness, as if someone pressed the pause button and all move-ment, all life, is abruptly switched off. Except for one small, persistent sound – somewhere, inside the house, a phone is ringing. It goes on and on, stabbing into my brain like a red-hot needle, until I can't stand it anymore, and I try to shout, 'For God's sake, can't somebody answer the bloody thing?' And suddenly, the world comes back, sirens, getting closer, frantic movement around me. Someone is sitting on my legs, someone else holding my arms, and I realise I've been strug-gling to get up, get to Joe. One of my rookies is cradling my head, trying to stuff his jacket underneath it to stop me cracking my skull on the pavement.

'Please, sir,' he says, panic in his voice, 'stay still. The ambulance is on its way.' His face is white, and I'm pretty sure he's puked his guts up in the last five minutes.

'Joe?' I ask him. 'What about Joe?'

He looks away. 'Sir ... please, just don't move.'

His voice is unsteady – he's crying, but whether from fear or shock I can't tell. I glance down, wondering if I've been injured somehow, and if so, why I can't feel any pain anywhere. The front of my shirt is covered in blood – not just blood – there are fragments of something in the mess on my chest, like shards of broken crockery and other, unidentifiable lumps of matter. It takes a moment to process what I'm looking at – parts of Joe Bailey's skull, his brain. And it's all down to me. I let him go first, wanted him to take the credit, tick the right boxes for the next round of promotions.

'It should have been me,' I say to the rookie holding my head. 'Jesus fucking Christ – it should have been me.'


'Al?' A female voice, gentle, next to my ear. I blink, trying to bring the world back into focus, and look up to see Grace crouching beside me, an uncharacteristic look of concern on her face. 'Al? Wherever you are, come back to us. It's all over now. Everything's fine – do you hear me, Al?'

I realise I'm lying on the floor, in a hallway – Joyce's hallway. I push myself into a sitting position – too fast, and almost slump back again, but Grace holds me up. 'Chrissie?' She should be next to me, but I can't see her anywhere. A few feet away, by the front door, a body half blocks the exit, covered by a tarpaulin. 'Chrissie?' I say again, my stomach starting to churn.

'Chrissie's fine, Al. She's in the ambulance – where you should be.' She straightens up and offers a hand. 'Come on, Inspector, let's get you out of here and properly checked over. You had us worried for a minute or two. It took the paramedics a while to decide that none of the blood was yours. They thought you might have got yourself shot again!'

I get shakily to my feet and shoot her a look. 'Not a chance, Grace. Once was quite enough. Still,' I mutter to myself as we head towards the door, Grace propping me up with one arm while I regain my balance, 'it should have been me.'

'So you've been telling us for the last five minutes,' she comments wryly, 'but we can discuss that later. Right now, you're going to get yourself checked out – and that, Inspector Crow, is an order.'

As we cross the threshold into the open air, one of the forensic team brushes past us holding a clear evidence bag. In the bag is a hypodermic, the plunger pulled back – the syringe is fully loaded. For the fourth time in my life I can't hold back the tears.


I DON'T KNOW how long I've slept, but however long it is, it doesn't feel long enough. I wake as a constable sticks her head round the door of what I realise, as I groggily come to, is a side room off a hospital ward, and brings in a bulky parcel. 'The DCI said you might want to change your clothes before you see Mrs Crow, sir. I'll wait outside until you're ready, and take you along if you like. She's just on the next floor.'

'How long have I been here?' I ask, taking in the plastic sheet cover I'm lying on, the torn, blood-soaked shirt in a heap on the floor, and my trousers, which thankfully I'm still wearing, in an equally poor state.

'Since yesterday evening, sir,' the PC replies. 'The doctors patched you up, and DCI Helston asked for you to be put in here and left alone to get some rest. It's eight in the morning now.'

I nod, the hazy memory coming back, of being prodded, washed, stitched and wrapped like an awkwardly shaped parcel. 'Thanks, Constable,' I say, and she disappears outside.

I change quickly, throwing my bloodstained clothing into a conveniently provided bin bag, and taking care not to dislodge any of the numerous dressings plastered over my hands and torso to cover the gashes from the glass in Joyce's loft window. The PC assures me there is no trace of blood left on my face or in my hair, and I follow her through the maze of corridors to the lift, up to a quieter ward with a number of side rooms.

'Go on in, sir,' the PC says, with a smile when we stop in front of a door, 'she's expecting you.'

I take a deep breath and turn the handle. Chrissie is sitting up, and when she sees me, her face lights up in a dazzling smile, and she holds out her arms. I don't know how long we sit there, wrapped in a tight hug, not a word passing between us. We might as well have been frozen in time, until I hear a polite cough behind us and turn to see Larson in the doorway, holding little Ben in his arms, Joyce hovering just behind him, dabbing her eyes with a handkerchief. We part as if we were teenagers caught out behind the bike sheds at school. Larson puts Ben down, and my grandson rushes at us like an express train and lands on the bed, bouncing with excitement.

'Look, Daddy – it's Granny and Grandad – you said we could have ice cream because we're in hospital. Can they have one too?' He looks at me, serious now. 'You want an ice cream, don't you, Grandad? I've had one already, but if you say yes, I can have another one to "keep you company". That's what you said, isn't it?' He glares at Larson as if challenging him to deny it.

Joyce steps in. 'Your dad did indeed say that, and we're going to get some right now. Come on, Ben, let's leave the grown-ups alone for a while, and see what we can find, okay?'

Ben whoops with delight and dashes back to his great-grandmother. 'Laters,' he singsongs, pulling at Joyce's arm.

Who the hell taught him that one, I think, and hard on that thought, and what the hell does it matter?

Larson comes forward and gives Chrissie a hug before stepping back and saying, 'I've just heard from Carol Dodds. Rosie is being released in a couple of hours. She pushed through the paperwork like you wouldn't believe! I think she had some help from DCI Helston as well. Anyway – Inspector, I thought you might like to come with us. I'm taking Ben of course, but I'm sure Rosie would like to see you, if you're up to it. What do you think?'

During the drive to the prison, I let Larson talk, while Ben, in the back seat, equipped with headphones, watches a cartoon on his father's iPad. 'Joyce and Ben were upstairs when Radcliffe broke in,' he says, shaking his head at the sheer luck of it. 'Ben had a bit of a sniffle, so she'd taken him up for a nap and given him a dose of Calpol – that's why he didn't wake up. She heard a commotion downstairs in the kitchen, and Christine screaming for someone to get out of the house, so she grabbed Ben and made it up into the loft before Radcliffe managed to force her way in. It's a miracle Radcliffe didn't think to search the loft – maybe she thought an old woman with a toddler couldn't possibly get up there.'

'She didn't know Joyce,' I murmur, smiling to myself.

'No,' he agrees, 'and she didn't know Chrissie or Rosie either.' He hesitates and then says, 'I tried to come after you, you know. They wouldn't let me. They just bundled us all into a van with an armed guard outside – there was nothing I could do. I wish ...'

'There's nothing you could have done,' I say quickly. 'I'm not sure I did anything much either. It's okay, son. You did your bit, and you can be proud of that. To tell the truth, you would have just got in the way.'

His fingers tighten on the wheel. 'My name is John,' he

growls, through gritted teeth, 'and you're probably right. I would have just been in your way.'

We've reached the prison, and he pulls up opposite the gate, switches the engine off and turns to me, frowning. 'Anything else you'd like to say, Inspector?'

'Just one thing,' I say, trying my hardest to look offhand, 'I'm probably not going to be an inspector for much longer. My friends call me Al. That okay with you, John?'

We've just managed, between us, to unload Ben from the back seat and untangle him from the headphones when the gate opens, and Rosie appears, blinking in the mid-morning sun. Carol Dodds emerges behind her, carrying a briefcase and a large carrier bag, presumably containing Rosie's things. She puts a hand on Rosie's back, says something and points towards us, gives her a gentle push.

'Go on,' I say to Larson, 'I'll wait here.'

I watch as Ben dashes across to his mother, squealing with excitement, and she scoops him up in a tight hug, at the same time reaching out to grab her husband's hand, pulling him into the embrace. As I watch them, Dodds strolls towards her car parked a few feet from ours. When she reaches it, though, she keeps on going, and without a word places the carrier on the ground beside me. Our eyes meet, and she nods, her mouth quirked in a slight smile. Then she walks back to her car, gets in and drives away.

When I look back to Rosie, she's coming towards me, alone, at first slowly, and then at a run. I try to move, but somehow my legs aren't listening, and I stay rooted to the spot until she reaches me, throws her arms around my neck and buries her head in my clean shirt. She tries to speak, but can only manage gulps for air between shuddering sobs as the tension suddenly pours out of her, the tears soaking through my shirt and threatening to dissolve the plasters over my newly stitched cuts. I hold her in my arms, stroke her hair, kiss the top of her head. 'Hush, sweetheart,' I whisper in her ear, 'it's all right. Everything's all right now.'

---

THE GEORGIAN HOUSE in Clifton that Joyce and Chrissie have bought between them from the proceeds of their former houses is big enough for even the most boisterous gang of five-year-olds to run wild without causing too much damage. Even so, as the door closes on the last party guest, a collective sigh of relief runs through the sitting room. Rosie comes in and flops into a chair, looking as if she's just come back from a 10K run.

'How did it go?' Chrissie asks her, getting up and passing her the wine bottle and a glass.

'Pretty well, considering, I think,' Rosie replies, filling the glass and downing half of it in one slug. 'Four tantrums, one grazed knee and three sick from too much cake – but not on the new carpet,' she adds quickly. 'Ben had a great time, so I suppose it was all worth it.'

'Of course it was,' Joyce puts in. 'It's not every day you're five. And don't worry about clearing up now. As you're staying over, we can all muck in in the morning.'

Rosie smiles her thanks and turns to me. 'Can you stay too, Dad? Ben wants you to help him build a police station with the Lego you brought him, and it's too late tonight. John's giving him his bath and putting him to bed before he sneaks more ice cream and makes himself sick again.'

'I don't see how I can refuse,' I tell her, 'if it's all right with your mother?' I raise an eyebrow at Chrissie, who laughs.

'Of course it is, Al. You know you're welcome anytime.'

We sit in silence, enjoying the calm following the storm of Ben's party, until the silence is broken by the soft trill of my mobile phone. I pull it out of my pocket and study the screen.

It's Grace Helston, who, despite my fears of being forced into retirement, is still my DCI. 'Sorry,' I say, 'I need to take this,' and make my way out of the sitting room into the now deserted kitchen. There's no sign of a tremor in my hand now – not since a couple of months after the death of Anna Radcliffe. I still have the occasional problem with what Rogers calls 'flashbacks' – usually following sudden loud noises, like fireworks or thunder, and, of course, gunshots – and every so often a leg gives way and I lose my balance, but it's getting better all the time. The misplaced sense of guilt, Rogers tells me, may never go away. I press the 'talk' button and put the phone to my ear.

'To what do I owe the pleasure, Grace?'

'I'm sorry to trouble you, Al, but some information has come in to us this afternoon, and I thought it was something you needed to know.'

I listen quietly while she talks, thank her and hang up. I'm still standing there, the phone in my hand, when Rosie comes in to find me.

'Christ, it's a mess in here,' she says, surveying the war zone of dirty plates, plastic cups and half-eaten food piled up on every surface. 'Dad? What is it? You've been in here ages.' She comes up to me and squeezes my arm. 'Are you okay? Was it that call? Who was it? What did they say?'

I nod, dust off a couple of chairs, and guide her to one of them, then sit in the other. She takes my hand and waits. 'It was Grace,' I tell her, 'Grace Helston, you remember?'

She nods. 'Of course. What did she say?'

I take a deep breath. 'A report came in this afternoon of a traffic accident on the M62 just outside Leeds. It was serious – four fatalities, a couple in their sixties driving a Ford Fiesta were hit by an Aston Martin going at speed – apparently almost twice the legal limit. The couple in the Aston died as well – a young woman in her twenties, and a man, early fifties, later identified as Terence Markham, wanted by the police on several counts of fraud and money laundering. There's no doubt, sweetheart. Terry Markham is dead.'

She's still for a minute and then leans over and kisses me on the cheek. 'You want me to tell Mum?'

I shake my head. 'No, love. It's a nice night. I think I'd like to take her for a little stroll, up to the observatory, perhaps, take in the view. What do you think?'

She smiles. 'I think she'd like that.' She gets up and goes to the door, then turns, and in her smile I see that all the little worry lines that have been there since the day she was arrested, over a year ago, seem to have disappeared. 'Thanks, Dad,' she says. 'It really is all over now.'

# ABOUT THE AUTHOR

H J Reed lives and writes in Bristol, where she graduated with a PhD in psychology and began a long career lecturing in psychology and criminology, both in mainstream universities and in the prison education system. Her evenings were spent writing novels and short stories in various genres and styles, and pondering on the strange workings of the criminal mind. After a number of publication successes, she gained an MA in creative writing and went on to teach literature and the arts. Now, she is able to follow her lifelong passion and write crime fiction full time. When she is not writing, she can be found being taken for long muddy walks by a middle-aged, temperamental toy poodle, or in far-flung foreign cities thinking up new plots.

Did you enjoy *Her Last Chance*? Please consider leaving a review on Amazon to help other readers discover the book.

www.hjreed.com

# ALSO BY HJ REED

**DI Crow Series**

Her Last Chance

The Killing Ground

Made in the USA
Monee, IL
27 July 2023

39997451R00173